Encyclopocalypse Publications
www.encyclopocalypse.com

Special Thanks

Sean Duregger
Troy Savoie
Adam Monreale
Leah Dawn Cole
Shannon Marie
Danika Meyerson
Ernie Shell

And my lovely wife, Lauren
For putting up with me
You rock

CONTENTS

Introduction   ix
Jesse D'Angelo

Foreword   xi
Jeff Strand

Prologue   1
1. Release   7
2. Breaking Bread   15
3. Ice Cream   21
4. Sandbox   31
5. Cooper Auto   43
6. Test Drive   51
7. The Whiskey Thief   59
8. Release The Beast   67
9. Snake Bite   71
10. A New Day   79
11. Something Inside   87
12. Energy   93
13. Buzz   99
14. Skinner   107
15. Captive   115
16. Questions   123
17. Crosstown Traffic   131
18. Answers   141
19. The Pack   157
20. The Tunnel   165
21. Licking Wounds   173
22. Back For Blood   181
23. Cargo   191

24. Growing Pains — 201
25. Road Trip — 211
26. Home — 219
27. Male Bonding — 231
28. Family — 245
29. Not A Monster — 253
30. Big Boss Man — 263
31. Blood River — 273
32. Clash — 285
33. Captives — 295
34. Mother's Embrace — 309
35. Hard Rain — 319
36. Brothers — 325
37. Inferno — 335
38. Sunset — 343

First look at Blackbirds Dance — 377
Also by Jesse D'Angelo — 385
About the Author — 387

INTRODUCTION

JESSE D'ANGELO

When I first released *Skinner* in 2021, I feel it got lost in the shuffle. I had just started publishing books independently and I thought it would be a great idea to release my first three all on the same day. After all, *Lady of the Lake* and *Skinner* were done, and I had enough short stories to compile *A Collection of Tails*, so why not put out all three at once? That way I'd start off already having a small catalogue. Well, that turned out to be a little overly ambitious, surprise surprise.

There was more I wanted to do with *Skinner* but just didn't have the time. I wasn't entirely happy with the cover, felt that my prose needed another pass of editing, and I wanted to include art as well. But of course I just *had* to put it out right away and had no idea how to market a book, and I was left feeling underwhelmed by the result. I loved this story and envisioned a grand saga unfolding in future books, and I just felt like it deserved more than what I had put out.

Now that I have the pleasure to be working with the

wonderful, twisted minds at Encyclopocalypse, I have the opportunity to finally do it right. I have gone back through with another pass of editing, fixing all typo's and other small issues that bothered me. I have spent months creating exclusive new artwork for the gallery and a new cover. That plus a couple extra goodies and I finally have *Skinner* the way I originally intended in this new special edition release.

I've loved werewolves and were-creatures since early childhood, and have always wanted to take the idea and mix it into an epic story filled with action, romance, and hard-hitting horror. When the story began unfolding in my mind, I realized this would have to be more than one book. This would be a saga, spanning at least three books.

I don't like to do things small.

Currently, the second installment, *Blackbirds Dance*, is on the way, and it will raise the stakes even more. I can't wait to show you all what's in store for Will Shaw and where his journey takes him. In the meantime, I want to thank each and every one of you who picks up this book from the bottom of my blackened, shriveled heart. I put everything I've got into what I do, and if people enjoy it, it really does mean the world to me.

So grab a drink, sit back in your favorite chair, put your feet up, and let me take you on an adventure...

—Jesse

FOREWORD

JEFF STRAND

This foreword would be easier to write if I had a more exciting story about meeting Jesse D'Angelo. Like, maybe we foiled a bank robbery together. Or he walked over to my table at a restaurant and made direct, unblinking eye contact as he took a nacho right off my plate—the biggest, cheesiest one—and ate it in front of me, daring me to say something.

Instead, it was more like this: "You live in Chattanooga? *I* live in Chattanooga! You're published by Encyclopocalypse Publications? *I'm* published by Encyclopocalypse Publications! We should go get breakfast or something."

And so we did. My strawberry waffles were quite good. Jesse was surprisingly alert and coherent for a guy who'd very recently procreated and was surviving on two non-consecutive hours of sleep a night. It was not deep, philosophical conversation (see: lack of sleep) but he talked about how he felt the need to deliver his very best work, every single time.

As breakfast ended and he had to return to his family duties, he gave me some of his books, packaged in a sparkly red gift bag. I was excited and nervous to read them. I wasn't nervous because of the subject matter—trust me, I can handle the splattery stuff—but from the standpoint of "Please, please, please, let them be good!"

This isn't a new experience. When I become friends with a writer, I also hope to be a fan of their work. It's not always the case. I had a great conversation with a guy I sat next to at an event, we traded books, and his was...it was *really* bad, okay? (If you've ever sat next to me at an event, I'm not talking about you. I promise. As long as your book doesn't have the title misspelled on the spine, I'm not talking about you.) And I've been on the other side of the equation. I saw a post from somebody that was basically, "Jeff Strand was such a cool guy when I talked to him, so it was really disappointing that his book was such a piece of crap!" (I'm not sure if that's better than "Jeff Strand is a fantastic writer; too bad he's a dick.")

Anyway, I started to read Jesse D'Angelo's novella *Dying Sheep*, and...yes! This guy could write! One chapter in, I knew he was the real deal, and relief washed over me. Because perhaps I knew somehow that he'd ask me to write the introduction to *Skinner*, and how awkward would it have been if I didn't enjoy his work?

Super awkward.

So welcome to the brand-new edition of *Skinner*! Do you like action? No? Oh, uh, well, I'm not gonna lie—this book is action *packed*. Like suspense? You don't? Really? Okay, then I'll have to apologize on behalf of Mr. D'Angelo, because this book has suspense pretty much from the first page to the last.

Seriously, it's one hell of a ride.

Strap yourself in, but no seatbelt, helmet, or other cautionary measures are going to protect you. Just hold on and hope you survive...

For the children
And the heroes who fight for them

JESSE D'ANGELO

SKINNER

THE SAGA BEGINS

PROLOGUE

NASHVILLE, *Tennessee*

A MOTORCYCLE ROARED THROUGH THE CITY.

The hard rain that night discouraged all but the die-hard tourists and townies from coming out. Variations of Country and Rock music boomed from every open door and window as the sleek, black Ducati Monster-1200 danced around every obstacle. Its female rider was clad in black. A black figure on a black bike, they were one.

The streets glistened.

Up ahead, she saw streaks of red as the taillights of her prey swerved through traffic. Horns blared. It was a red, older model Suburban. A dirty, scratched-up old beast. Behind the wheel was another kind of beast, and she couldn't let him get away.

Her black-gloved hand cranked the throttle and the bike jumped forward. She felt the rumble and vibrations shoot up her legs and through her spine. She raced around the other cars and trucks on the road, their horns and engines shrieking, feeling the whoosh of air as she passed within inches of them.

The Suburban ran through a red light and a group of young pedestrians jumped out of the way. Tires screeched as its driver yanked the wheel and fled left onto another street. The black bike zigged and zagged, dodging around vehicles and pedestrians as she closed the distance to her prey.

Rain slapped against her visor and her tires spun and struggled to maintain their grip. She lost sight of him. Traffic up ahead was stopped. She angled the handlebars left and shot up a small stone staircase leading to the entrance of Fannie Mae Dees Park.

She swerved into the open plaza, favoring a shortcut over the cluster of metal below. Dog walkers and hand-holding lovers huddling under umbrellas jumped aside as the rider roared up the walkway. She reached the top of the next hill, past the famous tile-mosaic dragon coming up through the ground, and turned left onto another pathway meant only for foot traffic.

The bike sprinted down the dark trail, the world buzzing with kinetic energy, blurring by.

She steered right and plunged into a wooded area. The tires blew through the muddy, earthen hill, stabilizing as she cut straight into the woods below, her headlight stabbing out into the darkness. Uneven ground bumped beneath her tires as she navigated through the trees and rock formations.

There were no street lights and the wan illumination of the half-moon was blocked off by the canopy above her. The Ducati jumped and dodged and sped through the trees. Up ahead stood even thicker woods and a giant boulder, a rock larger than most houses.

She didn't even think about it.

Shifting down one gear, she angled her wheel up, hitting the sloping face of the boulder. The wheels bumped and her grip held strong as the bike leapt up the steep rock. Rain pelted down, and without precise concentration, she would slip and plummet to the muddy ground.

Her eyes were focused laser beams; her grip held strong. She reached the top and the mechanized beast let out an angry roar. She did not let up, shooting the machine forward, down the other side of the boulder and back through the trees.

Up ahead, she saw an opening in the leaves, a bright, urban glow and the sounds of the modern age. She shifted gears again, speeding up. She would not let him get away. Not a chance. The Ducati blasted through the gap in the trees and bushes, over a wall twenty feet above the street below, zipping into the light.

She sliced through the rain, sailing high above the traffic. Pedestrians and drivers gasped as she flew overhead. The rider stayed calm, gently making adjustments and aiming her vehicle to land. A white Ford F-150 passed beneath her, providing the best ramp she could improvise at the moment.

She pushed the front wheel down hard, smashing into the front windshield of the truck and onto the hood. Aluminum crumpled and safety glass smashed. The bike was back on the pavement in the blink of an eye.

The driver of the Suburban saw the black Ducati burst back onto the street right behind him. Desperation gripped his face as he sped up. She was gaining.

On the seat beside him, a nickel-plated Smith & Wesson .38 snub-nose was loaded and ready.

"God damn it! Leave me alone!" He shouted.

The man steered off the main street, smashing past an orange Kia as he fled the busier urban center. She was right behind him. He frantically turned and the Suburban's left two wheels came up off the wet road.

His eyes were focused more on the assailant behind him than on the road ahead. He smashed up the stone steps of the town square, hydroplaning across the slick concrete surface above. The slipping Suburban knocked aside two sets of patio coffee tables and chairs.

Before he knew it, he was sliding sideways off the edge of a stone staircase, heading down onto a lower street. Forward momentum turned the vehicle over, sending the Suburban rolling sideways down the stone steps. Glass shattered and metal smashed as the once-mighty machine somersaulted to a pathetic end at the bottom of the stairs.

"Fuuuuck... God damn it!"

The man sat still, the world buzzing around him.

The windshield and windows were gone, and the rain pelted through. He unbuckled his seat belt, then snatched up the .38. He could still hear her machine outside, revving, growling and getting closer.

With a grunt, he kicked the driver's door open and instantly crumpled onto his hands and knees. His right leg was badly broken. He gritted through the pain and pulled himself away from the wreck as the rain poured down.

The woman on the motorcycle came to a halt behind him, scooping out her kickstand and climbing off the bike. She began to follow, her hips swinging with attitude in their black leggings.

"What?" he snapped. "What do you *want?*"

She took her time, slowly closing the distance.

"*Leave me alone, god damn it!*"

She pulled a Glock-19 Gen-5 from her jacket.

He turned to face her, waving the .38 in her direction and fired indiscriminately. *Pop-Pop-Pop* went the small-caliber firearm, and the shots went wild.

She didn't even flinch.

Instead, she lifted her own weapon with fluid grace and fired one controlled, well-aimed projectile. The nine millimeter bullet sliced through the raindrops and pierced the man's wrist just beneath his grip on the pistol.

He gasped in pain and dropped the .38. His mouth gaped as the deadly silhouette approached.

"Wh-Who are you...? *Nng!* What do you want?"

"Just be happy they found that girl alive, Hopkins," she said. "We'd be having a much different conversation otherwise." Her voice was smooth and strong, muffled and echoing within her black helmet.

"You're not a cop! Who are you?"

She raised the Glock again and fired off another shot. Blood exploded from the man's right knee cap and he howled in wet agony. The puddle of rain water he lay in was turning red with his blood. She stepped closer, fully confident and in control.

"Tell me where you got her, Hopkins."

"F-From Arthur!"

"I know about Arthur. But where is *he* getting these kids from?" She loomed over him, gun clenched. The man wept.

"I don't know, I swear! I-I just call Arthur when I want one! I never hurt her, I didn't! We were just party-ing, and-and..."

"She's *eight* years old."

"Look, I-I'm sorry, *okay?*"

"So that shit's all you got for me, huh? After all this... Arthur. A name I already know. You got nothin' else?"

"Um, his right hand guy's name is Jim. Th-They operate out of Chattanooga Billiards! D-Downtown Chattanooga! That's all I know, I swear!"

She hovered over him, circling, the approaching sounds of police sirens in the distance. She cocked her head, looking at him. "Okay," she said. She raised the Glock again and fired the next round into the man's crotch.

Indescribable pain burned through his manhood as the bullet blasted it apart, spouting a geyser of hot, dark blood. He let loose an unbridled scream of agony and despair. Blood and tears intermingled.

"*You fucking bitch! Ahhhhh! What do you want, huh? Why are you doing this? Oh, God!*"

She raised the Glock and leveled the sights at the center of his forehead.

"*Fuck you! Fuck you!*"

She pulled the trigger.

1

RELEASE

CHATTANOOGA, *Tennessee*

FIRE. TEETH. CLAWS.

POPS AND CRACKLES. LAUGHING AND HOWLING. TIP-TOEING DOWN THE STAIRS. CHOKING ON SMOKE.

GOING DOWN. FIRE. INTO THE LIVING ROOM. BLOOD. LAUGHTER. EYES ACROSS THE ROOM THROUGH THE SMOKE.

YELLOW EYES. SMILING. REACHING OUT A HAND. A CLAW.

"HEY, BUDDY. COME ON IN…"

WILL SHAW SPLASHED COLD WATER ON HIS FACE.

It was early morning, still dim and gray in the cell he had called home for the past five years. He stood at the sink, studying his face in the mirror, his body covered in a sheen of cold sweat. It wasn't a dream. Not this time.

To call it a dream would be inaccurate. It was a permanent fixture in his psyche, a vision, coming to him in flashes, unrestricted to his nighttime slumber. In the middle of the day, at any given time, there could be a flash. It would hit him suddenly, like a surprise knife attack —

EYES. TEETH. BLOOD. SHREDDING. ANIMAL.

THE IMAGES AND MEMORIES WOULD SHOOT THROUGH his head like an electric jolt and be gone just as quickly. It had been this way his whole life. Will accepted them as primal figments of his subconscious and went on with his days. But at night, in his dreams, the visions were stronger and more prolonged.

At least some of it was not mere fantasy, he knew. There had been a fire; his family had died. He was only six years-old at the time, the lone survivor. But it was all too vague and confusing to make sense of.

Melvin Owens, his cellmate, snored lightly as he always did from the top bunk. The sound had actually grown to become a small comfort to Will in these past few confined years. But today was the day. He was getting out. No more Melvin. No more snoring. No more gray, cinderblock walls. His five years were up.

He would be free once again.

Will grunted and ambled over to the toilet. He urinated in the small stainless-steel bowl, eyes still half asleep. He was thirty-eight years-old and stood at six-feet even, with an athletic build and close-cropped black hair. His skin was a warm bronze, his features decidedly American Indian. High, sharp cheekbones. Dark brown eyes set deep beneath a serious, chiseled brow. A strong, stubbled chin with flecks of gray.

His Cherokee blood flowed hot and strong. He was a pretty boy and a ruggedly handsome man at the same time. His nose had been broken long ago and hadn't healed right, leaving it slightly offset. His smile opened up two large dimples in his cheeks that never failed to win over the ladies.

Soon, guards would come with his release papers. He'd be taken to processing, his clothes and valuables returned. And then he'd be out. But had he learned his lesson? Could he control his temper? Could he restrain the beast? He thought back to that fateful night five years ago.

There was a bar. There was a girl. There was an obnoxious asshole. There were a few too many drinks. Will remembered having a pleasant time until the asshole tried to cut in and make a move on his girl.

He remembered it escalating too quickly. Whatever words exchanged were of no consequence; just predictable, drunken provocations and the male-dominance ritual of hierarchy. The asshole had grabbed him. Thrown a punch. Missed.

Will could have backed away. He was well trained; ten years in the Army and a lifetime of studying martial arts. He had nothing to prove. But his pulse raged and the animal wanted out.

He remembered striking back, landing a clean punch on the boozer's jaw. A flurry of drunken blows were thrown between them, with Will getting clipped a couple times himself. They went to the floor. Will was on top. He loaded up his right elbow and dropped it into the man's face. And again. And again.

He forgot how many times he hit the poor bastard, but he'd surely been knocked out by the first elbow alone. By the time Will stopped himself, the drunkard's jaw was shattered, his face mangled. He had to eat through a straw for the next six months and required major reconstructive surgery.

Will had taken it too far. His sentence: seven years hard time; out in five for good behavior. The counseling sessions in the penitentiary helped. The Paroxetine PTSD medicine helped. But the animal was still there. Always there. Clawing at the insides of his eyelids. Hungry for meat.

Waiting to be set free.

———

WILL WALKED DOWN THE LONG, GRAY CORRIDOR, back in his own clothes. Faded blue jeans, service-issued boots, plain black t-shirt, gray button-up, black leather jacket and his old backpack. Less than fifty dollars was in his wallet, along with his Tennessee State driver's license and credit cards that had long ago been cancelled. Keys to an apartment that was no longer his.

His simple black sunglasses were tucked into his shirt as he walked—no, strutted—down the hall. The door to the outside world grew closer. Two prison guards followed him in escort.

They reached the door.

"This is it, Will. Good luck to you, man." The guard unlocked the door, letting the sunshine stream into Will's eyes.

"Thanks, Jenno. Shoemake. You guys take care."

Will stepped across the threshold. He walked out into the expansive parking lot, employee vehicles to the left, visitors to the right. He looked up at the sky. Tennessee. Only a few small tufts of white, cotton clouds accented the atmosphere.

In Tennessee, that meant it was going to rain.

He took only three steps before an obnoxious-orange, 2016 Dodge Challenger with black racing stripes caught his eye. Leaning against the passenger door was a familiar face.

Handsome and scruffy, and nearly fifty pounds over-weight after years of duties as a husband and father, Jackson Cooper held his old acoustic guitar with a devious smile. Will smiled as he approached his friend. Jackson immediately launched into song —

"Drivin' 'cross the heartland! Just a red-blooded all-American man! Lookin' for a pretty girl, to give me what I neeeed..." He sang with an intentionally twangy, over-the-top Southern accent, strumming the chords of an epic Country ballad. Will couldn't help but laugh.

"I met her at a truck stop! In daisy-dukes and a halter top! I took 'er back to my place, and I blew all my seeeeeed!

Country girl, oh Country girl! You really really rock my world! Country fuckin' Country! American Grrrrrl!"

"I see you've matured a lot since I been away," Will said in his easy Kentucky drawl. He approached Jackson and they hugged, laughing.

"Damn, redskin, you got old!"

"Still look better than you, white boy! Look at that gut!"

"Yeah yeah, fuck off. How you doing?"

Will looked around, took in a deep breath. "I'm free, bro."

"Yes, you are, motherfucker! We gonna get you a job, we gonna get you some pussy... *Ow!* Come on, you hungry?"

"Always."

"Well, come on, get in!"

"Is this your mid-life crisis car, or your 'I have a little dick' car?"

"This is my 'fuck you, you're jealous' car. Come on!"

Jackson popped the trunk of the Challenger and Will tossed his bag inside. Jackson gently slipped his guitar into the trunk and slammed it closed. He ran around to the driver's door, bristling with excitement as he jumped in.

"What do you want, huh? Uncle Larry's? Sugar's? Taco Mamasita?"

"Uncle Larry's. Definitely."

"How about some beans? Ohhh, how I do love beans! Thick, fat, juicy beans! Oh, don't get me started on beans, or I'm liable to be yappin' till the sun comes up!" Jackson

contorted his face and cackled in his best old prospector voice, recalling an old movie quote he loved to recite.

Will shook his head, laughing.

"Oh, here," Jackson pulled a king-size Snickers bar from his pocket and tossed it to Will. "Little something for later on. I remember how much you love this shit. How you stay in such good shape, I have no idea. Bastard."

"Just drive, Jax. Jesus."

His old friend howled and pulled out onto the street, leaving the monolithic penitentiary in the rear view mirror.

2

BREAKING BREAD

"YOU WANT SOME MORE POTATOES, WILL?"

"Oh, no thank you, ma'am. I'm good."

"My God, stop calling me ma'am! Make me feel like an old lady," Annie Cooper said, sitting back down at the dinner table.

Jackson scarfed down a forkful of mashed potatoes and grilled chicken as Will sheepishly laughed. He wasn't used to hospitality, or a warm family meal. Children were another element he was unaccustomed to, so six year-old Dominic watching him eat felt a bit uncomfortable.

Jackson took a large swig from his bottle of Bud, then went back to work on his chicken with the table manners of a German Shepherd.

"Mm. Good food, babe," Jackson said, chewing. "Dom, isn't this good?"

"Yes," the little boy mewled, peeking out through a thick mop of dark hair.

"Say thank you, Mommy."

"Thank you, Mommy."

Annie smiled. She was pleasant on the eyes, but by no means a stunner. A plain, brown haircut was pulled into a ponytail, her features unadorned by makeup or jewelry. She had just finished her shift at the registration desk of the local hospital and come home, having just enough time to prepare this dinner. Hers was a quiet heroism, never complaining or seeking praise. She was a southern good girl. *How she wound up with a degenerate like Jackson,* Will wondered, *is anyone's guess.*

The simple dining table was placed in the center of the simple dining room. A warm earth-tone was painted on the walls, adorned with family photos and nice furniture, but nothing fancy. These design principles spread throughout the house, simple and nice, but nothing fancy. Other than the family photos, it was interchangeable with any American family home. Will wondered how long he would have to stay here as he swallowed another mouthful.

Silence lingered.

A warm and furry form brushed past Will's leg, and he looked down to see the family cat, Fromage, vying for attention. The chubby calico was fond of Will's scent, rubbing against his legs with a rolling purr. Will smiled and reached down, petting the little guy.

"Looks like Big-Cheese likes you," Annie chuckled.

Dom continued to stare at Will, fascinated by the stranger. Will turned to the boy, baring his teeth in a mock snarl and making the child laugh.

"You remember me at all, kiddo? Remember your Uncle Will?"

"No."

"You were just a baby the last time you saw Will, buddy. I think you were only one-year-old." Jackson nudged Dominic, smiling. "That was right before Will..." Jackson stopped himself, feeling foolish. Will continued to eat, uneasy. Dominic looked back and forth at both of them, his sponge of a brain demanding input.

"What happened, Daddy?"

"Ummm... Well, you know how Daddy was in the Army? Well, so was Uncle Will. That's where we met," Jackson spun the story like a pro. "Well, sometimes Army men get deployed overseas, have to go away for a long time."

Will cracked open his bottle of Paroxetine, popping the nightly pill into his mouth and flushing it down with a glass of water. Even thinking about the war was making him feel anxious, and that meant it was time for a pill.

"Where did he go overseas?"

Annie was growing uncomfortable with this line of questioning and wisely interjected, "So, Will. Are you looking forward to working at the dealership with Jackson?"

"Oh, yes ma'am... Uh, sorry. Annie."

"Uncle Will knows even more about cars than Daddy!" Jackson boasted to a very impressed Dominic. "You're gonna make a hell of a salesman, bro. You'll start making money hand over fist. That, plus your pension from Uncle Sam, you'll be set. You'll be out of here and in your own place in no time. *Bachelor paaaaad!*"

"Thanks man," Will humbly said. "I do appreciate it.

Thank you, Annie." She smiled politely and nibbled at her food.

"Of course, it's no rush, bro," Jackson said. "You can stay here as long as you need to."

"Yes, of course," Annie felt obliged to add. She was really trying. She cleared her throat, uncomfortable. "I got some cherry-cobbler from the store, you guys. Will, would you like some?"

Will's eyes went wide. *Sugar!*

"Oh, wow! Yes ma— Uh, thank you, Annie!"

Jackson shook his head as his wife passed the store-made cobbler over to Will, who gratefully carved out a slice. "Human trash compactor," Jackson said. "I swear to God."

"What's a bachelor pad, Daddy?" Dominic interjected again, and the three adults at the table chuckled uneasily and shifted in their chairs.

AFTER DINNER, JACKSON LED WILL UPSTAIRS. HE entered the guest room and turned on the light. Will glanced around at the simple, square setup. A small bed in the corner was positioned across from a chest of drawers, a twenty-inch television on top.

A cozy rug lay atop a stained-wood floor. Heavy drapes closed over a single window and a medium-sized closest was empty and ready for him to fill. A room all to himself.

Not much.

But much better than prison.

Will smiled and let out a sigh, putting his bag down on the bed. He strolled around, nodding his approval, not knowing what to say. "Thanks, man" would have to do.

"Oh, please," Jackson scoffed. "You know it, bro. The TV has basic cable, Netflix, Amazon Prime, I think Hulu... Uh, there's some towels for ya' in the closet. Bathroom's across the hall. I'm sure you want to take a shower... Just remember not to drop the soap!" Jackson just couldn't resist.

"So funny, bro! You're just *so* funny!"

"I know, right!" Jackson held up his hands. "Hey, you haven't even asked me about them. What the hell, bro?"

"Asked you about what?"

"Your babies."

"...My babies?"

"Ugh. Dude!"

Jackson crossed over to the bed, bending down onto one knee as he flipped up the edge of the blanket. He reached under the bed and grabbed hold of something. He pulled hard, and out slid a large, black pelican case. A durable, high-impact polymer shell, with heavy duty hinges and nail-tough hasps.

Will gasped in recognition, his eyes going wide.

"Oh, my *babies*!"

Jackson hefted the case up onto the bed, flipping open the clasps lining its edges. He threw open the lid, revealing a small arsenal, snugly sandwiched between custom-cut foam sheeting.

Waiting patiently there for Will was his Sig P365-X Macro 9mm, his Colt 1911 .45, his DPMS AR-15, his .380 Ruger LCP 2, his nickel-plated .38 snub-nose Smith

& Wesson, two concussion grenades, two combat knives and extra magazines.

"They missed their daddy."

Will laughed as he picked up the Sig, pulling back the slide and making sure the chamber was empty. He subconsciously let out a sigh of relief.

"I don't know how to thank you, bro."

"Sell lots of cars. Make me some money."

"10-4 on that, brother."

"Well, I'll leave you alone with your babies. Let you turn down the lights, put on some mood music, light a few candles..."

"Fuck off, Cooper." Will laughed.

"Bust out some scented oil..."

"See you in the morning."

3

ICE CREAM

THE JUNKYARD APPEARED to be deserted.

Burned-out shells of vehicles lined the periphery, along with spare parts, ramshackle structures and unrecognizable shapes jutting out from the dirt. An old fence topped with razor wire encircled the property. One block over stood a distillery. Two blocks up was an abandoned factory that used to produce copper piping.

Directly across the street was a lube shop/used tire emporium. The industrial area was dead; the only life being the dance of moths and mosquitos around the halogen lights. All was quiet and dark.

It was nighttime in Clarksville, Tennessee.

Headlights rounded a corner.

The vehicle rumbled down the pothole-ridden street, rolling through the streetlights and the shadows. It was a panel van; old, gray, nondescript. It grumbled to a halt in front of the junkyard gate. A moment later, the gate came to life, sliding open to allow entry.

The wheels lurched forward and the van pulled

inside, passing old wrecks, machinery and mountains of spare parts. It approached a series of trailer homes and corrugated metal structures tucked deep inside the maze of metal.

Inside the main office, a light was on. The van's engine cut and the two front doors swung open. Annette stepped out of the driver's seat. In her youth, the boys probably called her beautiful. Now, the angles of her face were severe. Thin, sharp lips. Crows feet were deepening. She was tall, blonde and middle-aged, an icy glare in her vacant eyes.

A man in his early thirties hopped out of the passenger side. Strong and handsome, he'd adopted the nick-name Moonshine after a few too many crazy, bonfire parties. With curly-brown hair and a beard, he stepped over to the sliding back door and pounded on it twice.

"Come on. Time to get out." He spoke with a thick southern twang. He slid the door open and looked into the dark back seats, where four small figures had huddled together. He could only see two of them, the tops of their heads trembling. The other two were hiding on the floor.

"Come on, now. Don't make us have to pull you out." Moonshine's voice carried the stern authority of a prison guard, or a rancher talking to his cattle. He was thickly muscled beneath his plain jeans and corduroy jacket. Muddy-old boots and a beat-up baseball cap completed the look of a man who would blend in and go unnoticed anywhere in the American south.

His blue eyes peered inside the van, growing impatient.

"Now!"

His fist beat against the door again, and a whimpering came from inside the van. Crying. One of the figures began to move, coming out from behind the seat and crossing into the light. It was a boy, barely eight years-old. With shorts and a t-shirt, he was dressed for a day at the park with his parents. His hair was a shaggy, sandy brown and tears had dried on his face.

Next came a young girl, six years of age. A blonde-haired, blue-eyed little cherub. Her face was scared and confused. They stepped out of the van and Moonshine lightly touched their shoulders, calling to the others still inside.

"Now, you two. Come on, we ain't got all night."

Two distinct voices came from the far back, shivering, whimpering, crying. They had burrowed themselves in deep to the darkest pocket they could find. A muffled plea came from within.

"P-Please, mister..."

Annette rolled her eyes, crossing to the back of the van and unlocking the tailgate.

"I got 'em, 'Shine."

She popped open the tailgate, and found the last two tots, balled up together in the far back. A brother and a sister, they were seven and nine years-old, each with raven-black hair. They had been playing out in the streets, unsupervised.

Seeing the older woman with the sharp features and the icy eyes, they gasped and let out a desperate cry. She reached in and pulled them out, grabbing each by an arm and dragging them around to where her partner waited.

"Good work, babe." Moonshine slapped Annette on the ass and smirked, leaning in for a quick kiss.

"Is this where the ice cream is?" The little blonde girl asked. Moonshine beamed an acidic smile and nodded his head as he began pushing them forward.

"That's right. Chocolate, strawberry, whatever you want."

"I want to go home," The little black-haired boy cried. Annette tightened her grip on his arm and dragged him and his sister along. The single light source in the small, pre-fabricated office loomed ahead.

The two adults pushed the four children forward to the door. As they stepped up the metal stairs, the front door swung open on squealing hinges. A man stood in silhouette, his mouth twisted into a crooked smile, a yo-yo dancing up and down in his hand.

Diminutive and in his early forties, TJ wore glasses and a bowler's hat, tight jeans and an old t-shirt with a faded band logo. He smiled, chewing gum, eyeing-up the catch of the evening.

"What's up, ya'll? Welcome to the party." TJ stepped aside, allowing Moonshine to lead the children inside. "And look at you, Annette. Such a way with kids, huh?" The two siblings shivered.

"Please, lady! We just want to go home!" The boy tried his best to comfort and protect his little sister, but Annette shoved them along with her callous grip.

"Shut up," she said, betraying no compassion in her thick drawl. The door slammed and locked behind them as they entered the dim, seedy room. A few folding chairs and tables, a few posters on the walls and a mini fridge adorned the cold space.

At the far end was a desk. At the desk was a man. He reclined in his chair, resting his big, black boots on the desktop. He sat in a haze of blue smoke, puffing on a fine cigar.

"Hey, Mase," Moonshine called out from across the room. The man at the desk did not answer right away. He held the smoke into his lungs, a wry smile on his tanned, handsome face. His hair was long and black, with streaks of gray. His aging and chiseled features were of American Indian descent. He released the smoke from his lungs, adding to the already sizable cloud in the room. He stood up with a smile, his black eyes gleaming.

"Hey there, kids. Welcome."

Mason stepped forward, the office shaking with his heavy footsteps. His voice was a low, rumbling bass tone. He stood six feet-three inches, with a thick and powerful build. His hands were large, strong and dark. His neck and fingers were adorned with American Indian jewelry. His eyes scanned from child to child.

"How are ya'll doin' tonight?"

"Please, mister," the shaggy-headed boy pleaded. "Please don't hurt us!"

"Oh now, why would I want to do that?"

"I want ice cream," the blonde girl added, oblivious.

"Well, I think we can do that. TJ, get this little darlin' some ice cream." TJ crossed over to the mini fridge, pulling out a small, portion-sized tub of vanilla ice cream and a plastic spoon. He cracked it open and handed it to the little girl. She looked down into the small cup, disappointed.

"But I want chocolaaate..." she said.

TJ ignored her request. He looked up into Mason's dark eyes. The four adults shared a look. Mason smiled.

"Any word on our new friend?" Mason asked.

"She's still sniffin' around," Annette sneered. "But we'll take care of that bitch."

"Mm."

"So uh, what do you think, boss?" Moonshine asked, hopeful.

"I think you need a shower, Moonshine," Mason said. The two alphas shared a look, the subordinate grumbling beneath his breath. "Any trouble?"

"Naw. Just a little attitude from this one." Annette shook the dark-haired boy, pointing him out. The child snarled and struggled against her steely grip.

"I want to go home!" The boy said. "I want to see my momma, now!"

"See what I mean?"

"Mm. I like his spunk," Mason said.

"Yeah, he's a firecracker," Moonshine rolled his eyes.

"Well," Mason said, eyes wandering between the kids. "Arthur said his clients are all looking for girls right now. And little blondies always fetch a good price..."

"I want chocolate..." The little girl repeated.

"And I'm sure he can do something with this one too," Mason pointed to the little black-haired girl as she trembled.

"Can we have one of the boys?" TJ drooled. "I'm hungry for some fresh meat."

"TJ, come on, now," Mason shook his head. "Don't scare 'em, you asshole. They been through enough... Take this little guy. I'll take care of my new friend here." Mason smiled at the kids. The black-haired boy continued to struggle, enraged.

"You ain't doin' nothin' with me! Nothin'!"

"Shhh, don't you worry. It's okay. Nothin' bad is gonna happen." Mason's eyes flicked back up to Moonshine and Annette. "You lovebirds go ahead and put the two girls back in the van," Mason said, circling them. "TJ, lock this little stud up in the back trailer for now. Get to him later. Call Arthur, tell them you're on your way."

"Yes, sir," Moonshine grumbled in compliance.

He and Annette smiled and led the little black-haired and blonde girls back to the door of the office. The older brother fought with all his rage as Annette passed him over to Mason's grasp.

"No! Nicki! Let her go! Leave my sister alone!"

"Tyler!" the little girl screamed, reaching out to him as she was forced back out through the door. The blonde child needed less prodding, more concerned with her ice cream as she poked it with the plastic spoon.

"But, I wanted chocolate..." she whined as she was led outside. The shaggy-haired boy whimpered and cried, repeating "Please, mister" over and over again as TJ led him outside and around the corner to another trailer. Mason smiled and called after them.

"Come back with the money. Then we'll have us a little party!" Mason laughed and slammed the door, locking it. The child in his grip screamed and cried, thrashed and punched at Mason's solid stomach, as the two of them were left alone.

"Let me go!" he cried. "Let me go! Nicki! *Nicki!*"

Mason put on his approximation of a sympathetic face, pulling the boy around to face him and holding him in place with a hand clamping down on each arm. Mason knelt down, eyes scanning the boy.

"Now... Tyler, is it?"

"Fuck you!"

"That's not very nice, little buddy."

"Fuck you, I said! What are you doing to my sister? What are you gonna do with me?"

Mason sighed. "Well, your sister is going over to a friend of mine's place. Don't worry. She'll be just fine. Promise."

"I want to see my sister!" the boy cried, terrified.

Mason rubbed the boy's arms tenderly, speaking in a slow and tender tone, like an uncle explaining the facts of life.

"Now, Tyler. I need you to be a big boy now, okay? I need you to be brave."

"Please, mister! Let me go!"

"Listen. You been to the doctor, right? You ever have to get a shot, or the doctor has to do somethin' that hurts, but they tell you it's for your own good?"

"Y-Yeah..."

"Well, this is like that, y'see. It's for your own good. And it'll just hurt for a second, I promise. And then the pain will all be over."

"W-Why are you doing this?"

Mason mused, searching for an answer.

He realized that he didn't even know.

"Why?... Well now, that is the question..."

"P-Please mister! I'm scared!"

"I know," Mason said. "And I'm sorry. I wish it didn't have to hurt... But after tonight, there won't be no more pain. No more fear. I'm gonna see to that."

The child squirmed and wept, urine streaming down his legs as he heard the sincerity in the man's voice. The big hands delicately stroked his shoulders and hair.

"Shhhhh. Don't be afraid, Tyler," Mason said. "We're just gonna play us a little game, you and me. Now, I want you to close your eyes."

"P-Please, mister..." the child sobbed.

"It's okay," Mason said. "Go ahead. Close your eyes."

The boy obeyed, squeezing his eyes closed, tears streaming down his face. Mason knelt down, getting closer. He licked his lips, bringing his voice down to a whisper. His eyes focused on the child's throat, observing the enticing throb of his carotid artery.

"That's good. Now just hold still, buddy. You're doin' so good. Just keep your eyes closed..."

Mason's countenance began to warp and drift, like heat rising over a highway in the summer. His black eyes wavered, warped, an electric yellow overtaking his irises. Human teeth flickered into fangs and he opened his mouth, drawing in closer.

"Here we go, buddy. I promise it won't hurt for long..."

4

SANDBOX

AFGHANISTAN, 2003

THE MISSION HAD BEEN COMPROMISED.

Infantry forces had blown it, giving away their positions and taking heavy fire. Sand kicked up around them as they took cover behind whatever refuge the third-world village could offer. The American Rangers were pinned down, ants in the dirt as a swarm of hornets descended around them. Blood spattered the ramshackle walls. RPG's zipped past their heads, throwing orange plumes of fire into the sky.

The Afghan sun beat down.

Sargeant Will Shaw controlled his breathing.

He was five-hundred yards away, on his stomach, looking down the barrel of his M110 7.62mm rifle, taking cover behind a formation of rocks. His desert camo was worn and filthy. The sniper rifle was spray-painted in hues of mottled tans and browns to match the terrain. His hair and beard were unkempt and dust-caked. Not a spec of gray lived on his chin. He was young and in prime physical form. His trigger finger was ready to squeeze.

"Talk to me, Jax."

"*Shitshitshit!* Umm..." A young, thin, Corporal Jackson Cooper fumbled with his M151 Enhanced Spotting Scope, aiming at a group of hostiles on a rooftop, firing on the other Americans. "Uh, we got three ugly fuckers due-west. Fifteen degrees north of our position. Five-hundred yards."

"Got 'em," Will said, adjusting his aim.

"God damn it! What the hell happened?" Corporal Rick Velasco stood guard behind Will and Jackson. The stocky Mexican-American held his M249 SAW light machine gun with trembling hands, keeping an eye out for any hostiles trying to flank them and take out their sniper team. "Who gave up their position?"

"Doesn't matter now, does it?" Will said. "We gotta get our boys out of there. Jax?"

"*Ohhhh, we're fixin' to shoot some guyyyyys... Shoot 'em in the fucking heeeaaad...*"

"Jax!"

"Sorry... Uh, two degrees right."

Sweat rolled down Jackson's face and his hands trembled. Will adjusted his aim, zeroing in on a particularly rank-looking Jihadi terrorist. He let out a breath, staying calm. He wrapped his finger around the trigger and began to squeeze.

KILL.

Will obeyed the voice, squeezing at the end of his exhale, sending an armor-piercing round hurtling across the Afghan landscape. Seconds passed and the three-man sniper team collectively held their breath. The round struck the wall beside their target, kicking up fragments of dust and stone. A miss.

"Shit! Come on, Jax."

"Sorry, sorry! Okay, ummm..." Jackson struggled to focus, trying to ignore the pounding of his heart and wondering why the hell he had decided to come to this armpit of the world. *"Gonna shoot some guyyyys, they're gonna be fucking deeeeaaad..."*

"Jax!"

"Sorry! I sing when I'm nervous!"

"Fucking pendejo," Velasco grumbled.

"Fuck off, beaner." Jackson focused. "Okay. Four degrees up. Two degrees right."

Will complied, sending death with a squeeze of his finger.

Seconds passed, and this time, Will saw a burst of blood through his scope. The Taliban foot soldier staggered as his chest exploded, covering his buddies with gore.

"Hit! Target down!" Jackson reported. Will chambered another round.

"How the fuck are we gonna hit the HVT now?" Velasco mused more to himself than his teammates.

"Fuck the HVT," Will said, his eye not leaving the scope. "The mission is blown. We have to get our guys out of there land get to the extraction point."

"But how did they know...?"

"Who cares, Velasco? It was a trap! The target was probably never even here! Jax!"

"Uhhh, ummm…" Jackson zeroed in on the next gunman on the roof. "T-Ten degrees left. Wind from the east, three knots."

Will took aim and fired.

Two-thirds of the man's head disappeared in a cloud of cranberry mist.

"T-Target down…"

"Yes!" Will chambered another round.

"Ohhhhh my god… ohmygodohmygoddddd… Killing guys, killing guuuuys… Fuckfuckfuuuuuck…"

"Nice! Good shot, Will!" Velasco said.

Jackson's eyes went wide as something caught his attention through the scope's lens. Three filthy, bullet-riddled pickup trucks were speeding away from the combat zone. Heading their way.

"G-guys…? W-We got inbound…" Jackson pointed a trembling figure. "Three trucks, twelve o'clock… They're onto us!"

Will peered through his scope, finding the raging combatants cutting a trail across the dunes in their direction.

KILL. SHRED FLESH. DRINK BLOOD.

"Shit…" Velasco said.

"We're fucked, Will! We're stranded out here!"

"God damn it, Jax! Don't Paxton-out on me!"

Velasco's hands gripped his M249, his teeth grinding. Jackson dropped his head, eyes squeezing shut and mumbling to himself.

"What the fuck am I doing here?" Jackson cringed. "I could be working for my dad at the car lot right now... *Fuck!*"

Will turned to face Jackson, his brother-in-arms, as tears rolled down his cheeks. Will smoothed out his voice, lowering his tone to soothe Cooper's shattered nerves.

"Jax, help me out here, buddy."

"I just wanna go home..." Jackson cried to himself.

"We'll get you home, Jax. Don't worry. We'll drink black-and-tans, go to a nice titty-bar... How 'bout that?"

Jackson looked up at Will. "T-Titty-bar?"

"Yeah, man. Bad dance music, black light, big titties in your face..."

"B-Big titties in my face...?"

Clouds of dust kicked up across the desert floor. The three pickups were closing in, no longer tiny specs to the human eye. Velasco saw them coming; they would soon be past the ridge.

"Guys, we need to fall back..." Velasco begged.

"It'll be okay, Jax," Will continued. "Let's just finish this, okay? Come on, man. Shake it out."

Jackson nodded, shaking his head and letting his cheeks go slack. He took a few quick, deep breaths, calming himself down.

"*Shake it ooooout, shake it ooooout... Big titties in my faaaaace...* Woo! Okay..."

"Okay, let's get these fuckers, Jax! Come on!"

"Okay," Jackson said, psyching himself up. "Uh,

driver. Far left vehicle. Two hundred-fifteen yards out. Fifteen degrees left, five degrees down. Uh, wind from the south-east, three knots."

"I'm takin' it," Will said. He squeezed the trigger.

The shot missed.

"Keep tracking down," Jackson said, following with his specialized optics. "Five degrees down, steady!" Will fired again. Missed.

"Come on, man!" Velasco shouted.

Hitting a moving target, especially from this distance, was no easy feat. Will controlled his breathing, squeezing the trigger as he aimed at the windshield.

BLOOD. FANGS. CLAWS. ATTACK.

THE SHOT RANG OUT AND THE BULLET SLICED OVER the rocky hills, smashing through the windshield and turning it red. The truck swerved, rolling up a ledge and flipping over onto its side.

"Hit!" Will announced.

The other two vehicles were closing in.

Will and Jackson worked on taking out the second, but they were close enough for Velasco to see the faces of the men coming to kill them. The Mexican warrior clicked off the safety on his weapon, preparing himself for battle.

Will took another shot. And another.

One slug hit the windshield of the second truck, the other dug into the hood. The vehicle did not stop, and they were too close now and moving too fast. They would be coming around the ridge seconds later.

"Guys," Velasco said. "We need to fall back! Find cover!"

"Y-Yeah," Jackson agreed. "Come on, Will..."

Will snarled and took another shot. And another. One of the enemy warriors was hit center-mass, falling from his perch in the flatbed of the rusty-old truck. They moved into range and opened fire on the American team.

Buddabuddabudda!

Fully automatic PKM's tore into the ridge in front of Will, and the three men hunkered down low. Will rolled away from the long rifle and picked up his M4. He pulled back the slide and clicked off the safety. The demon in his head would have its wish. There would be blood.

"Fall back!"

The two pickups roared around the ridge and up the embankment as the three American fighters ran for the cover of a nearby gulley. The sounds of automatic fire and Arabic screaming filled the air. Lead sprayed all around them and they fired back, superior aim taking out two of the hostiles.

The Americans ducked into the deep crack in the earth as rock bits and sand exploded all around them. Islamic fighters spilled out of the trucks, swarming around the gulley and closing them in.

Velasco returned fire as he backed up, his two comrades leading the way. He took down two more hostiles, but an enemy bullet sliced through his right thigh in the process. He howled and slid to the ground, jammed into the bottom of the crevice.

The enemy pushed forward, and the young Chicano scooted around a large boulder for cover, reloading his magazine.

"Rick!" Jackson noticed that their security officer had been hit and was no longer following them. Before Will knew he was gone, Jackson had already run to Velasco's side, kneeling down beside him to apply first aid.

"Shit!" Will doubled back, finding a cover spot and taking aim at the uglies as they closed in. His rifle screamed out in short, controlled bursts, and they returned fire.

Jackson took stock of Velasco's condition, noting that his femoral artery must have been hit. He was bleeding like a fire hydrant. Without thinking about himself, Jackson dug into Velasco's medical kit and began to prep a tourniquet.

"*Nnng! Fuck you, bastards!*" Velasco raged and emptied out his clip behind him, growing weaker by the second. Jackson worked fast, ignoring the approaching danger around them. The sound of the gunfire blended into the general din of high-pitch ringing that filled the air.

"Hang in there, Rick! I got you, buddy!"

A grenade flew at them.

It landed less than ten feet from Jackson and Velasco.

The corporal acted on instinct, grabbing his friend and heaving the two of them further down into the chasm. The concussion of the bomb shook the ground as shrapnel dug into every surface.

Jackson screamed as he took two pieces of jagged metal in the back, trying to protect his brother. But it was too late. Velasco was hit by the fragments as well, and his leg continued to bleed. His eyes grew dim and his body went limp.

"No, Rick! Rick!"

The Taliban fighters swarmed in after the explosion cleared the way, fast closing on their position. Jackson struggled to raise his weapon, feebly aiming at the cretins and opening fire. One short burst caught an Islamic fighter in the gut and he went down. Two more took his place, and Jackson was out of ammo. He struggled to reach for a new magazine.

They trained their sights on the wounded warrior.

Their chests erupted in blood.

Will charged forward, abandoning his cover and unloading on the ruthless enemies. His aim was true, cutting down three of them at once. They collapsed to the rocks, their blood cooking in the sun, each thinking they were headed to the paradise that had been promised to them.

Four more were coming.

"Jax!"

"I'm okay!" Jackson tried to be stoic, though his body was racked in agony. "Velasco's down!"

Will's rage boiled.

He ran forward as the oncoming foes charged at him, matching fire with fire. Bullets zinged past his ears, and he didn't care. One grazed his side, and another through his arm. Grains of sand and grit stung his eyes. He did not care.

He charged forward.

Two more went down, choking on their own blood

and bile. The last two took cover behind a boulder, reloading their tools of death and bickering in Arabic. Will tried to flank them but one fired over the edge of the rock, keeping him back.

"F-Fire in the hole!" Jackson had pulled a grenade of his own, yanking out the pin. Will stood at the ready, watching as Jackson hurled the explosive. It landed right in the nook protecting the last two men.

They screamed.

The bomb detonated, blowing fire and rock debris everywhere. One of the Taliban fighters died instantly. The other staggered from their destroyed hiding place, his left arm hanging by a strand of sinew and dragging on the dusty ground. Will raged.

BLOOD. KILL. RIP. EAT.

WILL CLOSED THE DISTANCE TO THE DELIRIOUS warrior. He unsheathed his Glauca B1 Tactical knife and grabbed the man by the collar. The terrorist's eyes fluttered, thick blood running into them, spilling down and collecting in his unkempt, black beard.

Will snarled, his eyes raging.

He pulled the man in close, eyeballing his throat, watching the pulse throbbing in his carotid artery. He imagined tearing into that soft, brown flesh, ripping it away and feasting on it. Breaking his neck and then tearing open his chest with claws and fangs.

. . .

KILL. MEAT. PREY. FEAST.

"WILL?"

It was Jackson's voice, jarring him back to reality. The corporal had crawled out of the gulley and could see what was happening. He watched with confused eyes. Will realized that he was poised to rip out a man's throat with his teeth. To slice him open and dine on his innards. The very thought shocked and horrified him.

What the hell is wrong with me? he thought.

Will blinked away the horrible thought. He looked back at the face of the man before him, a man who would have collapsed were if not for Will holding him up by the collar.

Will raised his knife and brought it down hard. It sliced between the man's ribs and into his heart, causing him to sputter and gasp. Will grimaced in his face as he twisted the blade, opening up the wound and yanking it back out.

The jihadi collapsed to the rocky ground, bleeding out and dying within seconds. Will caught his breath.

"Will?" It was a woman's voice.

"WILL?"

With a jolt, Will shot up in bed, his sheets dripping with sweat. He was in a dark room, a strange place. Was he in prison? Was he at war? Annie called his name again, and Will turned to see her standing in the doorway.

Annie wore her favorite robe, her morning hair still uncombed. Early morning light came in through the window of the guest room Will now called home. It took him a few seconds, but he remembered where he was.

Jackson's house.

"You okay?" Annie asked.

"Yeah... Just dreaming."

Annie nodded in understanding. "Jackson has them too... Can't ever really get away from it, can you?" Will shook his head. "The thing that really gets to me is when I think about my mom, and having to take her off life support," Annie went on. "I mean, I think that's what she would have wanted. I know it is. But I still wake up in the night thinking about her. Wondering if I did the right thing... Can't get away from it."

Will nodded.

"But you know what can make everything right in the world again?" she asked.

"What?"

"Banana pancakes."

Will chuckled, running his fingers through his hair.

"Well, come on down for some breakfast when you're ready. Jackson's waiting for you. Big first day on the lot today!" Her eyes were kind and patient, and Will nodded his appreciation.

"Thanks, Annie."

Annie smiled and left Will to himself. He stared off into the darkness, catching his breath.

He whispered, "Nope... Can't ever get away from it."

5

COOPER AUTO

"SIR?"

TEAR THROAT. HOT BLOOD. CLAWS. SHREDDING. ANIMAL.

"Um, sir...?"

Will blinked away his daydream. The diminutive man in front of him was a customer. Mr. Something-or-other. They stood on the lot of Cooper Auto, surrounded by row after row of pre-owned automobiles and motorcycles. Will wore beige khakis and a tucked-in, black Cooper's polo shirt adorned with a name tag.

He suddenly remembered he was trying to sell the man a car. The customer tapped his foot as he awaited Will's return to the conversation. Will had lost his place.

"What was I just saying?" Will said.

"The extended warranty."

"Right, right. It's the three year, thirty-six thousand-mile basic, or the five year, sixty-thousand mile powertrain."

"And you said you get about nineteen miles to the gallon?" the customer asked, gesturing to the Honda Odyssey before him.

"In the city," Will said. "Twenty-eight to thirty on the highway."

"Right..." The man rubbed his chin and pushed his glasses back up the bridge of his stubby nose. He paced in front of the pre-owned minivan, scrutinizing it. "I'm still torn, because I would also love something more sporty, y'know? Like that gray Mustang?"

"We can look at that again if you want. But you did say you have a wife and two kids, right? Well, I think this Honda would be much more appropriate for your needs."

The man paced around, squatted, circled and photographed. He asked every question he could think of. Will answered the questions to the best of his ability, but a part of him had drifted away again. He looked around. Other customers and salespeople strolled the lot.

The sun was oppressive.

Jackson was over by the office, laughing and shaking hands with new customers as only he could. Jackson had the gift of gab. He had this talent that Will admired, of being in the moment, focused on the person he's talking to. Making them feel like he cared.

Making them feel special.

But Will's mind was prone to wander...

. . .

RUNNING THROUGH TREES.
MUSCLES FLEX. CLAWS DIG IN.
UP HIGH. PREY PASSING BELOW.
READY TO SPRING.
BLOOD. RIPPING.
TEARING.

"Okay..." the customer said. "I guess I have some more thinking to do. Thank you." The man turned to walk away. Will followed behind, making one last feeble attempt.

"Well, would you like me to show you something else?"

"No, I'm good. Thanks for your time, Will."

The man smiled politely and kept walking. Will stopped following. He was both upset and relieved.

"Okay then, you, uh... You have a good day, now."

Back in the main showroom, Will poured himself a cup of coffee. He mixed in a single creamer and way too much sugar. Jackson made eye-contact from across the room, flashing an exaggerated grin and pointing at it, as if to say, "Smile!"

Will forced a smile and rolled his eyes. This was out of his wheelhouse. Having knowledge and passion about cars did not make him any better at selling them, he learned.

He tossed a few M&M's into his mouth and strolled through the showroom, sipping his coffee. His eyes glanced left and right at the other salesmen, buzzing around attentively, doting on the prospective customers. Will made no such effort, content that simply being there was enough, letting them know that he was available if they needed him.

He passed a black Mustang GTE. A blue Escape. A white Land Cruiser. He caught sight of one of the more obnoxious salesmen, Mark, approaching a young lady as she strolled around a blood-red Mitsubishi Eclipse.

WOMAN.

FROM MARK'S BODY LANGUAGE, WILL COULD TELL that he was turning on the charm, using his favorite jokes and lines, trying to hook a good catch. Whatever she said in return, Mark deflated, smiled and nodded politely, then walked away to leave her be.

Will chuckled. She had too much class and intelligence to fall for his rehearsed charisma and heavily-applied Drakkar Noir.

From across the room, Will could tell that she was lean, classy and beautiful. A young, dark-skinned black woman with short, natural hair.

She wore chic, black leggings and boots, topped with a dark purple blouse and a leopard-print scarf draped around her shoulders. Will tried not to stare as he walked by.

. . .

HIPS. EYES. LIPS.

The flashes were now coming to him with increasing frequency and persistence. Every time he blinked or let his mind wander in the slightest, fractals of beasts glimmered through his eyes. Sometimes they were violent and frightening; sometimes they were empowering. Now, it was sexual.

Will continued moving, giving her a polite smile as he walked by. She returned the gesture with a slight upturn of her full, red lips. Will reached the end of the showroom, ambling. He looked around, tapping his foot, sipping his coffee.

It had been a long five years.

Five years without a woman. Will tried to control his throbbing heartbeat, to ignore her, to just be cool. But his radar picked up movement coming from behind, and soon, her intoxicating aroma found him as well.

SCENT. ANIMAL. FUCK.

"So," she said. "Are you gonna ask to show me a car, or what?" Her voice was sweet and smooth, with a slight underlying purr, like the rev of a muscle car. Will turned and smiled, flashing those winning dimples. His brown eyes made contact with her brown eyes.

"Hi! Um, yeah. Sure. I didn't want to intrude. Figured Mark was already helping you."

"He was trying," she said.

"Aha, okay." Will laughed. "Well, what are you looking for?" She smiled at him with a sultry gaze, her full lips not parting into a full grin.

"Something hot and fast," she said.

Will's pulse picked up. He swallowed hard, trying to maintain his cool. He tried to avoid looking at the flowing curves of her face or the lean lines of her athletic body. He stammered, gesturing back to the Mitsubishi she had been looking at before.

"Well, uh... Would you like to know more about this? This Eclipse is pretty sporty."

"It's all right. But I'm looking for something a little... meaner." Her accent told him that she was no southern girl. New York, if he had to guess.

They walked past the Mitsubishi, strolling around the showroom.

"Okay. Well, I think I can help you find something. I'm Will Shaw, by the way." He extended his hand and she shook it. Her grip was strong, yet smooth.

"Janae Jones."

SMOOTH SKIN. FIVE YEARS. FUCK.

Her movements were sleek and silent as they moved around the showroom. Her footsteps should have clopped across the tiles, given the heeled-designer boots she wore, but she may as well have been walking bare-foot. Will gestured to cars as they passed.

"Well, I don't think you're looking for an SUV. Honda Civic, Ford Fusion... No. What do you think of this Mustang?"

"Not quite my style."

"Okay, no problem. We have a lot of options. Are you looking for something new or pre-owned?"

"New."

"Okay."

They continued to stroll.

She noted his long stride and his handsome, chiseled face. He tried to ignore the voices and flashes in his head. If he looked at her longer than a second, her deep eyes would entrance him and her lips would start his mouth watering.

They approached a roped-off display of the new Lexus convertible sports car, the LC. It was a beautiful, black, polished piece of engineering with chrome trim accents and a $101,000 price tag.

"Tell me about this one," Janae said.

"The LC?" Will said. "Well, it's a beautiful machine. Brand new. It gets about twenty-six miles to the gallon in the city, thirty-four on the highway. It's got keyless ignition, a backup camera, heated seats, cooled seats... Um, Bluetooth, a Wifi hotspot..."

Will led Janae around the car, pointing out its features as they took in the panoramic view. She smiled, her eyes following him instead of the car.

"She's a mean beast," Janae said.

"Oh, is it a she?"

"Most definitely."

"She uh, definitely has some sexy curves."

Janae held eye contact, leaning towards Will, causing his heart rate to climb even higher.

"Well, Mr. Shaw? How about you get the keys, and you and me take her out for a little test drive?"

WOMAN. BEAST. PULSE RACING.

6

TEST DRIVE

WILL WALKED to the small alcove in the back of the dealership to get the Lexus key from Amber, the assistant manager. Behind her desk was the lock-box containing copies of keys to every vehicle on the lot. She smiled at Will with shy, plump cheeks as he stepped up to the desk.

"Hey, Will."

"Amber, can I get the key for A-25, please?"

"Sure thing."

Jackson swaggered in from around the corner, his curiosity piqued and his eyes wide. "A-25? The Lexus? What kind of fish did you hook, Shaw?"

"Not sure yet, brother."

Will turned his gaze across the showroom where Janae waited patiently. Jackson's eyes lit up and he pulled in closer to whisper in Will's ear. "Holy shit, bro! Dark chocolate! She's hot! You givin' her a test drive?"

"That's the idea," Will said. Amber passed him the key and the log-out book for him to sign.

"Okay," Jackson said. "Well, you remember the route to take her on, right? Down Broad Street to 4th, onto the 153 — "

" — Off at Market Street, then back around. Yes, mother."

"And don't let her go too fast."

"Okay, boss."

"And don't fuck her in the car."

"Jesus..."

"And if you do, I want pictures."

THE LEXUS ROARED AS JANAE LAUNCHED IT OUT onto the street. Will's body tensed and he held on tight. The polished, black machine flashed down Broad Street, Janae piloting it like a stealth fighter. She up-shifted, slid around the slower cars in her way and sped down the road with a smile.

"She's smooth," Janae said. "Handles well."

"She's a 471 horsepower with a five liter V-8 engine. Rear wheel drive, ten-speed transmission with the new magnesium paddle shifters, which I really like... Um, okay. Slow down, now. Up here we're gonna turn left at the light, then — "

Janae accelerated as the light changed from yellow to red, blasting through the intersection and heading straight. Will tensed up again, his right hand gripping the door handle, his left hand gripping the seat.

Janae smiled, enjoying his discomfort.

·   ·   ·

RUNNING. JUMPING.
CHASING PREY.
SALIVATING.

"You okay over there?" she asked.

"Just fine. Could you maybe just slow down a li — "

"Let's make sure she got some pipes on her," Janae interjected, turning on the radio and cranking up the volume. Will's ears were instantly assaulted by an aggressive Hip-Hop top-20 hit.

Janae winced.

"Ugh," she said. "No thank you."

She shuffled through the radio stations, stopping at the soothing, yet uptempo sounds of Mozart's Symphony no. 36 in C Major. She smiled, letting out a sigh of relief.

"Yeah, there we go! That's m'boy, Wolfie!" She weaved past more slow-pokes, saturating the whole street with her symphonic musical choice.

"Jesus, Lord," Will said, but she couldn't hear. She hit the brakes and turned right, sending the sporty coupe down a back alley at breakneck speed. She steered them through to the other side and back out onto the street, cutting off a stream of other cars and causing them to brake and skid, leaning on their horns.

She laughed, letting Will see her perfect, sparkling-white teeth.

Her hands gripped and caressed the wheel.

"Yeah," she said. "I'm likin' this right here."

"What?" Will shouted, unable to hear over the music.

She turned the music back down as she launched them up an on-ramp, heading south on 153. According to Jackson's rules and following the planned route, they were supposed to go north, but that was the least of Will's problems.

The needle climbed on the LCD speedometer and Will began to fear for his life. Eighty, ninety, over one hundred miles-per-hour, they sped. Janae looked over at him with a playful and demure smile.

"Let's get some ice cream," Janae said.

She rocketed down the highway to the sounds of Amadeus, pushing the vehicle past one hundred. Other cars blurred by honking their disapproval. Will had given control of a two-ton metal monster over to a madwoman.

He envisioned them twisted within burning wreckage, blood and oil and broken glass everywhere. He envisioned having to explain a demolished, luxury sports car to his friend, who had trusted him with it.

"Can you... please slow down, Ms. Jones?" He managed.

"Here's the exit," she said.

From the far left lane, she cranked the wheel to the right, sliding across four lanes just in time to duck down the ramp. The sportster whipped off the ramp and cut in front of oncoming traffic in the lanes below. Baskin Robbins was up ahead on the left, less than a block away.

LEGS PUMPING.
STRENGTH. SPEED.

FREEDOM.

"Shit!" Will hung on as she yanked the wheel to the left, sending them across three lanes and into the left-turn lane. The light was red and cars were coming, but Janae didn't stop, gunning the gas pedal and shooting left across the intersection. The oncoming cars swerved and honked at her reckless driving, barely avoiding a multi-car collision.

Janae steered the Lexus into the drive-thru lane, slowing to a smooth halt in front of the order menu. She turned to acknowledge Will, smiling.

"I like it fast," she said.

"Yyyeah."

A teenage voice crackled through the speaker system: "Hello, welcome to Baskin Robbins. May I take your order?"

"Yes, just a minute," she said, then turned to Will again. "Is it okay if we eat in the car?"

Will released a loud, nervous laugh, shaking his head. She had no problem driving the vehicle like a lunatic with a death wish, yet she would politely ask permission to eat behind the wheel. Will waved his hand in a gesture that said, "Go right ahead," and so she did.

"Okay, I'd like the mint chocolate chip, please," she said.

"Cup or cone?"

"Cup." She glanced over at Will.

"What do you want?"

The Lexus rested in the parking lot, its engine idling. Janae enjoyed her mint chocolate-chip ice cream, licking it off the plastic spoon with her tongue and lips. Never one to turn down sweets, Will enjoyed his double-chocolate chunk.

He watched her, wanting to taste those lips more than any frozen dessert. He kept cool, maintaining his poker face as he ate.

"So, uh... How do you like the car?" he asked.

"It's beautiful. I love it."

"Great. Were you looking to purchase today, or...?"

"No, I won't be purchasing. I just wanted to go for a ride." She scooped up more of the cold snack, savoring every bite. Will's eyebrows wrinkled in confusion.

"Oh... So you just wanted to fuck with me and put my life at risk, then."

"And to get ice cream."

"You're unbelievable, you know that?"

"What's the matter, Will? You don't like going fast?" Janae scooped up a spoonful of mint chocolate chip, licking and slurping it into her mouth. Her eyes held on his.

Her heat radiated.

"Well, yeah," he said. "I like going fast sometimes."

"So, what's the problem?"

"I just... I don't know. Feel a little taken advantage of."

"Oh, I can take advantage of you if you want me to,"

Janae said. "Or you can take advantage of me." Will stammered, feeling a hot erection growing in his pants.

"Okay. So it's like that, huh?"

"Mm hm," she said, finishing off her ice cream. She rolled down her window, eyeballing the trash can several yards away. *Too far to throw it,* Will thought.

She launched her empty cup and spoon through the air with a snap of the wrist. The items swooshed perfectly in the trash. She snapped her fingers.

"Are you a drinking man, Will?"

"Used to be. It's been a while, just about five years."

"Too bad. I was hoping to come across a man today who would invite me out drinking."

"Oh, is that what you want? You want to go out for drinks?"

"I thought you'd never ask." She smiled at him.

"Well, uh..." he fumbled with his words. "Maybe this coming weekend, uh, if you want? I could pick you up, and w-we could go out somewhere...?"

"Tonight," she said.

"Uh, well I can't really do it tonight, you see..."

"Ten o'clock. Meet me outside The Whiskey Thief. And don't keep me waiting."

7

THE WHISKEY THIEF

JACKSON HAD BEGRUDGINGLY GIVEN WILL the keys to a red Acura from the lot, on the provision that any sexual conquest made that night would be relayed to him in explicit detail. Will wore his best blue jeans, a nice button-up black shirt and his leather jacket.

He'd also borrowed Jackson's rattlesnake-skin boots, deciding the moment he put them on that he was keeping them. Jackson would just have to deal.

Will drove the Acura into the heart of downtown Chattanooga, looking for a parking space. The nighttime streets bustled with hipsters and families, rich and poor. The city was a balance of old and new, with horse-drawn carriages and cobblestone backstreets, tourist trams, a grand aquarium, modern art museum, a glass blowing storefront, an axe throwing store, even an outdoor rock-climbing wall overlooking Broad Street.

The pavement glistened from a recent rain. Music sources from multiple restaurants and bars created a layered soundtrack to the night. The aromas of fresh-baked pizzas from Lupi's intermingled with cigarette smoke and the sweet smell of donuts and ice cream from Clumpie's.

Depending on how one looked at it, it was either a very small city, or a very large town.

After some circling, Will found a parking spot on Walnut Street. He checked himself in the mirror. Still looking studley. He cut the engine and headed out onto the sidewalk, the evening air unusually cool for Tennessee this time of year. He felt alive. He was free, healthy, out on the streets and surrounded by life.

And he had a date.

Will smiled as he walked in Jackson's boots, clip-clopping on the pavement. Young couples walked past, groups of friends laughed as they spilled out of bars and restaurants, and all around him, life buzzed.

Just a block ahead on Walnut Street was The Whiskey Thief, situated in the Edwin Hotel, its terrace positioned over a luminous view of the Walnut Street walking bridge and the shimmering Tennessee River.

"Okay, here we go."

Will's heart pounded as he walked through the lobby and boarded the brushed-steel modern elevator, going up. He'd been through war, and prison, but this terrified him.

A beautiful woman. A bar. Alcohol.

This combination had gotten him in trouble before. But it had been so long. He needed this, needed to feel human again. Will took a few deep breaths as he exited the elevator and approached the bar inside, nodding politely to the friendly hipster doorman with the over-groomed beard.

"Evening, sir. Welcome."

"Thank you," Will said, striding though the doors.

The young and stylish mingled with the rich and upperclass in the lush, tastefully designed room. There was a deep maroon couch that wrapped around half the periphery, accented by red leather chairs and stained wood. The walls were adorned with staggered oak panels and red brick, decorated with sparse but tasteful modern artwork. Candles and soft lighting complimented the slate floor and the brown, paneled tiles on the roof. Will was in awe and he made his way through the room.

Two young bartenders happily served the bustling crowd, each wearing the uniform of an old fashioned button-up shirt and suspenders. Will's eyes scanned around but the person he was looking for was nowhere in sight. He checked his watch to verify that he was on time.

He continued moving as smooth, relaxing music played at a comfortable level, allowing the bar patrons to speak without having to shout. He made his way to the grand wall of windows, peering out at the balcony over-looking the city below.

Will made his way out onto the patio, taking in the panoramic view of the urban center and river stretching out before him. Cool breeze ran its fingers through his hair.

Several other parties sat at the tables, drinking, laughing and admiring the view. His eyes pushed past the other bar patrons, seeking out the farthest corner, and that's when he saw her.

Janae sat alone at a small table in the corner of the patio, away from the clamor. She reclined in her chair, facing the door, posed and waiting for him. Her legs were crossed. She wore a short, shimmering-gold dress, showing off her smooth, long legs and small, firm cleavage.

Her high-heel shoes bore a tiger-stripe print pattern, as did her purse. Her eyes were accentuated by tasteful blue mascara, and they were focused on the handsome Cherokee as he approached.

WOMAN.

HEART POUNDING, WILL PLAYED IT COOL, STEPPING up to her table with confidence. He smiled, putting those dimples to work.

"Is this seat taken?" he asked.

Janae glanced down at her watch, a sleek, 24-carat gold ladies' timepiece. He was one minute late. She looked back up at him with her smoky eyes, then gestured to the chair across from her. Will smiled and sat down.

"Thanks," he said. "You look very nice."

"Thank you," she said, and signaled to someone at the other end of the patio. Will turned and in a moment, a waiter approached the table from behind him.

"Hey guys," the waiter smiled. "Ready to order?"

"I'll have a Kettle 1 Cosmo," Janae said. "And you?"

Will hesitated. He'd been dry for five years. Still, he was free, he was alive, the night air was perfect and he was with a stunning, alluring woman. If there was ever a time to have a drink, this was it.

As long as I don't have too much, I'll be fine. With a smile, he turned to the waiter.

"151 bourbon on the rocks, please. And a water."

"Okay, I'll get those right out!"

"Thank you, sir."

The waiter went back inside to get their drinks, leaving Will and Janae to size each other up.

"You're so polite," she said. *"Thank you, sir.* Such a southern gentleman."

Will laughed. "Yeah, well between that and the Army, I can't much help it."

"Oh, really? And what did you do in the Army?"

"I was a sniper in the Rangers. Can't really get into the specifics of where, but you know... Reached the rank of sergeant. I was enlisted for ten years, honorable discharge. Then I ran a firearms and hand-to-hand combat training course for a while, teaching police, military, you know..."

"Interesting," she said. "So how are you now selling cars?"

Will's throat tightened. He would have to come clean, at the risk of scaring her off. "Well," he started. "I got into some trouble a few years ago. Had to do a little time. Just recently got out, tryin' to get back on my feet."

"Really?" Janae asked, uncrossing her legs, shifting in her seat, then switching legs and crossing them again. "You were in prison? What for?"

"Seven parking tickets."

"Oh, wow. That's a lot."

"Yeah, they really threw the book at me. I think it's because I'm Indian. Racist assholes."

Janae chuckled, her eyes enjoying his face. The handsome and symmetrical features. The short beard stubble. Those dark eyes. Her gaze held strong, and Will knew he should be honest.

"No, I uh... I got into a fight. Hurt the other guy real bad. So, uh... I was inside for five years."

"Oh, wow. What happened?"

"Oh, you know. There was a girl, there was a bar, there was too much alcohol..." Will looked around his current surroundings. "And there was a guy who was just asking for it. And I, uh... I lost control. Let the beast out."

"Oh, really?"

Janae's interest was piqued, leaning in further and holding eye contact. The waiter returned, carrying their drinks on a serving tray.

"Here you go," the waiter said in his most jovial tone.

"Thank you, sir."

"If you guys need anything else, you just let me know!"

"Thank you."

The waiter left them alone, heading back to check on the other patrons in his section. Will reached to his jacket pocket, remembering suddenly that he had forgot his Paroxetine back at the house. *Shit,* he thought. *Ah, don't worry about it. I'll be fine.* He smiled, playing it cool.

Will looked down at his drink. His old, favorite drink. He rotated the glass in his fingers, listening to the clinking ice as it kept the strong amber-colored spirits cold. He hesitated.

"You afraid you're going to let the beast out?" Janae smiled, gently swirling her drink.

"Kind of. It's been a while."

"Well, you didn't kill the guy, did you?"

"No, but I hurt him pretty bad. He was in the hospital for months. I definitely took it too far."

"Yeah, but if you didn't kill him, I'd hardly say you 'let the beast out.' Have you ever killed anyone? I mean in combat?"

Will tensed up. Paused. "Multiple."

"That doesn't count," she said.

"Oh, really?"

"In war, you're just doing your duty. It's not cold-blooded murder. You're not taking an innocent life. You're just following orders."

"I guess."

RIPPING. TEARING. BLOOD.

"SOUNDS TO ME LIKE YOU'VE NEVER *REALLY* LET THE beast out. You got it all under control... Go ahead, drink up." Janae held out her glass, offering a toast. Will took a deep breath, finally raising his glass.

"Okay, here we go," he said. They clinked glasses and Janae took a sip. Will hesitated a moment, holding the liquor in front of his face. *Fuck it.* He put the glass to his lips and let the cool alcohol burn down his throat. There was that familiar flavor, that comfortable heat in his chest. He savored that sip, letting out a sigh of relief.

"So, what are you, a psychologist or something?" Will asked with a playful chuckle.

"No," she said. "Why do you ask that?"

"Well, you're talking about 'the beast within' and all that. Do you have firsthand knowledge?"

"Sure," she said.

"And you've set your beast free?"

"Of course."

"I see. And how exactly do you do that?"

"One way is to kill. To take an innocent life."

"Is there another way?"

She smiled, her sultry eyes speaking volumes.

"Aha, I see," he said, his pulse speeding up as he took another sip of bourbon. "So, you uh, you live around here?"

"No," she said. "I'm staying here at The Edwin. Just in town for business."

"Okay, cool. And what exactly is it that you do?"

She smiled and took another sip of her Cosmo.

"Whatever I want."

8

RELEASE THE BEAST

BEFORE THEY COULD UNLOCK the door to Janae's suite at the Edwin Hotel, their lips were pressed together and her back was against the wall. Will's hands kneaded her supple hips and his tongue slid into her mouth. She kissed him back, her hands fishing through her purse for the room's key card.

She turned from him to swipe the card across the sensor, and he closed the distance, pressing up behind her and kissing the back of her neck. She gasped, feeling his strong hands gripping her.

"Oh my god," was all she could say.

The door buzzed open and they spilled into the room, kissing and groping and breathing and gasping. They stumbled forward, using nothing more than their peripheral vision to guide them. Will was on fire, ravenous. She was intoxicating.

His mouth moved from her lips to her throat, his hands exploring her firm, brown skin. She pulled off his leather jacket, letting it drop to the floor. Her hands moved from his chest down to his stomach, to the front of his jeans.

WOMAN. BURNING UP. HOT BLOOD.

THEY STUMBLED INTO THE BED, FALLING BUT catching themselves with a hearty laugh. She ripped his shirt off. Her gold dress fell to the floor. Will marveled at her tight body, clad now only in lacy black panties, her small, perky breasts requiring no bra.

Will kissed her all over.

Both hearts pounded.

Her fingernails bit into his back, and he loved it. She trembled and shook in his hands, her fingers running up to his head, tracing through his short, black hair.

"Yes," she breathed. "*Yes*, Will. Do it to me. Do it."

The panties came off, falling to the floor.

Will's hand traced back around to the front, and his fingers reached between her legs. She threw her head back with a moan, happy to let him do anything he wanted.

"You like that?" he asked.

"Yes!"

He continued, and now it was her hand at his belt buckle, unfastening him. The top button came undone. Then the zipper. Will gasped as she slid a hand inside. The pants fell to his feet and he did an awkward little dance to kick them away from his ankles.

She backed into the bed and sat down. He stepped

up to her and she pulled him in. Will's head fell back and he groaned as she went down on him.

WOMAN. SO GOOD. YES.

SHE SUCKED, STROKED, TWISTED AND LICKED. WILL had forgotten how good this felt. His body was taut, straining, but he had to be careful not to finish too soon. He stopped her, gently gripping Janae's arms and pulling her up.

"Your turn," he said, playfully tossing her onto the bed. She laughed as he jumped on top of her, kissing her breasts, her firm stomach, then worked his way down.

Janae's body tensed and she gripped on to the blanket. She squirmed, loving it, melting into his mouth. Her fingers caressed through his hair and gripped his head, pressing his face deeper into her.

He could barely breathe, but he didn't care. He felt her riding a wave of ecstasy and wanted to take her all the way.

She moaned and gasped and begged for more. He gave her more. The pressure and pace accelerated. She squirmed and writhed, her breathing and moaning working to an orgasmic crescendo.

Janae gasped for breath, her dark body glistening with sweat on the bedspread. "Oh my god" was once again all she could say. Will looked up, admiring her beauty and proud of his accomplishment.

He'd done it for her.

He still had it.

She looked at him with a satisfied smile.

"Do you want me to make love to you?" Will said.

She gripped him, looking up into his eyes, digging her nails into his skin.

"No," she said. "I want you to fuck me. *Hard.*"

Will obliged her demand.

9

SNAKE BITE

CASEY MADISON WAS GOING to be a doctor.

She was twelve years-old, bright and beautiful, and her mother promised her that she could be anything she wanted when she grew up. Her father never promised her anything, as he had bailed before Casey was even born.

She stood near the door on the Chattanooga electric trolley, waiting for her stop. Her thumbs were hooked under the straps of her *SpongeBob-Squarepants* backpack. Her hair was braided and accented with pink butterfly clips. Her shoes were rainbow Nikes and her clothes were simple, modern and tasteful.

Makeup was years away from adorning her milk-chocolate-hued cheeks. Casey's big brown eyes sparkled with the promise of a bright future and reflected the colorful lights of the city's nighttime attractions.

After school, she had gone to her piano class, followed by tutoring to help with those lagging History and English grades, then finally a trip to her friend

Kimmy's house for dinner and studying. Now it was late, and Casey was wiped out. The electric bus would drop her off in front of the old train station, and from there it was only a short walk across the historic museum of antique box-cars to reach her mother's house.

The bus slowed to a halt in front of the old train station-turned hotel and the doors squeaked open. "Bye," Casey said to the driver and anyone who might be listening, then hopped down the steps and onto the rain-slicked sidewalk. She pulled out her cell phone and texted her mother:

Be there in 5! — followed by smile and heart emojis.

She skipped a few steps down the sidewalk, navigating through a thin crowd of adults, then relaxed into a normal gait.

Casey walked up the grand stairs and past the front entrance. Crossing around the side, the back of the building had been transformed into a promenade of shops, abuzz with friends and happy young couples. There were restaurants, a bar, a comedy club, an ice cream shop, a giant pretzel stand and outdoor games lit by streetlights and Christmas bulbs strung through the trees.

Casey smiled as she made her way through the crowd of adults. The street was always so alive with activity, crackling with music and intoxicating aromas, and her curious eyes happily took it all in. Here or there she would she a homeless person off in the shadows, sleeping on a park bench or slumped against a wall, but they were few and seemed unthreatening.

Beyond the promenade of shops was the old train

yard, occupied by refurbished box cars, once used for shipping passengers across country. Now they were antiques that tourists could rent out as hotel accommodations.

The lights dimmed as she moved away from the crowd and onto one of the platforms between tracks. Behind her, a man leaned against a lamp post, watching the child's movements. He began to move, following her with slow, casual steps.

Casey made her way through the dark stretch between trains, admiring the Glenn Miller Gardens to her left, with its trimmed hedges, rose bushes and fish ponds. The sounds from the bustling promenade behind her faded as she passed between the trains, nearing her mother's house.

But the sound of one pair of footsteps behind her did not fade. The steps were slow and deliberate, going the same direction as her. She turned to look back and saw the man not twenty yards behind, cloaked in darkness.

She turned back around and continued walking. Her pulse picked up in tempo and she wrote it off as childish foolishness. *There's nothing to worry about*, she thought. She knew not to talk to strangers; her mother had given her the talk. She had even taught her how to kick and punch, so she could take care of herself, thank you very much.

Still, her heart beat faster. She dared not look back again, but rather picked up the pace. Casey figured she was just being paranoid. He was just a guy out walking, heading in the same direction as her. *There's nothing to worry about.*

"Hey, there."

The voice came from behind her. It was a deep southern drawl. Casey's heart pounded harder, and she chanced another look back. The man was closing the distance, hands in his pockets. His face slipped out of the shadows and into the light, smiling.

"Hey," Moonshine said.

Casey didn't answer. She walked faster, turning away from him. *There's something to worry about.* She struggled to maintain her cool, but felt the dark presence gaining on her.

"Hey, where're you going?" he said. "Are ya' lost? Do ya' need any help?"

She turned again as she walked. "N-No. Thank you. I'm fine." Her little feet propelled her forward, on the brink of breaking into a sprint. She could *feel* him smiling behind her.

"What's your name, huh?" Moonshine closed the distance. "Where you going all by yourself?"

"Please, just leave me alone..."

Her feet sped across a slick patch of oil on the already-wet ground, her balance failing her. She tried to right herself, but spun and tumbled, landing on her hands and knees. Her palms stung and she could tell she had skinned her left knee. The man came up from behind, his shadow closing in.

"You okay, sweetie?" he said, offering his hand. Casey shook her head, scooping up her bag and wobbling to her feet like a newborn deer.

"N-No, I'm okay. Thank you."

He reached for her arm. "It's okay, come here."

"No, please!" She pulled away.

He reached again, grabbing her arm. "It's okay."

"No!"

She wrenched away from his grip, tripping over her feet and breaking into a panicked run. The man in the shadows gave chase, reaching out with his big hands. She could see the street up ahead; her mother's house was so close.

"Help!" she screamed. "Somebody help!"

She was yards away from emerging onto the well-lit street, where she might hopefully find a cop or even a pedestrian to save her. But she felt an abrupt tug from behind and all her momentum was cut short as she was yanked backward. Moonshine had a firm grip on her arm and he grinned with menacing promise.

"Where exactly do ya' think you're goin'?" he cackled. Casey thrashed and struggled, shouting "*help!*" again and again. "Why don't you come with me, little darlin'? I won't hurt ya' none."

She fought him with all she had, but it wasn't nearly enough. He began to pull her back into the shadows, when a woman's voice boomed from the street —

"Hey! What are you doin' to that child?"

A van passing by had stopped in front of them, the driver seeing the struggle on the edge of the shadows. Casey screamed for help. "You let go of that child right now, y'hear! I'm calling the cops!" Moonshine froze, his grip holding strong.

The driver's door flung open, and a tall, middle-aged woman with long blonde hair jumped out. She crossed around to the passenger side, pulling a nickel-plated .380

from her jacket. "I *said*, you let go of that child right now!"

Moonshine's grip let up, allowing Casey to wrench her arm away. She ran the remaining steps to the samaritan standing beside her van, gasping for air. Moonshine stood empty handed, watching as the woman opened up the passenger door for the terrified child.

"Go ahead now, sweetie. Get in."

Casey did as she was told, jumping into the passenger seat without hesitation. The blonde woman held her aim at the man lingering in the shadows.

"Now, I'm calling the police," she said, pulling a cell phone from her pocket. "You just slowly lie down on your stomach and don't move a muscle until they get here. Go on, now!"

Moonshine hesitated, looking left and right.

"Do it, you sum'bitch!"

The man began stooping down to his knees, only to spring back up, darting away into the shadows.

"Hey! *Hey!* Shit..."

The woman lowered her pistol as she held the phone up to her ear. The attacker had vanished into the night. She closed the passenger door, then crossed around and got in behind the wheel. Casey struggled to catch her breath.

"Thank you," Casey gasped.

"No problem, baby. You just sit tight, now. I'm calling the cops."

Casey produced her own phone from her bag with trembling hands. The woman glanced over at her.

"What are you doin', baby?" the woman asked.

"I-I'm calling my momma."

"You don't have to do that, baby. The cops will be here soon. You just sit tight."

"N-No. My momma's house is just a few blocks up. She'll come down and get me." Casey began to dial, but a strong hand came down on the phone.

"That's not necessary, baby girl. Just relax, now. I got you."

Casey stared into the woman's eyes, confused. They were cold, gray eyes, set in an angular, harsh face.

"B-But... I have to... call my mom..."

Annette leaned forward into the light.

Her grip tightened. A glimmer rippled across the flesh of her face, like the heat of a desert mirage. Her features warped, displaced and shifted. Cold, gray eyes gave way to large black orbs with vertical slits.

Her harsh, angular face drifted into black and mottled neon-green, scaled skin. Reptilian fangs floated into existence, a paralyzing venom oozing from their hollow ducts. A smile split across her viper face and a forked tongue whispered out the words —

"Just relax, now. I got you."

10

A NEW DAY

DAWN PEAKED OVER THE HORIZON. The crimson streak stretched over the city of Chattanooga, and two young lovers cuddled, watching it spread. Will and Janae lay naked in tangled sheets, damp with sweat, glazed eyes staring unfocused out the window.

After an amazing night, they had finally caught their breath and allowed their high-octane engines to cool down. Her tired fingers circled around his chest, tracing through the dry sweat on his copper pectorals.

"You're incredible," she said.

"Well," he smirked. "I aim to please."

She laughed and cuddled up closer to him.

"Yeah, for an old man who's out of practice, you did pretty good." He pinched her side and they tussled, giggling.

"Old man, huh? I'll show you old man!"

"Oh yeah? You got energy for round four?"

"Well..." Will mused. "Maybe not just yet. Maybe just a little rest would be nice." They laughed again, snuggling in their blissful haze as the sky eased into orange hues.

"Guess it's been a while?" she asked.

"Yeah, five years..."

"Was there a girl back home?"

"What, you mean in Kentucky?"

"Yeah, a wife, girlfriend...?"

"Naw," Will said, shifting to put his arm behind her neck, letting her head rest on his shoulder. "Not for a while, anyway. I mean, I dated. But... Nothing too serious."

"Is that where your family is?" she asked.

"Yeah. We also spent a lot of time here when I was real little. My folks would take us to the old railroad museum, take us on the ferry down the river... But yeah, we lived in Harlan, Kentucky. My papaw's still up there."

"Your *what?*" Her eyebrows crunched.

"My papaw. Grandfather?"

She laughed. "I guess that's a southern thing."

"You've never heard that before? Papaw?" She shook her head, giggling. "Yeah, I guess not... He pretty much raised me."

"Oh yeah?" she prodded. "What about your parents?"

"They, uh..."

BLOOD. FIRE. LAUGHTER.

. . .

"They died when I was little." Will's eyes stared up at the ceiling, remembering. Her fingers continued to caress his chest, her eyes searching the emotions he tried to hide on his face.

"Oh, I'm sorry," she said. "What happened?"

"There was a fire. I was six years old. My papaw was the one who got me out, otherwise I'd be dead too."

"That's horrible."

"It's all right. I barely even remember."

"So, he's all you have left now? No aunts or uncles...?"

"I mean, I have a brother out there somewhere."

"Oh yeah? What happened to him?"

"HEY, BUDDY. COME ON IN..."

Will shifted, uncomfortable. "Um, I don't know."

"He didn't die in the fire?"

"No, they never found him in the wreckage. He's out there somewhere." Janae studied his face, watching as his eyes looked through the ceiling and into the past.

"You okay?" she asked.

"Yeah," he said.

"Were you two close?"

"No. I mean, yeah... I-I don't know."

"What is it?" she gently coaxed with a sensitive whisper and a delicate graze of her fingertips. Will took a deep breath and let it out, remembering what he'd always tried to forget.

"He wasn't... He was a sick person. He was violent, he was a killer. We're pretty sure it was him who started that fire, killed my parents..."

Janae lifted her head, intrigued.

"We were close when I was little. Playing games, chasin' toads in the woods, ridin' the trains... He taught me how to ride a bike. But he also liked killin' animals, liked it a bit too much. He would shoot squirrels with a slingshot, then he started shooting cats with a BB-gun..." Will swallowed hard, his jaw clenching. "He was almost ten years older than me. I remember one day he bragged that he killed a boy. Pushed him off a bridge and let the gators get him."

"Oh my God..." Janae's eyes were wide.

"And my papaw told me when I got older that he had killed a man, then set his house on fire. But the police couldn't make it stick, and he was set free... And I guess, this one night, he and my parents must have got in a fight, and he killed them. And then he..."

SMOKE. FLAMES. BLOOD.

"...He set the whole place on fire. And my papaw got me out of there. Took care of me after that." Will sat up in bed, unable to lay still any longer. His gaze penetrated the walls, the city, the present day. He could no longer see the rising sun, the glittering city, the beautiful woman beside him.

"So where is your brother now?" Janae asked.

Will chuckled, "It's not exactly like we kept in touch. I have no idea. Probably in prison somewhere. Or dead... He was a bad person, Janae. He's gonna have to answer to his maker one of these days, that's for sure."

Her fingers traced his back. "I'm sorry."

Will shook his head, forcing a laugh. "Yeah, well... What about you?" he asked.

"What about me?"

"I don't know anything about you. You know everything about me, and all I know about you is you have expensive tastes and a total disregard for public safety." They both laughed and he fell back into the pillows. She shrugged, trying to think of what to say.

"What about me?" she said. "I'm from The Bronx. I like ice cream. Fast cars. Hot, Native American guys."

"Yeah yeah, ha-ha. And what do you do?"

"Independently wealthy."

"Mm hm."

"No, seriously though..." Her voice dropped to nearly a whisper. "I was adopted into a rich family, so I don't really have to work. I can travel, collect art, have my little projects sometimes..."

"Mm. You don't want to tell me much, do you?"

She cuddled up closer, yawning. "No, it's not that. It's just been a long night. You wore me out. I really need to get some sleep. *We* really need to get some sleep. You got work today?"

"Later this afternoon."

"Mmmm..." she cuddled into him, yawning again. "Let's get some sleep. I'm spent." Her yawn triggered one from Will, his mouth stretching to its limit as he talked through it.

"Okay..." he yawned. "You twisted my arm... But you're not off the hook... When we wake up, I'm gonna start my interrogation..."

"Mmmm, okay, deal."

"We'll order some breakfast... And I'll interrogate you... It'll be... yeah..." Will was fading. They both drifted away as the sky turned gold, falling asleep as the rest of the world woke up.

Will dreamed of fire.

IT WAS JUST AFTER TEN IN THE MORNING AND WILL remained fast asleep. Janae zipped up her black boots and loaded the last of her toiletries into her Rimowa designer suitcase. She stood at the mirror, making sure she was slick and tight. Form-fitting blue jeans and a leopard print blouse clung to her figure, the whole outfit completed by an oversize pair of Gucci sunglasses.

She scooped up her suitcase, putting its wheels on the floor and extending the handle. She slung her purse over her shoulder. Heading for the door, she stopped, turning to look at Will.

He lay tangled in hotel bed sheets, his chest and legs exposed. His black hair was tussled and a slight smirk rested on his stubbly face. She couldn't help but smile at him.

Turning to the desk, she picked up the hotel's memo pad, scrawling a note on it for him. She tore the page off the pad and folded it in half, his name printed on the front, then placed it on the desk for him to see.

"See you soon, Will," she whispered, then slipped out the door.

Janae walked down the hallway to the elevator and pushed the button to go down. She pulled out her phone and typed out a text message as she waited:

Yeah, he don't know nothing, she typed.

11

SOMETHING INSIDE

WILL DREAMED —

"HEY, BUDDY. COME ON IN…"

INCHING FORWARD THROUGH THE SMOKE. YELLOW EYES AHEAD. MOM AND DAD ON THE FLOOR.

BLOOD EVERYWHERE. FLAMES. GLASS BREAKING. PAPAW RUNS THROUGH THE HOUSE, SCREAMING.

"WILL! WILL!" CLAWED HAND REACHING OUT. FANGED SMILE. "COME ON IN, BUDDY. I WANT TO SHOW YOU SOMETHING…"

WILL AWAKENED.

The old dream swirled in his mind. It took a second

to get his bearings and remember that he was in the Edwin Hotel, laying beside — Janae was not there. He looked around, finding the room emptied out except for his own belongings. He got up and went to the bathroom. When he came back in the bedroom, rubbing the crust from his eyes, he saw the note. Plucking it from the desktop, he read —

"Order some breakfast on my tab, hot stuff. I'll see you around — Janae."

Will's posture sank and he let out a sigh. He was hungry after last night, but he didn't want to linger in the empty, lonely space. Something inside him was buzzing, urging him to move forward.

Something was different.

He crossed over to the window, gazing out over the daytime Chattanooga skyline. The river stretched out, straddled by the Walnut Street walking bridge, then two blocks over by the Market Street bridge, which cars and trucks used to cross. The sun was shining freely, not a single cloud marring the sky.

Fresh air, life, freedom.

GET OUT.

WILL THREW ON HIS CLOTHES, PROPELLED BY A NEW sense of urgency he didn't understand. He felt a buzzing within, a vibrating frequency. The brights were brighter, the air fresher. His hearing was crystal clear, no longer crackling through old speakers, but remastered in glorious high-def.

His body felt strong, charged and rested. Sex had its way of making one feel recharged and renewed, but not like this.

Something was different.

He pulled on his boots and his jacket, then strode into the hallway, heading for the elevator. He pressed the button and stood waiting, only to feel compelled to keep moving. The thought of standing still in a confined tin can, even for a few seconds, was unacceptable.

He kept going, finding the stairs and flying down to the ground floor.

He emerged into the lobby, Jackson's boots clipping the tiles in a staccato rhythm. He reached the front desk, finding a young man slouched in his chair. His hair was tussled, his shirt ill-fitting and his name tag read *Matt*. Something caught Will's eye that he didn't like, or perhaps it wasn't his eye.

It wasn't something he could only see, but a tactile sensation he could also feel. There was a darkness around the young man, a muddy-gray color encircled him... Or was it inside of him?

As Will approached the counter, he could feel the color drain, the light dim and time itself slowed. Matt glanced up from his computer, his face blank, meeting Will's eyes for a brief moment.

"Morning, sir. How may I help you?"

GET OUT.

. . .

WILL FELT A DRAIN IN HIS ENERGY. THIS YOUTH didn't want to help him; didn't even want to be there. If he went somewhere else, he wouldn't be happy there, either. He hated life, hated himself, hated everyone and everything. His mask was made of rice paper. Matt thought to himself, *Oh come on, guy. Leave me the fuck alone.*

Will didn't hear the thought, but he felt it. It came to him like one of his own. *Maybe it is one of my own thoughts,* Will concluded. Surely, he hadn't read the kid's mind. He cleared his throat, struggling to focus.

"Um, yes. Has Janae Jones already checked out?"

Matt released a small sigh that he thought was imperceptible. But Will perceived. He waited as the hotel worker clicked his mouse, scanning his screen with disinterested eyes. Finding the answer, he looked back up at Will.

"She checked out, yes."

GET OUT.

"SHE, UH... SHE DIDN'T SAY ANY..." WILL STARTED. But it was pointless. He felt a black pull, his body weakening. The dead eyes of this front desk worker were almost hypnotizing, the energy swirling around him nothing but negative. No point. Get out.

"Never mind... Thank you."

Will bolted out into the streets and felt an immediate surge of energy and life. His eyes fought to adjust to the glare of the sun; he had gone out after dark last night and hadn't been planning on staying over, so he had no sunglasses. And no toothbrush; his teeth had developed a layer of grime.

But still, life. Energy. Fresh air. He had parked the loaner car around the corner from the hotel, but he felt compelled in the other direction, across the Walnut Street bridge.

Snakeskin boots carried him across the weathered, rundown boards of the walkway. Young couples held hands as they walked past; young mothers jogged by, pushing their babies in strollers. The mighty river surged below as Will pulled in deep breaths of crisp air. His senses were sharpened and focused, but it was more than that.

Each person he crossed had an essence to them, a color, a vibration, much like the receptionist at the hotel. The vast majority were bright, light and airy. Some seemed to have a tinge of blue, or a swirl of red, not that Will had any idea what that meant. All he knew was that he woke up alone, feeling different, sensing life as he never had before.

Has Janae drugged me somehow?

His mind raced, but it wasn't only his own thoughts in his head. As people walked by, he could hear their thoughts, or feel their emotions; he couldn't tell which. It was exciting, refreshing and stimulating, but it was also overload. *Too much.*

A dog walker passed by and the German Shepard began barking at him, smelling something it didn't like.

The owner pulled back on the leash with an expression of apology on her face.

GET OUT.

G*ET OUT WHERE?* H*E* THOUGHT. H*E WAS* OUT. H*E* reached the end of the bridge and turned around. The day was passing into afternoon and he would have to be at work soon.

Will had to get back to Jackson's house, shower, shave, brush his teeth, take his medicine, put his head on straight. Try to shake this insistent voice in his head, prodding him from the backseat.

12

———

ENERGY

WILL BOUNDED through the front door of the Cooper house and was greeted by the animated charms of *Hero Elementary* on the big flat-screen. Annie and Dominic had snuggled up into a nest of blankets on the couch, turning to greet Will with big smiles as he entered.

"Hi Will!" Annie said, and Dominic repeated.

"Hey guys..."

Will looked around, eyes bulging, sweat glistening on his face. Down the hall, he saw Jackson sitting at the kitchen table, talking on his phone. They made eye contact and Jackson's mouth lifted into a devilish grin.

"Will, close the door," Annie said. "Don't let Fromage out."

"Oh, sure." Will closed the door behind him and smiled as the orange Tabby walked by. "Hey, buddy," Will called to the cat, leaning down to pet him. But the animal turned with a snap and hissed at him, all the fur on its back standing up in alarm.

"Whoa. Okay, buddy. Easy."

"Be nice, Cheesy-Butt!" Annie called out to the cat.

Jackson hurried to finish off his business call, then strode down the hallway in his slacks, shirt and tie, greeting Will with a knowing smile and hand slap.

"Hey there, stud!" Jackson said. "How was your night?" His eyes narrowed and his smile twisted to the right. Will's head buzzed as he tried to behave normally. But his friend's energy swirled around him, a combination of fresh and earthy tones and dirty, mischievous intoxication. Will swallowed hard and searched for an answer to the question. Finally —

"Um, good."

"Just good? Okay... I was starting to worry. I'm fixin' to head off to the dealership pretty soon. Less than an hour." Jackson drew in closer, getting a whiff of Will's post-sex aroma and breath. "Yyyyeah. And I think you might want to shower first, bud." Jackson suppressed a laugh, slapping Will's shoulder.

"Uh, yeah... Shower sounds good."

"Dominic," Annie said. "Do you want to give Uncle Will his present?" The boy blushed and lowered his face, shrugging.

"Okay," Dom said, hopping off the couch and crawling over to a pile of arts and crafts products on the floor. There were several crude sculptures, each decorated and personalized. Dom picked up one and brought it over to Will, holding it out to him with a shy smile. "Here, Uncle Will. This is you."

Will took the small, wooden figure and held it up to see. It was made of several tongue depressors, with arms, legs and a head, held together with wood glue. A few rhinestones circled the neck to form a necklace, a larger one made up the belt buckle and the rest of the details were drawn in with magic markers. Leather jacket, boots, jeans and the best face the six year-old could draw, complete with black hair and a big smile.

"Oh my god," Will said, his heart melting. "Thanks, buddy." He knelt down and opened his arms, and Dom came in for a big hug. Will squeezed him, feeling his warmth, his innocence, his purity. The energy was entirely different from Cooper's, Annie's or anyone he had passed on the street.

Dominic's light was bright, undiluted, unconflicted. He was nothing but pure goodness, his essence untainted by the world. Will held him tight, feeling the boy's positive energy resonating through the wooden figure he had been given. "I love it, little dude. Thank you so much."

Will released the hug and Dom's big eyes lit up with his grin. The boy ran back over to the pile of supplies, pointing out the rest of his handiwork with pride. "I made one for everybody," Dom said. "This one's Mommy, this one's Daddy, this one's me, this one's Fromage and this one's Grandma Millie!"

Will stood back up, beaming. His fingers worked over the wood figurine in his hand, feeling Dom's energy continue to pulse through it.

"You did such a good job," Annie said. "Just put them in a box so they don't get broken when you take them to school."

"Okay, Mom."

Annie's energy was also clean, pure and good, but faded. It took on a champagne-colored hue rather than the beaming, pure-white of Dom's essence. Will's mind spun as he took it all in. Jackson stepped in and slapped Will's back, clearing his throat.

"Well, we need to go pretty soon," Jackson said. "Will, you want to shower up and get ready for work? We'll drive in together?" Will took a moment to answer, his eyes stupefied. Jackson tried to mask his concern, holding his smile tight.

Will finally nodded with a meek smile.

"Yeah... Yeah. Shower sounds good."

———

THE SUN WAS BRIGHT AND THE AIR BRISK.

Jackson steered the obnoxious-orange Challenger through the streets of downtown Chattanooga, stealing concerned glimpses over at Will in the passenger street. Will was showered and clad in fresh business clothes, yet he could not scrub away the curious symptoms that lingered from the night before. He sat still and silent, watching the streets blur past, his striped necktie strangling him.

"Dude," Jackson said, losing his patience. "Are you gonna tell me about last night, or what?"

"Huh?"

"Come on, man! You spent the night with that chick, right? How was it? Hot brown sugar! *Yow!* Did she suck your dick?"

"Jackson..."

"Was that dark-chocolate ass perfect, or what? I hope you got pictures!"

"Jackson..."

"Feet? She have nice feet?"

"*Bro!* Just... quit it, would you?"

Jackson took a long, hard look at his friend as they slowed to a halt at a red light. "Dude... What is going on with you? Are you okay?"

"Yeah, I'm fine."

"You sure? You on something?"

"What? No!" But Will did feel the effects of some mysterious drug. His head swam, his eyes saw the world in a new light and his blood didn't just pump, but rather charged through his veins. "I just... Didn't get much sleep last night. That's all."

"Because you seem like you're on something, bro. You sure you're okay to work? I don't want you in there if you're gonna be all..."

"I'm fine, Jax. Really. Just need some coffee, and I'll be good." The light turned green and Jackson drove on, a devious smile returning to his face.

"So, no pictures?"

"Christ." Will's hand came up to massage his temples.

"Don't hold out on me, you fuck! I want details! Was she all shaved down there, or did she have like, a little afro-landing strip? *I need to know these things!*"

"I swear to god, I hate you so much..."

"*YOW!!!*"

LET ME OUT.

13

BUZZ

DRINKING COFFEE WAS A MISTAKE.

Will's already heightened senses were now in high gear, pulsing and racing and twitching and jumping. Every light was blinding, every scent overwhelming. He walked the lot as zealous customers buzzed to and fro, looking at cars and discussing leasing options. Will did not engage. If a customer was casually looking at a car, he would leave them be, letting the other salesmen have first dibs.

His mind could not focus. If he was not thinking about the strange way his body felt, he was wondering what Janae might have drugged him with. *Is this ecstasy? LSD? Meth or Molly? And how can I possibly find her now? She didn't even give me a phone number.*

The hours passed.

Sunset painted watercolor streaks of yellows and purples across the sky. A few customers had approached him with questions, but his demeanor was so quiet and non-engaging, they all moved on to continue their browsing without him. Jackson hadn't failed to notice.

As he laughed and shook hands and made deals, he kept his eye on the big injun through the windows. He watched as Will strolled around aimlessly, deep in contemplation. *We're gonna have to have a talk soon*, he thought. This just wasn't going to do.

Will found himself in the bathroom, looking down at the palms of his hands. They were the same as always, but somehow, they were different. *Is there something beneath them? Are they more than just hands?*

He realized he'd been staring for five minutes, the water running in the sink. He turned the tap off, then looked back up at the mirror. There was his face. *Is there something beneath my face? Is there another person there, another face?*

LET ME OUT.

THERE WAS AN URGENCY IN HIS BODY, AN UNKNOWN vibration. A surge of energy. A strange communication with a part of himself he never knew. Will stared into his own eyes and knew he wasn't crazy. There *was* another face behind his face. There *was* something in him that needed to be let out.

He felt pregnant in an unsettling way, except it was not the swell of a baby in a womb. It was a swelling of his whole body, something inside every bit of his being, something that wanted not to simply come out of him, but to overtake him.

Will's head shivered with an ancient resonance, his muscles flexing with electrical charges.

LET ME OUT LET ME OUT LET ME OUT!

"Hello? Will, you in there?"

It was Jackson's voice, followed by a knock on the door. "Come on out. I got something for ya!"

"Um... Just a second."

Will pulled his gaze away from the mirror, forcing himself to ignore the urgent pressure from within. He unlocked the door and walked back out into the showroom, where Jackson met him with a smile. He playfully jabbed Will's shoulder and put an arm around him, leading him out towards the lot.

"Got a nice, easy one for you out there, bud. Married couple. They want a nice little sedan, they brought a trade-in, and they are ready to buy. They're right out here." Jackson pointed to a mild-mannered man and woman waiting outside.

"I don't know, man," Will sighed. His blood simmered with an unknown rage, an alien presence knocking at the back door of his mind. Jackson stopped walking, turning to face him. They were right beside the black Lexus that he and Janae took their test drive in.

"Brother," Jackson looked him in the eye. "I'm trying to help you here. You need to make some sales. You got this job because you're my boy, but I can't just keep you here if you're not gonna move cars, y'know?"

"Yeah..." Will leaned against the driver's side of the Lexus and felt a streak of electricity shoot through his hand. It was her, Janae. He could feel her energy, her essence, still imprinted on the car. Jackson continued to talk, but Will's mind was elsewhere.

He could feel her, smell her, see her.

He reached in deeper, placing his hand on the steering wheel, and the feeling became even stronger. She had touched that wheel. He could see her now, wearing a black suit, looking very conservative and professional.

She was somewhere in the city, outside, beneath neon lights. She was talking to someone, but Will couldn't focus on who, or what was said.

"You feel me, man?" Jackson concluded. "Come on. Now go out there and get that sale! Make that money, playa'. Okay?"

"...Uh, yeah. Okay. You got it, Jax."

"You can do it. Go, go, go!"

Jackson spun Will back around, severing his connection with Janae as his hand pulled away from the wheel. The two men walked outside into the cool southern night, and Jackson turned on his best salesman-smile. The husband and wife turned to face them, their demeanor as meek and plain as their appearance.

"Mike! Beth!" Jackson's delivery was rehearsed, polished and professional. "I want to introduce ya'll to m'boy, Will. This guy knows more about cars than anyone I know. He can answer all of your questions and is more than happy to help you out."

LET ME OUT! I WANT TO RUN!

WILL SHOOK HANDS WITH THE HUSBAND AND WIFE. Their energy piqued his anger. It was slow, dim, sedentary and muddy in color. It was the energy of...

Prey.

I WANT TO EAT!

"NICE TO MEET YOU," THE HUSBAND SAID.

"Hello..."

"I'll just leave you guys to it," Jackson said. "Will, I'll see you back inside." He smiled and waved as he left them to talk. Will struggled.

"So, uh..." Will said, "how can I help you?"

"Well," the wife said. "We're looking for a Civic, or maybe an Accord. Something that gets good mileage."

"Red or silver if possible," the husband said.

"Uh huh, okay."

MEAT! BLOOD! FREEDOM! LET ME OUT!

. . .

WILL FELT THE HINGES COMING LOOSE, THE WALLS crumbling around him. Something was breaking out. He could feel it inside of him; the strength, the hunger, the sheer animal presence within. He could feel its breath on the back of his neck, its claws tearing at his insides to escape.

Sweat glistened on his brow and his hands wrung together. The husband and wife were oblivious as they prattled on about the kind of car they wanted, the cars they didn't like, their son who was in school, studying divorce law.

"Okay... That's cool..." Will struggled to get the words out. His mouth wanted to open up wider than his entire head. His fingers wanted to be blades. His mental wall continued crumbling, shards of invisible stone falling all around him.

Something was definitely coming through.

"This one is pretty nice," Mike said, pointing to a silver Honda. Beth shook her head, hands on her hips.

"Yeah, but it's an '08. We want something newer."

I DON'T CARE! LET ME OUT!

"YEAH, BUT IT'S A GOOD DEAL. ONLY FORTY thousand miles."

"I don't know, sweetie. It's got a dent in the side..."

LET ME OUT! LET ME OUT!

"Well, can we get a good trade-in value for it?"

"Sir, does this one come with GPS and Blue-Tooth?"

LET ME OUT! LET ME OUT!

Will trembled and shook.

Sweat glistened on his face. Something was coming, and it couldn't be stopped. He had to leave, go anywhere but here. Had to run far, far away. Mike took a look at Will, saw his distress and reached out a hand to his shoulder.

"Hey, buddy. You okay?"

"Don't touch me!"

Will yanked his arm away and fire was in his eyes. Mike and Beth yelped and grabbed onto each other, feeling a cold shiver run through their bones as Will's voice boomed.

Everyone on the lot turned to see.

Will snarled through his teeth, his eyes flashing yellow, his body tense and ready to attack. These two creatures before him were soft, fat, slow and weak. Prey. How easy it would be to slash them apart and feast on their bloody meat.

. . .

LET ME OUT! LET ME OUT!

"*Stay the fuck away from me!*"

Will felt people watching him from all around. Jackson ran outside and watched in terror as he beheld the madness in his friend's eyes.

The flashes of yellow. *Couldn't be...*

Will staggered back, fighting the urge to jump on these two delicate morsels and tear into them. He had to go, had to run.

"*Just stay the fuck away!*"

And with that, he sprinted into the night. His feet pounded the pavement. He flew down the sidewalk and across the street. He had to get away from people, as far away as possible. Nobody could see.

Something was coming.

14

SKINNER

WILL'S LEGS PUMPED.

His heart drummed with increasing fury.

He sprinted across the street, cars whinnying to a halt as he blurred past their headlights. He blasted down 4th Avenue, up Market Street and made straight for the Tennessee River. There was no plan other than to get someplace private.

Something was about to happen, and he had no idea what. He felt an urgency, a new consciousness threatening to force its way out. Something inside demanded release, swelling within his entire body. His arms, his legs, his eyeballs, his mouth, his ears.

Something was coming out.

He blew past a group of pedestrians, leapt over a row of bushes and shot off the main road. He dashed down an alley, his skull vibrating, his body pulsing. The sounds and smells of the river ahead called to him and he descended out of the street lights toward the surging water.

His feet staggered as he navigated down the dark embankment, tripping over uneven terrain. Chiseled stone steps gave way to natural formations of craggy rocks and soil, and Will felt a cool breeze of moist river air meet his face.

There before him was the great Tennessee River.

Its current flowed by peacefully, the lights from the city and the half-moon reflecting in its rippling waves. Will looked left and right, gasping for air.

The Market Street bridge stretched across the water to his left, the Walnut Street bridge to his right.

He staggered toward the underbelly of the concrete structure, where no light reached and no human beings were present. Shrouded in nearly complete shadow, Will finally stopped. He ripped open his collar and pulled loose his necktie.

"God... what is... happening to me...?"

LET ME OUT.

LET WHO OUT? WILL THOUGHT. WAS IT A DEMON, AN angel, perhaps some new madness? What was it? What did it want from him? And how could he let it out?

JUST FALL BACK, WILL.

FALL BACK? HOW? SURRENDER? WILL'S MIND RACED.

He didn't know what any of it meant. Only that the time had come. He had to have faith, to give his trust to whoever or whatever this thing was.

To fall back, to surrender.

He closed his eyes and held out his hands, finally allowing his body to relax, to shift his balance backward, as if a net would catch him. He felt a strange warmth from behind, a vacuum pulling him into a warm bed to sleep. He felt a dream-like state envelop him as he slowly began fade out, and something else began to fade in.

There was no pain.

A shimmer ran across Will's face.

A warping of light like a desert mirage. Like heat rising from a scorching highway, Will began to warp away, and something else began to emerge into being.

It was covered in short, glistening-black hair. Its arms and legs were massive and muscular. Fingers glimmered away to reveal mighty claws sheathed in padded paws. A powerful, agile tail lashed out from the base of his spine.

Yellow eyes flared.

Powerful feline jaws warped into place. His large, predatory physique flexed and stretched, balanced on two haunched legs. His clothes did not tear away, but simply disappeared along with the rest of his human form. The mirage shimmered to its conclusion, taking less than thirty seconds from start to finish.

Standing on the riverbank, reflected in the ripples of the running water below, Will Shaw could no longer be mistaken for a human being.

He was a massive, black jaguar.

He looked down at himself. The faintest spots of a

rosette pattern appeared in his coat when he turned the right way in the light. His claws flexed, somewhere between paws and hands, with extended fingers and opposable thumbs. His snout wrinkled as he snarled.

He was a beast, an animal, a predator.

He wanted to...

RUN.

WILL LAUNCHED INTO MOTION.

His spring-loaded haunches shot him forward, sprinting down the riverbank at speeds he could not believe. His powerful fangs snapped at the air as he raced along the water, a silent, black shadow. Over rocks, fallen trees, bushes and uneven ground, he flew.

He was master of the night. He was free. He basked in this new, unbridled power as the city sparkled up above, oblivious. He stopped, not winded in the slightest after sprinting over a mile.

He looked down at his paws, flexing his digits and making the smooth, crescent claws slide out. A sense of peace came over him. He was not lost, but found. He was still somehow Will Shaw, just the other side of him who had never come out to play. This was another facet of a gemstone, and now he understood a more complete sense of self.

He was Will Shaw, but he was also... Beast. Animal. Predator. Will threw back his head and roared. His primal voice reverberated and echoed across the river.

Here he was, and the gods needed to know it.

HUNGRY.

Yes, Will thought, *I must find prey.* The thought of tender meat and hot blood made his mouth water. He kept running, staying down by the river, not daring to venture up into the city streets. His realm was the shadows. Up ahead, he smelled something.

Flesh. Prey.

He slowed his stride, falling down onto all-fours in order to creep better. Several yards away, erected by the embankment was a small tent and camp-site. A puny fire burned, and a man and his dog huddled before it.

Will crept closer.

The man was filthy, old and feeble. He would make for an easy kill. His dog was a small mutt and would cause no issues; one swipe of his claws and the little thing would be out of the picture.

Then he could dine on that sweet flesh, pink and smooth and juicy. He would slash it open, tear out chunks of viscera and indulge in its savory flavor.

Will stopped behind a tree, watching the scene before him. The old man sang an unintelligible song to his pet, rocking in a torn-up old lawn chair. Cheap whiskey was on his breath.

The dog peered off into the shadows, uneasy. It sensed another animal out there with them. It quivered and growled, knowing they were not alone.

"It's okay, boy..." the old man said. "What is it?" He looked around into the darkness, the flickering fire-light catching in his eyes and whiskers. Will crept forward, preparing to pounce.

He would crush his prey's windpipe between his teeth, break his neck and drink his blood. Then he would tear him open and eat, eat to his heart's content. He moved out into the open, slowly raising back up onto his hind legs as he moved forward.

The dog finally saw the looming black creature approaching and panicked, barking in fear. The old man turned and saw the beast as well, teeth glaring, claws flexed and ready to shred tender meat.

Will bolted forward.

The old hobo had no time to react as the animal was on him in an instant, knocking through the fire, sending embers swirling into the air. The yapping dog flew out of the way with a yelp. The man was on his back, scream-ing, looking up into the black face of certain death.

"Jesus Christ! No! Oh God!"

Will snarled as he held the man down, taking a good, close whiff as the little dog barked incessantly. He smelled the whiskey, the filth, the body odor. But there was something else. There was the energy.

It circled the human like a fog.

It carried within it guilt, deep sadness and a strange, simple-minded purity. The energy was a mossy-green color. It was natural, elemental and clean, despite his outward stink and grime. There was an honesty and nobility to the man. Will knew... This was wrong.

"Oh, please! Please God, help me!"

Will let up on the pressure, releasing his grip on the poor, old riverman. His mouth still watered, still craved bloody meat, but he stepped back. The old man looked up, confused tears in his eyes. The dog continued to bark.

With a snarl, Will bolted away, heading farther down the river. *What is this? A beast with conscience?* Will didn't like it, but it was something deep within him that wouldn't allow the attack.

He ran until he was well outside of the city limits, the sparkling lights of civilization far off in the distance. He stood on the bank of the river, surrounded by boulders and dirt, and let out a roar to the heavens. He saw his own tail and chased it in frustration, spinning in circles.

He saw the flowing river water and ran into it, splashing around in a fit of anger. *What is this I'm feeling? What is happening to me? What am I going to do?* His feline mind raced as somewhere in a dark corner, his human self floated in a peaceful sleep.

He thrashed waist deep in the river, feeling the cool water running through his black coat. He started to walk back onto dry land when something under the surface brushed past his leg. He looked around, his big, wild eyes scanning the water, but finding nothing.

A massive set of jaws launched up at him.

Will jumped back, narrowly missing the attack of a ten-foot alligator looking for a meal. The scaly predator circled and lunged again, and the black cat felt its bite close down around his right forearm. Will snarled in pain and jumped back, but the gator was strong. It whipped back and forth, trying to pull Will down below.

Will roared and flashed the claws of his free left

hand, digging them into the throat of the amphibian. The two beasts thrashed and rolled in the shallows, neither letting go. Will felt the sharp teeth piercing his arm, hot blood flowing from the wounds.

He yanked with all his new strength, pulling the leviathan out of the water and smashing it down to the rocky soil.

He dug the claws of his feet into the creature's lower belly and legs, using the leverage to rip his left hand across its throat. The claws tore deep, and thick lizard blood oozed from the wound.

The gator finally let go of Will's arm and feebly tried to escape. Will was hooked in, tearing deep into the creature, and as he held it down, he could feel its death throes as it bled out.

Will roared in victory, bearing his long, sharp teeth. He tore the alligator apart, watching its guts spill onto the riverbank. He ate, feeding on its flesh, drinking its blood. He filled his gullet and emptied his mind.

All was good in the world. The wind was cool and pleasant. The moon was calming and dim. Will reclined, a black jaguar lounging on the shore of the great Tennessee River.

The night was his.

15

CAPTIVE

CASEY'S EYES FLUTTERED OPEN.

Reality warped around her as she slowly emerged from a fog. Sounds bent and twisted, and she realized they were voices she was hearing. She cleared her throat and groaned. She was lying on a bed. The soft cushion and blankets invited her to close her eyes again and drift back into dream-land, but now her dreams were populated by monsters.

Snakes.

She felt a throbbing pain in her left shoulder and slowly pulled herself up, rubbing at it. She looked down and saw a stain of dry blood, inspecting it further to find two small puncture wounds. She rubbed her shoulder as her mind began to settle, looking around to take in her surroundings.

It was a humble bedroom, simple in its design and decor. A small bed and a dresser filled the space, and two rounded windows were framed on either side of plastic walls. She realized that she was in a mobile home.

A whimper came from behind her, and Casey whipped her head around to see two more children, huddled in the corner between the bed and the back wall.

"Hello..." Casey said.

One of them, a little boy of ten, raised a trembling finger to his lips, indicating for her to shush. He was a blonde ragamuffin, and the girl he cradled in his arms was raven-haired and even younger. Her face was streaked with tears.

They both bore the same bite marks as her.

Casey's world settled into focus. She had been bitten. She had been taken. She was a prisoner. Someone had poisoned her and these other two kids, and she had no idea where they were or how much time had passed. One thing she was sure of: her mother was already panicking.

Casey stayed silent, scooting to the edge of the bed as she tried to zero-in on the voices she heard through the wall. It was a group of adults talking, and their voices were unfamiliar. She crept to the thin, faux-woodgrain door, angling her head to hear better.

A man's voice commanded silence from the others. It was deep and throaty, clearly the leader of the group.

"And what about our friend out there?" he said. "Has she found him yet?"

"She has. It's just a matter of time."

"Ahhh, Will..."

"I don't like this, Mase. She's getting too close. We should go back to Kentucky."

"You're not scared of 'er, are you?" the leader said. "Come on, now. I been lookin' forward to this for too long."

"Yeah, 'Shine," a woman's voice said. "There's four of us and only one of her."

"And if she finds us, she might bring the others!"

Casey's pulse sped up, as did her breathing. She recognized the woman's voice on the other side of the door. *"Just relax now, I got you."*

Snakes, monsters.

Casey's shoulder throbbed. She remembered the pressure of the bite, her head swirling with fog and her consciousness fading away. She remembered the tall blonde woman with the cold eyes, and the way her face... Changed.

This can't be real, can it?

"Do we have product to move, or not? Ya'll got a new girl, didn't you?"

"Yeah, bro. You're gonna like 'er. She's a pretty one."

"Well? Let me see 'er then!"

The sound of footsteps approached and Casey backed away from the door, tripping as she bumped into the bed. The doorknob turned and the door swung open. A man not much taller than Casey stepped in. He wore thin glasses and held a spooled yo-yo in one hand, ready for play. He chewed a piece of bubblegum with a wet, smacking glee.

TJ smiled in appraisal of the young girl before him and adjusted his bowler hat. Casey froze on the edge of the bed, noting the increased whimpering and squirming of the two younger children behind her. TJ stepped up to Casey, holding his hand out, the smile on his face off-center.

"Come on, sweetie. It's okay."

Her first instinct was to scream, but she knew that would frighten the other kids even more. She hesitated, but pushed herself back up onto her feet, making a massive effort to appear stoic. She inched forward, jittery and trembling, her head held high.

TJ took hold of her arm and guided her the rest of the way through the door. She winced at his touch, reflexively pulling back, but it was no use. He was taking her through that door.

"Here she is," TJ said, his boyish voice almost a giggle. "Fresh candy! Trick or treat!" TJ yipped and laughed at his own bad joke, and none of the others joined in.

TJ held onto her arm, displaying her for the others to see. Moonshine and Annette sat on the dirty, beige couch, his arm around her as she nuzzled into him, running her fingers through his hair.

Across from them, another man sat at the small, pitiful excuse for a dining room table. Mason reclined against the wall, his legs crossed, enjoying the show. He raised a beer to his lips and drank, smiling at his new princess.

"Hello there," Mason said.

Casey did not reply. She trembled, but stood her ground.

"What's your name?"

Casey did not reply.

Annette answered for her, "Casey Madison."

Casey glanced at Annette, afraid to look her in the eye. The older woman gave her a little smile and waved with her fingertips. Moonshine leered with the same look he had when he chased her through the dark train platform the night before, then gave Annette a kiss on the cheek.

"Bring 'er here."

TJ walked over to Mason, the young girl in tow, dropping his yo-yo down into a spin and pulling it back up. Casey winced again as he pulled at her arm, the wound throbbing. Her sanity and dignity relied on staying calm; to panic and cry would be too gratifying for these heathens.

TJ presented her to Mason, still spinning his yo-yo up and down. Terrified, Casey stood her ground.

Mason smiled and slid forward, placing his beer down on the table. She turned her head, not wanting to look at him as he drank her in from head to toe.

He leaned in close, breathing her scent.

"She's a pretty one, right?" Moonshine said. "Arthur should pay top dollar."

Mason continued to smell her, inspecting her wounded shoulder. His eyebrows furrowed. Something was different about this one. She was beautiful, and strong, and intelligent, but there was something more.

"Annette bit you, huh?"

Casey did not reply.

"Just the usual," Annette said. "I didn't want to take the chance. Don't worry, Mase. I only gave 'er a little. Just enough to knock 'er out."

"Mm hm," Mason nodded. "Did you not realize that this one is special?" He looked away from the girl and focused his dark eyes at the couple sitting on the couch.

Their bewildered expressions answered the question for him.

"Well, yeah," Moonshine said. "She's beautiful. She's..."

"*No,*" Mason snapped. "Not just that. This one is *special.* Could you not tell?" Mason put his face right up against the child's neck, smelling her scent.

Casey shuddered and trembled, closing her eyes. A single tear ran down her cheek. TJ stopped playing with his yo-yo, glancing over at Annette and Moonshine, all three of them baffled.

"*Look!*"

In a single, rapid motion, Mason spun Casey around, grabbed the back of her neck and pushed her forward, standing and advancing on his three cohorts. He towered above them all, his grip firm on the child's neck, holding her out for all to see. TJ, Moonshine and Annette all inched forward, taking a closer look, and smell.

Annette's eyes went wide with shock.

"Is she...?"

"Yes. And you *bit her.*"

"I-I'm sorry..."

"We can't take her to Arthur now," Mason said.

"Oh shit, Mason," Moonshine stammered. "We had no idea!"

"You idiot! None of ya'll could tell?"

"W-Well, we ain't got the gift like you do, Mase. We can't see things and know things like you —"

"It's got nothin' to do with psychic abilities!" Mason barked. "You couldn't pick up her scent? *None* of ya'll could tell?" Mason glared at his three cohorts, and they shrank beneath his burning glare.

"This has never happened before," Moonshine said. "This is... I-I don't know how this happened..."

"You weren't paying attention."

"Well, what do we do now?" TJ asked.

"We have to get rid of her," Annette snapped, fear and panic in her arctic eyes. Mason snarled and the four of them erupted into an argument as Casey remained pinched in his grasp. She dared to crack her eyes open, putting all her effort into being as calm as possible. Over the din of voices, she opened her mouth and took a calculated chance.

"S-Sir...? Sir?"

They all stopped as Casey finally spoke. Mason relaxed his grip slightly and sank down onto his haunches, turning her slightly so he could see her sweet face.

"Yes, little one."

"Whatever you're thinking of doing... P-Please don't do it. If you want money, I'm sure my mom will give you whatever you want. I-I'll do whatever you say. I won't run, I won't scream... Just please... Please don't hurt me."

Mason nearly swooned, admiring her courage. "Oh no, little one. We won't hurt you. You're our responsibility now. You're one of us."

16

QUESTIONS

QUESTIONS SWIRLED and raced in Will's head.

The very fabric of his reality had been slashed with a straight razor. Every truth had crumbled, every grip on sanity slick with oil. Taboos and superstitions once thought the stuff of children's stories and fairy tales could no longer be written off as invalid.

They might be as real as the forces of gravity, or the Earth's rotation around the sun. If even those truths were still to be believed. Up was down and fantasy was reality. Will blinked hard, remembering last night, and knew it was not a dream.

He had become a cat.

Will sat on the bank of the river, his clothes and shoes wet but still intact. His wallet and keys were even still in his pockets. *But how could that be possible?* He thought. It was early morning, the air was cool and the city of Chattanooga was beginning to wake up around him.

His right forearm ached with dull pain. He rolled up his sleeve and found several round puncture wounds spanning from elbow to wrist. The lacerations were fresh but shallow, and they had stopped bleeding. Still, even though his arm was wounded, the sleeves of his shirt and jacket had not a single rip or puncture.

How is that possible?

Questions.

Will pushed himself off the rock he'd been sitting on, standing and stretching the morning out of his muscles. He had awakened on the shore of the river several minutes earlier, his clothes dirty and damp, but otherwise no worse for wear.

The events of last night spun and danced through his foggy mind, dreamlike, but much too real.

He *had* changed. He had felt the strength and the fury and the speed of the animal, seen his hands as paws and heard his voice as a beastly roar. He had almost killed a man, and he had killed and eaten an alligator.

One glance at the disemboweled carcass several yards away confirmed that. He had eaten its flesh and drank its blood, and loved it. Yet his suit had not a single drop of blood on it.

How was that possible?

He had to get back to Jackson's house.

The strange buzz and heightened sensations from the previous day had diminished, as had the strange, urgent voice within his head. He had gone through the change, and somehow that had released the pressure of these surging stimuli.

But he could still feel it in his head. The animal. It was there now, closer than ever, waiting behind the veil for him to call upon it.

Questions swirled, and at the heart of it all was Janae. He had to find her. She had somehow caused all of this. She had done this to him. But first, Jackson's house. A shower, fresh clothes and his medicine were in order. It would be a long walk, so he set off up the embankment, away from the river and back up onto the streets of men.

———

JACKSON STRUMMED HIS ACOUSTIC GUITAR AT THE kitchen table, singing to little Dominic as the child fussed over finishing his breakfast. He played simple chords as lyrics materialized in stream-of-conscious fashion.

"...Because boys who don't eat their eggies
Don't grow up big and stroooong
Superheroes eat their veggies
Yes, that's why... I sing this sooooong
No candy till you finish breakfaaast
And put your plate in the siiiiink
Then you can watch cartoooons
Um... Or take a bath so you don't stiiiink..."

Annie chuckled at Jackson's antics as she straightened up the kitchen. Dominic laughed out loud, wanting more musical silliness from his father.

Jackson continued to play, but stopped as he heard a key turn the lock in the front door. The whole family watched as a frazzled Will Shaw walked into the house.

Jackson's jaw tightened and his heart began to beat a heavier tempo. Will stood in the doorway, disheveled and dirty. He and Jackson locked eyes, neither knowing quite what to say, but each feeling the thick tension hanging in the air.

"Hey guys," Will said as he closed the door behind him, making his way to meet them in the kitchen.

"Hi, Uncle Will!" Dominic beamed at his new adopted uncle. Jackson and Annie shared a look, but said nothing. Fromage was under the kitchen table, rubbing against his favorite peoples' legs, but stiffened up when he saw Will coming. The cat hissed, bolting out of the room to find a hiding place.

Will forced a smile as he entered the kitchen, masking the anxiety that came when he'd gone too long without his pills.

"Hey, what's up?" Will said.

"Hey, man." Jackson barely glanced up at him.

"You guys mind if I get something to drink?" Will said, not waiting for them to answer before going to the fridge and pulling out a carton of orange juice. "Long night. Had to walk home this morning." Will poured himself a tall glass of juice and powered it down, then refilled the glass right away.

"Uncle Will, why are you so dirty?" Dominic's question was the kind of straightforward honesty one would expect from a child. Will chuckled, once again observing the pure, bright aura that surrounded the boy. He took another swig of juice, laughing.

"Oh, I just, uh... Just had a long night, buddy. Fell down a hill, got a bit dirty... But I'm fine!" Will could tell Jackson and Annie were uncomfortable, but that was the least of his concerns. "I, uh... Really need to shower. Take my pills. I'm just gonna... Yeah." He crossed out of the kitchen, heading up the stairs.

Jackson took a deep breath, deciding some words were in order. He had told Annie that Will had run off last night, and she understood. He and Will had known each other for years, seen one another at their worst... And he had never seen Will like that before. *Those eyes.* He didn't want his wife to know just how worried he was.

"Hey babe..." Jackson said. "Why don't you, uh... Take Dom to the park for a while, okay?"

"Well, we were gonna go out later, I thought?"

"Look... I need to have a little talk with Will. Can you just...?"

"Okay, sure," Annie said, crossing over to her son. "C'mon, booger. Let's go out for a while, okay?"

"But I wanna watch *Rainbow Rex!*"

"I know, baby. We can watch him later. Come on."

Annie coaxed Dominic out of his seat and slipped into her shoes, scooping her purse from the counter. She and Jackson shared a concerned look. When a man who took nothing seriously had such a dour expression on his face, Annie knew not to question him. She got the boy's shoes on and hurried him out the door, the two of them waving to Jackson on the way out.

He waved back and said his goodbyes, deflating when they were finally gone. He closed his eyes and let out a long sigh, apprehensive about the conversation to come. He cleared his throat and put his guitar down on the back of the couch, then climbed the stairs, where he could already hear running water coming from the guest bathroom.

Will stood at the mirror, his jacket and shirt crumpled on the floor. He ran his right arm under the tap, cleaning out the row of tooth marks embedded in his skin. Jackson entered the doorway and his eyes went wide.

"Dude, what the hell happened to you?"

"Don't ask."

"Are you kidding me? Of course I'm gonna ask! The way you acted last night, and now *this?* What happened to your fucking arm?" Will chuckled at Jackson's question and figured it couldn't hurt to answer with the truth.

"Uh... I was bitten by an alligator?"

"Oh, good! Okay!"

Will cracked open his bottle of Paroxetine and tapped a single pill into the palm of his hand. He threw it in his mouth and chased it with a flush of orange juice.

"Are you gonna tell me what's going on, or what?"

"Brother," Will tried to find the words. "I don't know. Please, just... I need to take a shower. I need to figure some shit out."

"That's not good enough, Will! You scared the shit out of everyone at the dealership last night! You ran off, disappeared for the night, now you come back like *this?*" Jackson took a step closer to his friend, all humor and jovial sarcasm gone from his voice. "I took you into my *home*, bro. With my fucking *family*, okay? I gave you a job, vouched for you! I... I'm trying to do everything I can to help you here! But this shit? This is just scaring me!"

"Don't be scared. I would never hurt you."

"That's not good enough, bro. This is *me*, Will. We had each others' backs for years! We've seen the worst of the worst. But I've *never* seen you act like this, bro! You gotta *talk* to me. What really happened to your arm? Tell me the truth."

"Jackson, I really... I just..."

"Are you on drugs?"

"No, man. Just this shit I'm taking here."

Will walked past Jackson and into his bedroom, stripping down to his boxer briefs and leaving his dirty pants and shoes on the floor. Jackson followed, not letting up.

"That's just your shit for PTSD, right? Is that what this is? Are you taking too much, or you haven't been taking it enough, or..."

"Jax, listen... It's not that. I don't know what it is. Something's happening to me, and I... I just don't know. That girl the other night, she..." Will looked up as he searched for the words, his eyes finding the note she left him in the hotel. He had taken it out of his pocket yesterday and left it on the counter by his bed. He crossed over to the counter and snatched up the small piece of paper.

An electric charge sparked through his fingers as the note touched his skin. Will staggered back as his synapses flooded with stimuli. Sights, sounds, aromas and feelings, his senses were shocked with new information, and it all involved *her*.

Janae.

He could feel her, smell her, hear her like a stuttering radio transmission. It was just like the night before, when he put his hands on the Lexus she had test driven. Images flashed through his eyes of city streets, buildings, people; he had the distinct feeling that he was seeing what she was seeing. But it was faded, weak and barely more than blurred whispers and skipping reflections.

"Whoa."

"Will? What's wrong? You were saying, that girl the other night? What about her?"

"I think... she gave me something."

"Like she spiked your drink or something? Have you been poisoned? Are you sick? Bro, come on, let me take you to the hospital!" Will held up his hand, gesturing for Jackson to calm down. "*Dude!* You are acting really weird! And did you see your eyes last night? I could've sworn they turned fuckin' *yellow*, bro! Now, I'll help you, but you gotta work with me here, man!"

"Jax... It's nothing like that. I just gotta find that girl. Just let me take a shower and bandage up my arm. Then I need to go out and find her."

"Well, how are you going to find her?"

"I'll start at the dealership."

"*What?* Why the hell would she be there?"

"She wouldn't. But something's there that she touched."

17

CROSSTOWN TRAFFIC

WILL SAT in the passenger seat as Jackson drove to the dealership. He was clad in his favorite blue jeans and leather jacket, and had made sure Jackson hadn't seen him conceal his Sig X-Macro in its holster. Will tapped his foot and rubbed his hands together.

Jackson shot concerned glances over at his friend every few seconds. It was a Saturday afternoon and neither was scheduled to work, but as Jackson was the boss, he felt it necessary to at least wear his dress slacks, shirt and a tie if he was making an appearance.

They pulled into the dealership lot and Jackson slid into his parking space. Will was out the door before the car stopped. His eyes scanned the lot, hungry. Business was slow, but a few of the employees who witnessed his episode last night gave him uneasy looks.

"Where's the Lexus LC I took out the other day?"

"It's in the service department," Jackson said, climbing out of the car. "Getting refueled and detailed. Why?"

Will was striding for the service department before the words finished leaving Jackson's lips.

"Shit," Will said. "They haven't already cleaned it yet, have they?"

"Um, I don't know, bro. Why?"

"Shit."

Jackson chased after Will, putting on a forced smile as he waved to the staff members who were watching them. "Hey, guys! Afternoon! *Sell sell sell!*"

Will bounded through the doors of the service department, a luxury spa for automobiles. Mechanics in greasy-gray coveralls worked on engines, changed tires, washed cars and drove finished vehicles out onto the lot. The sounds of hoses spraying, bolts being tightened and men talking and laughing echoed through the expansive space, along with Stevie Wonder's *Superstition,* which boomed through a small, filthy CD player.

Will walked through the rows of cars, finally zeroing in on the sleek, black-and-chrome jewel on wheels. A bald Peruvian man in coveralls was polishing its finish to a mirror shine. Will ran up and nearly pushed the man away in a huff.

"Stop!" Will said.

"Who the hell are you?"

"Shit!"

Jackson shifted his weight from foot to foot, hands in his pockets, smiling through closed lips. "Um, Leo, this is Will. Remember, my friend I said would be coming to work with us?"

"Oh, yeah..." Leo looked Will up and down. "It's, uh, nice to meet you." Leo held out his hand for him to shake, but Will was already circling the car, his eyes scanning it up and down, oblivious to all else. He waved his hand in a dismissive gesture at them, his eyes never leaving the Lexus.

"Go on, now... Go..." Will was transfixed.

Leo looked over at Jackson, who just shrugged sheepishly. Leo shook his head and stalked away, muttering something in Spanish. Jackson let out a sigh, keeping an eye on his friend.

"Glad to see you're ingratiating yourself to the rest of the staff here!" Jackson's sarcasm didn't even register with Will; his entire focus was on the car.

"Maybe it's not too late..." Will said, slowly approaching the driver's door with outstretched hands.

"Okayyy," Jackson said more to himself than Will.

His fingertips finally touched the door; Will ran them across the cool surface, tracing across the black finish and the sleek handle. A jolt of fireworks shot through his fingers, up his arms and into his head, ending in a ping of sparks on the roof of his skull. It was her.

Janae.

"Whoa!"

Will backed off a step, stunned.

"W-What is it, bro? You okay?"

Jackson's concern fell upon deaf ears as Will stepped forward again, this time pressing his hands firmly on the door. *Fireworks.* He saw her in his head, her bright smile, her dark skin. He felt her touch again, running across his chest, flashes of their night together.

He could see the inside of the hotel room, smell the sheets, hear the traffic outside. He was there again. Will smiled. The car being washed hadn't minimized the potency of whatever it was she left behind with her touch.

Mechanics walked past the scene, slowing down to observe Will latched on to the car in a state of psychic ecstasy. Jackson smiled at them, rocking back and forth on his feet, hands in his pockets.

"Hey, guys," Jackson said. "Carry on..." He approached Will, leaning in to get a look at his face, the big Cherokee's eyes focused somewhere miles away. "Hey, buddy. You okay?"

"Oh, yeah..." Will managed to get out.

"Yeah? 'Cause you look like you're about to whip out your cock and fuck the car." No sooner than Jackson spoke, Will opened the driver's door and plopped into the seat, grabbing hold of the steering wheel. Another jolt of current shot through his body, and Will's head rocked back in euphoria.

"*Oh!*" Will's groan was almost orgasmic.

"Buddy?" Jackson tried to keep his tone light. "Remember when I said you were scaring me back at the house? Well, now *this?* Uh... Are you okay?"

"Beautiful!" Will looked down and saw that the key-fab was in the car. He pressed the ignition button. The Lexus growled to life and began to purr and hum. Jackson jumped forward, grabbing onto the driver's door with panic in his eyes.

"*What are you doing?*"

"I have to go find her..."

"*Ohhhhh, no no no no no!* No way! Will! Snap out of

it, bro! You are not taking this car! No way! Come on, bro! *Out!*"

"I have to find her, Jax..."

"Will, do you know what the MSRP is on this car? I'm begging you, bro!"

"Sorry, Jax..." Will said, shifting the car into drive and beginning to roll forward. Jackson hurled himself around to the passenger side in an awkward and frantic dance, throwing the door open and jumping in.

"Oh, God help me!" Jackson said, closing his eyes in prayer and fastening his seatbelt as Will pulled the onyx machine out into the afternoon light.

"Get out of the car, Jackson."

"No fucking way! You are not stealing a hundred-thousand-dollar car off my lot, Geronimo! I'm going with you! Someone has to keep you out of trouble!"

"Suit yourself."

Will pulled across the lot to the exit, about to enter the flow of traffic on the main street. He closed his eyes, feeling the sensations shoot from the steering wheel up into his eyes.

"Bro, are you even okay to drive? You look like you're tripping balls!"

"I'm fine, Jackson."

"Well, where the hell are we even going?"

"To find her... Janae." Just saying her name, he could feel her smooth skin against his own, the warmth of her mouth. He smiled, pulling out onto the street and accelerating through the civilian traffic.

"And how do you plan to find her?"

"I can... See her. Feel her. I can't explain it."

"Oh, good. Okay."

Images, sounds and smells flashed through his mind. He saw her walking down a busy sidewalk. Wearing leather over a tiger-print blouse. She was following someone up ahead. A large African American man, tall and husky with a shaved head. She was keeping her distance, blending into the crowd.

"She's walking down the street..." Will said.

"Awesome."

"She's holding a cell phone to her ear... But she's not talking to anyone... She's pretending... Keeping her distance..."

"Will? Will? The road! *Will?* Jesus Christ!"

Jackson gripped hard into the seat as Will sped and weaved around other cars, his mind in two places at once. The Lexus drifted into the next lane over before sliding back again. Other drivers honked their raging disapproval. Sweat beaded up on Jackson's forehead, every muscle in his body tensed.

"Wait... She's getting on a bike now... A black bike... The man up ahead is getting into an SUV... Where the hell are they...?" The images sparkled through Will's mind as he tried to solve the puzzle and avoid wrecking the Lexus. "I think they're in East Ridge! No... I see planes landing... Is she near the airport?"

Will cut the wheel to the right and soared across two lanes of traffic. Oncoming vehicles skidded and nearly collided to avoid smashing directly into him. Jackson winced and cursed as they leaned on their horns. He couldn't resist turning back to wave at them as Will raced forward.

"Sorry! Sorry!" Jackson turned back to look at Will. "Bro, *please* let me help you. Where are you trying to go?"

"I think... Near the airport?"

"You *think* near the airport. Okayyy... Turn right on the next ramp then. Get on 58. Christ..." Will did as he was told, yanking the wheel once again and sending them zooming up the on-ramp. Will's grip remained tight on the wheel, feeling Janae in every breath.

"She's driving... She's close..."

Will swerved around other vehicles on the highway, picking up speed. Jackson felt the rumble of the concrete beneath the wheels, the rough jerk of every movement Will made. Jackson held tight as the G-forces rumbled through his guts.

"*Oh, I do not like this, no not one little biiiiit...*" Jackson sang. "*No, I do not like thiiiis... Shitshitshitshit-shiiiiiit...*"

"She's passing a sign... Shallow-something..."

"Shallowford Road?"

"Yeah, that's it!"

"Well, that's off 153-South. The exit's coming up ahead, but you'll have to get over —"

Will whipped the wheel left, then right, jolting past an old lady in a Buick, cutting off a soccer-mom in a Kia, then finally slicing around a lumbering eighteen-wheeler. He pushed the speedometer up past 90 and then leapt back across four lanes of traffic.

"*Shitshitshitshitshit!*"

"She's entering a residential — no! — A business district..." Will concentrated on the visions as he sent the

Lexus charging onto route 153. "She's parking... Looks like a strip mall or something... Warehouses around... She's getting off her bike..."

"You don't say!"

"There's a lot of cars parked there... Motorcycles... There's a sign... Billiard Club?"

"The pool hall? Chattanooga Billiards?" Jackson kept his eyes on Will, ready to grab the wheel at a moment's notice if necessary.

"Yeah, that's it!"

"Yeah, okay. That's off 64, off Shallowford. Not too far." Jackson tried to catch his breath. "The exit for 64 is coming up on the right in about two miles. Now, *slowly* start getting over into the right lane!"

Will chuckled at his friend. "Pussy."

WILL STEERED THE LEXUS INTO THE PARKING LOT OF the Chattanooga Billiard Club. He stopped the car. Jackson could hear his own heart beating.

"This is it," Will said. "She's in there." Parked off to the side was the sleek, black Ducati Monster-1200 he'd seen Janae driving. Will shifted in his seat, and Jackson caught a glimpse of the Sig concealed by his jacket.

"Will," Jackson said, genuine concern in his voice. "Please don't do anything stupid. I mean, it's a little late for that now, but y'know, don't do anything *even more* stupid..."

"I'm sorry about this, Jax. I really am. I can't explain

it. Just... Go. Take the car and get out of here. I'll be all right." The two men shared a silent look.

"Bro," Jackson said. "I can't just leave you here like this."

"Jax, just go... I'm sorry." And with that, Will was out the door, striding for the entryway to the pool hall before Jackson had time to stop him.

18

―――――――

ANSWERS

WILL STEPPED INTO THE DIM, ambient lighting of the bustling pool hall. Three rows of billiards tables stretched before him, leading to an expansive bar that spanned wall to wall. People laughed and drank and talked as they played pool, while others sat over to the side in the dining room, enjoying the games as they supped on selections of fried bar food.

He inched his way forward, his eyes surveying every crevice of the hall. His senses were on the brink of overload. Cigarette smoke clouded the air, AC/DC blared over the speakers and conversations were punctuated by the sharp clacking of billiard balls. Everyone in the room had an energy to them, visible and tangible, and it was all starting to blur together and coalesce into a sinus headache.

He walked down the center aisle, steering around the players and their pool cues. To the left, the aromas of greasy fish and chips, burgers and onion rings permeated the atmosphere. To his right, an enclave of pinball machines and video games played their own music and attracted their own crowd. But Will was only interested in one person there tonight, and he saw her as he approached from behind.

Janae sat at the bar.

Her open-back blouse revealed her firm muscles and brown skin. She sat upright with perfect posture, sipping on a martini. Will saw the energy she emitted for the first time and his puzzlement and curiosity was piqued.

The aura was different then anyone else's in the room. It radiated a warm, golden hue, and he sensed in it not only violence, but courage and virtue as well. It was a complicated essence, but definitely not sinister or evil. Will crept up behind her, teeth and fists clenched.

Janae smiled.

"I ordered you a bourbon. 151, right?" She didn't have to turn around to look at him. Will deflated, feeling foolish. He drew in close, his lips to her ear.

"Nice to see you again, *sweetheart*," he said.

"It took you long enough to find me," she said. "I was beginning to worry."

"Let's go somewhere and talk," Will said.

"We can talk right here."

"Somewhere *private*."

"Look, hot stuff, I'm working here. Okay?"

"Oh yeah? And what exactly is it that you — "

One of three bartenders interjected, "One bourbon 151 on the rocks." The drink was placed on the bar in front of Will, and he swallowed hard. It did look good.

"Sit down," Janae said. "Have a drink."

"I don't want a drink," Will sat down, glaring at her. "I want to know what the hell you *did* to me!"

Janae smiled, returning his gaze.

"Ooh, baby. You want me to talk dirty?"

"I want you to tell me what the hell is going on."

"I told you. I'm working."

"Yeah, doing what?"

"Watching someone. Waiting for someone."

Her eyes moved from the mirror behind the bar to a mirror off to the side. Will could tell he didn't have her full attention. He leaned in to her, putting his hand on her wrist with measured strength. She turned back to face him. His eyes were all business.

"Fine," she said. "Let's get a table over there. It's more private. Okay?" She nodded over to the dining area and Will saw a few open tables far enough away from other people.

"Okay. Move slow." Will stood up, hand firm on her wrist, and she followed, shouldering her purse and picking up her jacket. He began to lead her to the dining area.

"Don't forget your drink," Janae said.

Will sighed and scooped the glass of bourbon off the bar, carrying it with him. They negotiated through the crowd, finding their way to the back end of the dining room. Will released his grip and let her sit down. He followed suit, eyes not leaving her for a second.

She sipped her martini, eyes following someone behind Will. He turned to follow her line of sight, finding the man he'd seen in his visions. A large, husky black man with a shaved head, impeccably dressed. He was talking to a nordic-looking man with greying hair, who appeared to be the subordinate. Will turned back to face Janae, jaw clenched.

"Who is he?" Will said.

"His name is Arthur Wyckoff," Janae said. "He owns this place. That's his assistant, Jim Reid."

"Why are you following him?"

"Arthur is a bad boy. I've been shadowing him for weeks. Tonight he's meeting up with some... other bad boys."

Flustered, Will downed half of his bourbon in one gulp, nearly slamming the glass back down on the table. "So you *are* a cop." She glanced back at him briefly with a bemused smile.

"Not hardly." She took another sip of her drink, eyes flicking back over to Arthur.

Will's patience with her expired.

"*Hey!*" he snapped, hand slapping back down on her wrist. "Look at me! Okay?" Her eyes shifted back to meet his, and she was no longer amused.

"Keep. Your. Voice. Down. Don't you dare blow this for me, Will. This is too important."

"You better start talking and making some sense, lady!" Will hissed between gritted teeth. "You better tell me what the fuck you did to me! You better tell me what the *fuck* is going on! No more games!"

"Look," she said. "Arthur is about to make a very big deal here, okay? He's meeting with someone, an even bigger scumbag. We've been looking for this guy for years, Will. I can't blow it tonight."

"What deal, drugs? And who is *we?*"

"Please, you'll just have to trust me."

"Trust *you*? Are you fucking kidding me?"

"Will, you *cannot* ruin this for me tonight. Too much is at stake!" Her resolve was cracking, her icy demeanor melting.

Will had had enough. He'd tried to be patient, to sit down and discuss this over a nice drink, but now it was time to play hardball. His hand went into his jacket and pulled out the Sig, slipping the compact 9mm under the table and into her side. Janae cringed in frustration, recognizing the check-mate.

"Okay," Will said, guzzling down the rest of his drink with his other hand. "Here's what we're gonna do. We're gonna walk calmly to the door, we're gonna go outside, and we're gonna find us a nice place to talk."

Janae's eyes locked in on Moonshine and Annette as they sauntered toward the bar, approaching Arthur and Jim. They met and shook hands.

Janae trembled in frustration.

"Will, don't do this. Please, you have no idea..."

"Well then, you can give me an idea. You can tell me everything. Every fucking thing."

"I will, I promise," she said, eyes darting between Will and her intended targets. Arthur chatted up Moonshine and Annette, pouring them shots and chugging them down, then waved for them to follow him. Janae watched as Arthur led them through the employees-only door, heading up a staircase. "I'll tell you everything. Trust me. But please, let me finish this. I have to..."

"Let's go. Get moving. Stand up nice and slow."

Will pushed the concealed carry pistol into her ribs,

indicating for her to stand. She gritted her teeth and finally obeyed, eyes staying with Arthur and his associates as they disappeared behind the private door. Will threw her jacket over the gun to conceal it, nudging her forward out of the dining area.

"Nice and slow," he said. "Stay in front of me."

"God damn it, Will. You don't know — "

"Just move your ass."

Will and Janae inched through the bustling room, dodging around drunks, cowboys and hipsters. The lights, smoke, clamor and noise threatened to split Will's skull in two; he couldn't think as long as he was in there. He guided her forward to the door, the cool, fresh air welcoming them.

Off in the gaming section, a large man stood at a pinball machine, playing a game. His back was turned to the room. A well-worn cowboy hat hung over his grizzled face. He turned to watch as Will and Janae left the building.

Mason smiled.

———

THE FIRST TONES OF YELLOW IN THE SKY MARKED the beginning of the sun's descent. Will did his best to look casual as he led Janae outside, his left hand holding onto her arm, his right pushing the gun into her ribs. He looked around at the surrounding area, his eyes settling on a vacant retail space across the street that used to be an Italian restaurant. A *for lease* sign hung in the crusty-old window, and Will smiled.

Perfect.

"Come on," he said, walking her across the street at a brisk pace. The foot traffic outside was minimal, but there were still potential witnesses who could see them.

He angled her around the side of the building, expecting to find a side or back door. And there it was, a loading dock in the back, complete with large, steel-shudder doors and one regular entryway. A padlock secured the door to its frame, but Will was not deterred.

"Stand back."

He kept his grip on her arm but held her out of the way. Stepping back, he launched a powerful front-kick into the door. The frame shook but held strong. Two more crashing kicks came, each more vicious and angry than the last, and the door finally blasted inwards in a shower of splinters.

Will shoved Janae inside the filthy, dark, empty restaurant space. A few tables remained standing, along with a handful of chairs, but the place had clearly been gutted.

"Drop your purse on the floor. Do it!"

Janae complied, and Will pushed her face-first into a wall, spreading her legs with a rough kick from his boot. "Now, don't move." Keeping his firearm trained on her back, he frisked her with his other hand, not bothering to be gentle.

"I have a gun in my purse," she said.

"And *this* in your boot. Very nice." Will pulled out a folding knife, tossing it to the floor. "Okay, now turn around."

She did as she was told, facing him, her back to the wall. He stepped back, eyes laser-focused on hers.

Silence throbbed in the dusty, dark space. Neither said anything, each waiting for the other to start.

Will gave in first.

"Speak words."

"What do you want to hear, Will?"

"The truth. What the hell did you do to me? No tricks."

"I fucked you, Will. Better than you ever had before. That's it. You did the rest."

"Keep talking."

Janae sighed. "You're different, Will. You were born this way. You can't tell me you haven't felt it. Something inside just isn't right, is it? Someone else is in there, living inside your skin, isn't there?"

YES.

"No..." Will stammered.

"Bullshit. You know I'm telling you the truth. And while we're wasting time in here, some serious shit is about to go down, and you're gonna fuck it all up. Now I've got to get back over there," she snarled and marched forward, but Will stepped back in her way, his gun coming up again.

"_What the fuck did you do to me? What am I?_"

"You're a skinner, Will. You have been since the day you were born! I had no idea when we spent the night together. I had no way of knowing until you changed... Now, I *will* tell you more! I'll tell you everything! But right now, I have *got to* get back in there! I can't let them get away!" She tried to storm past him, but he grabbed her arm and yanked her back, slamming her against the opposite wall.

"What the fuck is a skinner? W-What do you mean? Who are you working for? What... How did..." Will's mind raced, flipped, somersaulted and backflipped within his cranium. Janae raged, lunging at him again.

"I don't have time for this, Will!" The crescent kick blurred through the air before he could register it, and the sharp crack of her boot knocked the pistol out of his hand and into the gloom. "Now get out of my way!"

She followed the kick with a punch to the solar plexus, followed by an uppercut, sending a shower of sparks through his eyes. Will staggered back but caught her again, hurling her back into the vacuous space. She skittered across the floor, snarling and righting herself into a crouched pose, ready to spring.

LET ME OUT.

"Damn it, Shaw! Stop it! You don't know what you're doing!"

"No, but you know," he said, stalking towards her. "And you're going to tell me everything." He reached out to grab her, and she sprung forward, unleashing a rapid combination of punches at him. Two he blocked.

The third connected with his jaw, jarring him back again.

Rage flooded his veins. A familiar feeling made itself known. A knock at the door. Another presence within, trying to break free.

LET ME OUT.

"WHAT THE HELL AM I, JANAE?"

"I'll tell you everything, I promise! Just — "

"What the hell am I?"

He lunged at her again, his years of fight training useless in this emotional and confused state. She dodged to the side, a curved blade to his blunt weapon. She countered with several more blistering strikes, connecting to his face and body. He caught her last punch, kicking her legs out from under her and sending her to the floor with a *smack.*

Janae was up in a flash, kicking again, driving him back. The rage boiled within him, overflowing. The loss of control was imminent. The knocking at the door had become a crashing battering ram.

LET ME OUT!

WILL SURRENDERED. IT WAS EASIER THAN LAST TIME. He gave in to it, allowing his human self to fall back into the floating ether, and something else to fall forward into his place. There was a blur, a glimmer, a refracting of light. Will slipped out.

The beast slipped in.

Within seconds, the change was complete, leaving Will standing nearly seven feet-tall; a powerful, muscular black jaguar, he glowered down at the puny girl before him.

His yellow eyes gleamed and his mighty jaws split open to release a roar of nearly industrial depth and resonance. So low and rumbling was his guttural growl, it would feel at home in a steel mill or the engine of a freight train.

He lashed out, backhanding Janae and sending her across the room. She smacked into the far wall, sliding to the ground with a wince of pain.

Will stomped forward, drunk on his own power. Janae brought herself back up into a crouching position, ready to pounce. Will closed the distance, an imposing and vicious animal. Long fangs salivated, ready to sink into dark flesh.

Curved claws flexed, ready to rip and tear. He bunched himself up, springing forward through the air, diving at her with a booming roar.

Janae changed.

Before Will's black beast could land on its prey, a glimmer ran through Janae's body. A warping of light and matter. A transition from one sphere of existence to another. Janae leapt up, dainty flesh hands reaching out to grab Will's wrists; by the time she planted her feet, feet had become paws. Hands had become claws.

She stood nearly as tall as him, a jungle leopard, tail thrashing, fangs gnashing.

She gripped his wrists, stopping his charge, looking into his yellow eyes with her sparkling greens, and roared right back at him. Will disengaged, jumping back a step and circling to observe her better.

Her gold and white coat glistened in the light, adorned with a pattern of black spots and rosettes. Her muscles were strong and slender, but not as bulky as his. She circled along with him, her movements sleek and smooth. The distinct thought occurred to him deep in his cat brain, that she was even sexier now.

"Will, stop it!"

The words did not come from Janae's mouth, now a maw of dripping fangs, but from her eyes. Will stopped short, surprised and confused. *How did she do that?*

"Will, I need you to calm down."

It must be some kind of a trick, the black cat reasoned. More trickery that he wouldn't fall for. He snarled and lunged at her again, swiping with deadly claws. She dodged left, dodged right, ducked under a slash and then circled him again.

"I know you're in there, Will. Please listen to me..."

Will dove forward, knocking her to the floor and pinning her down. He lunged at her throat, fangs straining for flesh. Janae pushed up, then slashed across his stomach with her own claws, knocking him off and jumping back to her feet.

"Will! Please listen to me! I know you can hear me!"

The black jaguar was on his feet again, four bloody claw-marks across his stomach. He snarled, inching forward. Janae circled and dodged, taking a non-threatening posture. Her claws retracted into their sheaths and she held them out to the side. Her green eyes were wide and pleading.

"Will, it's me, please! It's Janae. Stop. Please."

He heard her voice.

Will heard her voice, not the cat. He was still in there, still piloting this monster, if only from its deepest subconscious. His breathing slowed. His snarl faded into a confused wonder. Janae could see his posture was changing, becoming less threatening.

"There you go, Will," she said. "There you go. It's okay. Let's not fight. Just calm down... There you go."

Will stopped, catching his breath.

He looked at her, baffled. With a ripple of light, he saw her image warp. The leopard began to waver and fade, and within seconds, it was gone. The change was rapid and smooth, and Janae had skinned back to her human form as effortlessly as taking off a jacket.

The black jaguar towered over her, stupefied.

"Come back to me, Will," Janae whispered, holding her hands out. "I'll tell you everything. I promise. Just... Come on back. You can do it. Come on back..."

Will stood perplexed. Deep inside, he floated somewhere in a warm, comfortable and fuzzy place. He was a dreamer, becoming aware of the dream. He knew what he had to do, but didn't know how. He looked down at himself, at his muscular, black-furred body, at his paws, trying to solve the puzzle.

"Just let it go, Will. Just relax and fall back. Just let the change happen. Just fall back into it."

Will closed his eyes, took a deep breath. *Yes, just fall back. Surrender. Let the cat fall back. Let the cat fall away, slip away...* He felt a vacuum, a gust of wind. A transport from one place to another. Shadows and light bent around him, one reality drifted into the next.

Will Shaw was himself again.

Janae smiled at him. Will was amazed, dumbfounded. There was a pain in his midsection and he looked down to see blood staining the front of his shirt. He lifted the garment to reveal four shallow claws marks, oozing crimson blood. Janae cringed as she approached him, tenderly touching his face.

"Sorry about that," she said.

"What... What's happening to me, Janae?" Will whispered.

"I'll tell you everything. I promise."

She pulled him in to a tight embrace. Will wrapped his arms around her, holding on to what was solid and tangible. His whole world was spinning, and his rage had given way to wonder and confusion. They held each other tight for what felt like forever.

Clap. Clap. Clap.

"That was awesome!"

Will and Janae turned with a start as the gruff voice came from the shadows, followed by a large, well-built man in an old cowboy hat. He chuckled as he stopped beside Will's fallen pistol, picking it up with a smile.

"Sig. Nice."

Will's heart began to sink. A door opened within him, fear and dread peaking in at him from the other side.

Janae froze, all muscles tensed. They both watched as the imposing figure strutted through the maze of shadows.

His hair was long and black, with streaks of gray at his temples and chin. His physique was strong and thick beneath a redneck wardrobe facade. His skin was a leathery, dark copper. His eyes were deep in shadow. His features were chiseled from American Indian clay.

"Mason," Janae clenched her jaw in recognition.

The dark figure stopped, tipping his hat.

"Ma'am..." His eyes settled on Will and his lips pulled into a thin smile. "Hey Will," Mason said. "How ya' doin', buddy?"

19

THE PACK

FLASHES OF MEMORIES —

"WILL! COME ON!"

PAPAW SQUEEZES TIGHT. LIFTING OFF THE GROUND. RUNNING THROUGH SMOKE. OUT THE WINDOW. ONTO THE FRONT LAWN. HOUSE IS BURNING. PAPAW IS CRYING. WON'T LET GO.

LAUGHTER FROM WITHIN.

TURNING INTO A HOWL.

Mason stepped forward into a shaft of light.

Janae inched back, reaching out for Will.

"Will, come on..." Her words fell on deaf ears.

Will stared stupefied at the tall stranger before him in

the dim, empty space. His voice was familiar, his face almost like looking in a mirror.

But something was different. The energy around the man, that new element of consciousness that had become a fixture in Will's psyche, was unlike anything he'd seen. It was a swirling blackness mottled with the deep red of dried, old blood. The stranger stood in this blackness; it was a cloud lingering around him.

It felt tainted and sick.

"Who... Who are you?" Will said.

"I have to thank you for bringin' him to me, Ms. Jones," Mason said, circling them, Will's pistol in his hand. "Other than that, you have been quite a pain in my ass."

"Fuck you."

"Oh, come on," Mason said. "Fuck me? That the best you can do? I thought you were supposed to be all clever and witty. I'm disappointed."

"Yeah well, I'm happy to disappoint you, Mason."

"Mason..." Will whispered.

"Naw, you're just scared," Mason said, strutting around them. "You know what we're gonna do to you."

"Same thing you do to all those innocent children, you piece of *shit*?" Janae's words were a hiss.

"I don't know what she's told you, Will. But you can bet your ass it's a lie." Mason sauntered closer, within arm's reach. A creeping sensation moved through Will's guts as he looked into the man's dark eyes. "I've been looking for you a long time. Heard you joined the Army right after high school. Kind of fell off the map after that."

"Mason..."

"Then I heard you did some time," Mason said with an amused chuckle. "Not such a Boy Scout after all, huh?"

"You stay away from him, Mason! We are gonna take you and your whole little crew down, you—"

"Shut your hole, bitch," Mason snarled. "I'll deal with you in a minute."

Janae shot a glance over to her purse, on the floor less than ten feet away. Her gun was inside, and her keys. A muscle flexed in her jaw, her mind racing.

Mason's head cocked to the side, smiling as three shadows emerged from the darkness behind him. "Hey guys, welcome to the party."

Moonshine, Annette and TJ closed in, forming a half circle around Will and Janae. TJ snickered and cracked his knuckles. Moonshine chewed on a lump of dip. Annette fixed on Janae with cold, lifeless eyes.

"It's all done, Mase," Moonshine said. "The product has been unloaded."

"Thank you, 'Shine. And the money?"

"It's in the truck," Annette's voice was as cold as her eyes. She stared at Janae with contempt.

"*Product*. You fuckers make me sick." Janae's body was tense, seething at them as they closed in.

Will looked at each of the gang, veiled in shadows, finding them all to have a similar energy as Mason. Dark, twisted, sick. He barely knew Janae and had no reason to trust her, but it did not take long to decide which side he was on.

"Guys, would you take care of Ms. Jones for me,

please?" Mason said. "I think me and Will here need to have us a little talk."

"With pleasure," TJ said.

He began to change.

Waves of heat distortion flowed across TJ's body, and Will watched in amazement as the same warping of light flickered across Annette and Moonshine as well. Will and Janae inched back as the three cretins stretched and grew into inhuman beasts.

Moonshine's new form was a towering, brown wolf, snarling at them with dripping teeth and blue eyes. His coat was russet and beige, his musculature thick and full. There was no humanity left in his face; his head was all wolf, all predator. He stepped forward, ready to pounce.

TJ had morphed into something very similar, yet his back curved into an arching hunch leading to a cranium with a short snout and rounded ears. He yipped and snarled behind crazed eyes, a twisted convergence of man and hyena. His muscles flexed beneath a black-and-tan spotted coat, peppered with nicks and scars from a life of brutality.

Annette's human form had slithered away into something that truly made Will's stomach squirm. She had become the offspring of human and viper, her powerful form shielded with a pattern of black and neon-green scales, clawed hands and feet, and an extended, reptilian neck. A black tongue flicked between her dripping fangs, her unblinking, giant-black eyes staring at them like easy prey.

The serpent issued an evil hiss.

"Ho...lee...God..." The words barely croaked from between Will's lips as the three horrors closed in.

"Go ahead, guys," Mason said with a menacing smile. "Take 'er in the back and finish 'er. Scrape 'er fuckin' bones clean, 'Shine." The beasts snarled as they stalked toward Janae, Moonshine smiling through his wolf's muzzle. Janae's body was tense. She stood on her toes, ready to spring.

The gun in Mason's hand was trained casually at Will's midsection, confident in his dominance. He was within arm's reach. Will saw the barrel of the pistol, so close.

NEVER POINT YOUR SIDEARM AT YOUR OPPONENT FROM WITHIN A DISTANCE OF THREE FEET, PRIVATE! WAY TOO EASY FOR ME TO DO THIS —

WILL DIDN'T HAVE TO THINK ABOUT IT.

With his hand-to-hand combat instructor's voice ringing in his memory, his hand reflexively flew to the barrel of the Sig. He pushed, then pulled, then twisted. He used leverage and speed, taking Mason by surprise and knocking him back to the floor with a *thud*.

The gun was Will's again, and before he knew it, it was singing its favorite song.

Pop!Pop!Pop!Pop!Pop!

His shattered nerves did nothing to help Will's accuracy, but the lead slugs ripped through the air at their beastly targets, driving them away for cover. The viper-woman took a round in her side, grabbing the stinging wound as she took cover behind the dining counter.

Moonshine and TJ ducked behind stone pillars and Mason kicked across the floor to take cover behind the wall leading to the kitchen.

Janae lunged for her purse, rolling across the dusty floor and scooping it up in one fluid motion. Her hand reached in and instantly came out with a Kimber 9mm compact 1911 semi-automatic.

"Go! Go!" Janae pushed Will toward the front windows as the snarling beasts inched back out from their hiding places. A deep rumbling came from the kitchen area and Will looked to see what was emerging.

A giant wolf lurched on two feet, its coat black and gray. Mason. A Timber-wolf. His fur was peppered with scars. His eyes blazed yellow. They burned into Will's heart as he kept his pistol trained at the room.

"*Come on!*" Janae shouted.

She fired two shots into the front window, shattering the glass into a crackling spiderweb pattern. She wrenched a dusty-old chair off the floor with a grunt, hurling it into the bullet holes she'd punched through.

The chair crashed through the glass and onto the sidewalk outside, a shower of tinkling shards exploding outward with it.

She flew through the shattered window, Will close behind. The Ducati was directly across the street in the pool hall's parking lot, and she powered straight for it.

A handful of bar-goers milling around outside converged at the sound of gunfire and smashing glass.

They watched as the two figures ran across the road at full speed, guns in hand.

"Hurry! Get on!" Janae said, leaping onto the bike and starting it in one fluid motion. Will did not argue. She threw on her helmet, kicked the starter and revved the engine awake with a roar.

"Hold on!"

20

THE TUNNEL

JANAE AND WILL ZOOMED off into the sunset.

Still in his wolf-form, Moonshine ran over to Annette; she hissed and clutched her wound. The cold blood oozed from her scaly skin. Moonshine snarled, his fangs dripping. Mason and TJ were already running out toward the street, skinning back into their human selves.

"Move it!" Mason said, jumping through the window.

"You okay, baby?" Moonshine asked Annette.

"I'm fine! Come on!"

She lurched to her feet, and he helped her out of the dark restaurant and into the street. Four human figures emerged onto the roadway, watching the red tail-lights of the Ducati disappearing in the distance. Mason snarled and ran around the corner, where their panel van waited, jumping in and starting the engine.

"*Let's go!*" Mason snapped as TJ and Annette leapt into the back of the van. Moonshine jumped onto a red Harley Road-King and started up its growling engine. "Nobody lays a *fucking finger* on him, you got that?"

Moonshine didn't answer, revving the engine, fire in his eyes. *"'Shine, you got that?"*

Moonshine sped off down the street after Will and Janae, thirsty for blood. Mason hit the gas and the van screeched out of its parking space, joining the chase.

"WHAT THE FUCK WERE THOSE THINGS?" WILL SAID.

Janae swerved the bike around two cars as Will clutched her midsection. The last reds of the day sank under the horizon.

*"Shitshitshitshitshit!"*Janae swerved down a side street, heading for the freeway. "Saw my face... *Fuck!"*

"Hey, god damn it! What the fuck were those things?"

"They're skinners! Like us!" Even screaming, they could barely hear each other over the sound of the roaring motorcycle and traffic.

"What the fuck is a skinner?"

"Skinwalkers! Shapeshifters!" Janae powered the bike up the on-ramp, swerving around traffic as she surged up onto the highway.

"But what... How...?" Will's head spun.

"We're all born with an animal spirit, Will! But us skinners are the only ones who can *access* it!"

Will turned to look behind them. A motorcycle and a van roared up hard on their tail.

"They're coming!"

"HEY, BUDDY."

. . .

Will wanted nothing more than to turn his brain off. To stop the cacophony of thoughts and sights and sounds. Memories fluttered in his eyes as horns blared and brakes screeched.

Janae pissed off every driver on the road and caused multiple accidents in her wake as she charged ahead, cutting left and right. She streaked around a lumbering eighteen-wheeler, then cut right in front of it, speeding up. Will looked back.

Their pursuers were gaining.

Moonshine sped up, matching Janae's aggressive driving as he thundered after them. Mason, TJ and Annette struggled to keep up in the van, the boxy tin can nowhere near as lithe as the two motorcycles.

Mason snarled. He could tell that Moonshine was out for blood. "God damn it, 'Shine!" He said, punching the wheel.

Janae dodged and weaved.

She picked up speed, flying onto the exit for highway 153. The wheels left the ground as they shot up the ramp, flying, then smashed back down. Will held on tight. He looked back again.

The red Harley was right behind them. Moonshine came up within striking distance, weaving around to their right flank.

"Watch out!"

Janae barely had time to react as Moonshine sideswiped them. He lunged out with a knife in his left hand, missing. Janae and Will wobbled and weaved, but stayed on two wheels.

"*Shit!*"

Will held on with his left hand and drew his Sig. He squeezed off two rounds, and Moonshine ducked back and fell behind. He sheathed his knife, then pulled out a gun of his own.

"*Look out!*" Will shouted as Moonshine took aim.

Pop! Pop! Pop! Moonshine's shots went wild.

Janae surprised them both with a yank of the handlebars, sending the Ducati off the exit and towards Wilcox Avenue. Moonshine wobbled and swerved, but followed.

Behind him, Mason pushed the van forward to its limits, charging up towards Moonshine. He got right up against the Harley's back wheel and angrily pushed his weight onto the horn.

"*God damn it, 'Shine! I said don't hurt him, you dumb fuck!*" Mason nearly smashed into Moonshine's bike and knocked him off the road. Annette's cold eyes showed a flicker of worry as Mason threatened to crush her lover beneath the van's wheels.

"Don't kill him, Mase..." she cringed.

Moonshine threw up a middle finger behind him, aimed at Mason, then zoomed off out of range. Mason's teeth clenched and his eyes flared with yellow.

"Son of a bitch..."

Up ahead, Janae swerved around a pickup truck towing another pickup truck, nearly lost her balance, but kept blasting ahead. Concrete and cars and lights blurred past. She looked back to see Moonshine still coming up on their tail.

"We gotta lose 'em, fast!" she shouted. *"Before the cops show up! If they get a chopper on us, we're finished!"*

Will had no arguments with that.

Up ahead, Janae saw the Wilcox tunnel rapidly approaching. It was a tiny, round, concrete tube, decorated with colorful murals from top to bottom, and despite looking like it was barely big enough for one Prius to pass through, somehow it accommodated two lanes of traffic and a narrow walkway.

A steady stream of cars and trucks flowed through the extremely tight space, sideview mirrors under constant threat of being sheared off.

Janae braced herself and sped up.

Moonshine sped up. He aimed his gun.

Pop! Pop! Pop!

Janae sped and swerved. Will turned and fired his gun. The bullets went wild. Two cars crashed behind Moonshine, and Mason swerved the van to get around them.

Moonshine got alongside Will and Janae. He tried to shoot, but Will reached out and grabbed him.

"I'm gonna tear your fucking throats out!" Moonshine salivated, nearly transforming right there on his bike.

They struggled, yanking at each other as their bikes soared at high speeds. Will pulled Moonshine in, headbutting him and sending him back. Moonshine's gun went airborne.

"Hang on!"

Janae shot into the tunnel.

She zipped around cars in both lanes. Horns honked

and echoed within the tight, concrete tube. Moonshine raged forward, matching her zig for zag.

Janae saw two trucks ahead, approaching each other in opposing lanes. A small window to get through was closing between them. Her whole body tensed and hunkered down as she squirted through the tight hole, barely making it to the other side.

Moonshine was not so lucky.

The two trucks skidded and crashed into each other, creating a wall of metal in front of him. He hit the brakes and flew headlong into the side of the first truck with a bone-pulverizing smash, then crashed into the windshield of the other.

His Harley soared through the air, hitting the upper curve of the tunnel. Sparks blazed as the wrecked bike scraped through to the other side of the wreckage.

Janae and Will flashed off into the night.

Mason skidded to a halt.

All traffic was stopped. The passage was completely sealed off with the wreckage of twisted metal and broken glass. Annette looked through the windshield, her mouth agape.

Mason jumped out of the van. Annette and TJ followed as he approached the trail of wreckage leading to where Moonshine lay motionless in a streak of blood.

"'Sh-'Shine...?" Annette croaked.

Mason approached the scene, the sounds of car horns and screaming civilians mere ambient tones in the background. The faint sound of police sirens approached in the distance. On the ground were skid marks. Glass. Bits of metal. Blood.

The drivers of the two trucks that collided had gotten out, dumbfounded. They stumbled around the wreckage, trying to make sense of what happened.

"Hey man, you okay?" one truck driver said to the other.

"Yeah... What happened?"

"That bike just cut in front a' me! Came outta' nowhere!"

Mason followed the blood.

On the pavement in front of the massive wreck was a quivering shape. It was a man, or what was left of one.

Moonshine lay twisted and broken, choking on the syrupy blood oozing out of his mouth. His back was broken, and his skull cracked. His arms and legs were shattered. The flesh on the whole left side of his head was torn away from the skull like a half-peeled blood orange. The coppery smell of gore intermingled with gasoline and motor oil.

"S-Sorry... Mase..." Moonshine sputtered.

"Fucking idiot." Mason knelt down, sizing him up.

One of the truck drivers called out to Mason, "Hey man! We gotta call for help!"

Mason whipped his gaze up at the man with wolf-yellow eyes, snarling in a deep animal tone. The man's face drooped in fear and he ran the other way, dragging the other driver with him.

Annette stopped in her tracks, hands coming up to her mouth. Cold tears were in her eyes. TJ held onto her arm in case she passed out. The police sirens were getting closer.

"'Shine!... Oh my God, 'Shine!"

Annette tried to go to him, but TJ held her back.

"You know what I gotta do," Mason said.

"D-Do it," Moonshine gurdled through blood.

Mason reached down and gripped Moonshine's throat. As he squeezed, a glimmer ran through his arm. Bronze flesh warped away into a large, muscular limb, lined with gray fur. Strong claws grew through his fingers and dug deep into Moonshine's throat.

With one stiff yank, Mason ripped away the soft tissue and hot blood spouted from the wound. Moonshine's body spasmed, bleeding out onto the pavement.

Death came quickly.

Mason's arm melted back to its human state as he stood up and shook the blood from his fingertips. Annette sobbed as Mason casually walked past them back to the van.

"Let's go."

21

LICKING WOUNDS

THE SHOWER PRESSURE WAS STRONG, the water hot.

Will cleaned himself up in the room they had rented at the Red Roof Inn. He watched as his blood rinsed off of his body, flowing down through the drain. Hot water hit the four parallel scratches across his stomach, and he winced at the sting.

His ears still rang from gunshots. The aromas of gas, burnt rubber and human gore lingered in his sinuses. Images of monsters and devils danced in his eyes. Janae had gone out for supplies, leaving him alone with his thoughts. And memories.

"HEY, BUDDY."

THAT SMILE, THOSE EYES.

Will could not turn his brain off and he feared it

might explode at any minute. He held up his right arm, noting that the gator's teeth-marks were starting to scab over. The scratches in his stomach were fresh, but had stopped bleeding.

He turned the water off, convinced he had gone insane, but at least he was clean. He stepped out of the shower to towel off. It was time to take his Paroxetine, and he was glad he'd brought it with him.

He heard the front door squeak open in the main room and knew it was her. He wrapped the towel around his waist and stepped out to greet her. Janae was there with plastic bags in hand, locking the door.

"Hey," he said.

"Hi, sexy."

Janae tossed her jacket on the bed along with the two plastic bags. She pulled out bandages, sterile pads, hydrogen peroxide, cotton balls, Neosporin and tape. From the second bag, she produced a three-pack of Hanes plain-white t-shirts, tossing it to him.

"Oh yeah," she said. "And we can't forget these." She pulled one last item from the bag, a pack of Gummi-Worms, and threw that over as well. "Can't believe you eat that shit."

"Bite me," Will said, tearing into the packaging and throwing a sugary, rainbow-colored worm into his mouth.

"Let's get you patched up, shall we?"

Will stepped closer, looking at his wound.

"You think it'll need stitches?" He asked.

"Nah," she said, taking a closer look. "They're not too deep. And besides, we heal pretty fast." She began to arrange and open the wound-care products as she sat on the bed in front of him.

"And by *we*, you mean... skinners?"

"That's right."

"So, you scratched me when I was... That cat, the panther. And now I'm normal, and I still..."

"Your wounds carry over, yeah. If your spirit animal gets hurt or dies, so do you. And vice versa." Janae opened the peroxide and began applying it to a cotton ball.

"Spirit animal..."

"Yours is a black jaguar. Mine is a leopard. Everybody has one, Will. Every single human being on the planet has a spirit animal. It's connected to us, like... Tethered. It goes where we go, just on a different plane of existence."

"Jesus... *Ahh!*" Will cringed as Janae began to apply the stinging peroxide to his wounds. He popped another Gummi-Worm into his mouth, chewing. "But the skin-walker is a *Navajo* legend. They're supposed to be evil witches, or something. Not..."

"It's more complicated than that. A skinner is just a person who can connect with their animal spirit, to call it into this plane. Most of us go our whole lives not even knowing we can connect, never making the change."

"So then why is it that all of a sudden, this is happening to me? I'm thirty-eight."

"Well, there's a couple ways a dormant skinner can be awakened. One is to be bitten by a full skinner, of course. And the other..."

"To make love," Will finished, shaking his head.

"To *fuck*," Janae corrected.

She made sure to disinfect his wounds completely, then blew a stream of cool air on them. They made eye contact and smiled. "I've been tracking this gang for years," she said. "They never stay in one place too long. I traced them here... And then I found you."

"Tell me about them."

"They call themselves The Pack."

"And what are they into? Drugs?"

"Much worse. Human trafficking. Children."

Will's gaze hardened as he looked down at her. Her countenance was serious and grim, and he knew she was telling the truth. She opened the bottle of Neosporin and began applying it to his wounds as she continued.

"You wouldn't believe how many sick bastards are out there, Will. People looking to buy kids, sell them into prostitution, sell them overseas... Every year, hundreds of children, *babies*... Snatched up. Never seen again..."

"How are you involved in this?"

Janae sighed. "I was one of those kids, Will. Years ago. I was an orphan. Lived in foster care, going from house to house... Then one day these people came to the house where I was staying. They killed my foster parents, took me..."

"*What?* How did you get away?"

"A great man came and rescued me. Brought me home to a new family... He taught me the truth, showed me who I was."

"And who is that?"

Janae finished with the ointment, putting the tube aside and looking him in the eye. "There is a balance that has to be maintained. Skinners are supposed to be the spiritual guardians of this Earth, protecting that balance. We are not allowed to interfere with the natural world, to prey on humans, or let our secret be known. But sometimes, a skinner comes along and defies that balance, and we have to deal with them."

"So basically, you *are* a cop."

Janae smiled, opening the box of sterile pads. "Something like that," she said.

"So, The Pack... They're interfering with your balance."

"Their leader is... the darkest soul I have ever met," she said, starting to apply the pads over Will's wounds. "He's cruel, he's sadistic and he's utterly insane... His name is Mason."

"HEY, BUDDY."

"HE STARTED THIS LITTLE GANG ABOUT TWENTY years ago. He found other dormant skinners — sick fuckers like him — And changed them all. Brought them under his wing, started a little business." Janae taped the bandages in place, gritting her teeth as she relayed the painful story.

"Like most human trafficking rings, they abduct and sell children on the black market. But The Pack doesn't sell everyone they catch. No... They keep some of the kids for themselves... *To feed on!*"

"Oh my God," said Will, squeezing his eyes closed.

"I've been after them for years, and I've found too many dead children, Will... Too many. Little bodies torn to pieces... Buried in shallow graves, or just tossed over a bridge..." Tears burned in Janae's eyes as the memories came to her. "They are upsetting the balance and they're threatening to expose us all. And I for one am *not* about to let one more innocent baby die."

"That's why you were at that pool hall."

"That's right. Mason has *got* to be stopped. He's cold, he's brutal, he's fucking *evil*, he's..."

"HEY, BUDDY."

"My brother," Will finished.

Janae looked up at him, eyes wide. In just saying the words out loud, the truth resonated in him. Mason's eyes, his smile, his voice, the way he walked... It reminded him of his father. The fragmented memories of childhood fluttered in his head.

His father's cocky strut, his mother's booming laugh. Playing in the backyard with toy trucks, a toddler, with an older boy running around him, laughing. He had dimples too, and the same dark hair and skin.

He would burn ants with a magnifying glass and shoot his slingshot at squirrels and gophers. His mother would call out: *"Mason, keep an eye on your brother!"* Mason... Mason.

"He's my brother," Will repeated, opening his eyes.

Janae finished bandaging Will's wounds, standing up

to face him. "Are you sure?" she said. He nodded. "So that's why he's here. You were released from prison, and now he's looking for you. Trying to recruit you into his sick little gang. And then of course, I ran into you too, and we..."

"I'm glad you found me before he did," Will said.

"So am I."

She drew closer to him. Their eyes met, their lips wanting to kiss. She reached out and touched his hand, looking down at his arm, the bite wound still raw. "Here, bandage up your arm. Then put your clothes on."

"Wait, where are we going?"

"Back to the pool hall," she said, throwing her jacket back on. "Mason dropped off a van full of kids with Arthur, his distributor here. Those kids might still be there. It might not be too late."

22

BACK FOR BLOOD

JIM REID SECURED the final lock in the back door of Chattanooga Billiards and lit up a Chesterfield. He was a tall, sturdy, barrel-chested man, a graying military haircut and a close-cropped beard over a lantern jaw. It had been a long day, and it was not over yet.

Arthur had just brought in a new shipment of cargo, and now that night had crept into its deepest hours, it was time to unload. Jim paced in small circles and leaned against the driver's door of a parked, gray panel van, enjoying his cigarette under the single streetlight that illuminated the dank alley. The pre-dawn world was silent and all the lost souls had crawled back to their holes for the night.

The growl of a motorcycle passed through the dark.

A rider on the main street, the growl faded and finally cut out, leaving Jim in relaxed silence again. He took another drag from his cigarette and kicked at a bottle cap. The next sound that registered in his ears was footsteps. Two sets, coming closer, people walking on the sidewalk out front.

He expected whoever it was to just walk on by, like everyone else, but two silhouetted figures stopped when they reached the head of the alley. A man and a woman. They turned and walked toward him.

Jim's pulse skipped. He stopped pacing and played it cool. His nickel-plated Sig Sauer P320 reminded him of its presence in his shoulder holster. The two figures drew in closer. The man was tall with short-cropped hair and a leather jacket that accentuated his powerful shoulders. The woman was sleek and lithe, the streetlights catching in her short, punk-rock afro.

Will and Janae stepped into the light.

"We're closed," Jim said.

Janae smiled as she drew closer. "We're here to see Arthur." Will flanked Jim, hands crossed in front of him. Jim noted the serious glare in the eyes of the tall Indian.

"Arthur's gone for the night."

"You must be Jim."

"Uh... Do I know you guys?"

"No, Jim. But we know you." Her eyes were hypnotic caverns, drawing him into their depths.

"Look, get out of here, little girl. You too, chief. Don't make me have to fuck you up." Jim puffed out his chest as he stood his ground.

"Can I get a cigarette?" She asked, the edges of her lips pulling back into a heart-shaped smirk. Jim resisted, but those eyes kept pulling at him. He produced his pack of Chesterfields without even thinking, and passed her one.

"Light me up?"

Jim obliged, sparking his Zippo and lighting the smoke for her. She took a puff and exhaled a sensual cloud into the light. Will watched with fascinated interest. "Wh-Who are you guys...?" Jim said.

"We're your employers, Jim."

"Look, I work for Arthur. Ya'll better get out of — "

"And Arthur works for us," Janae said. "Go ahead and pass me your sidearm, would you?" Will shot a doubtful glance at her nonchalant request, but in an instant, the bewitched Jim had produced the weapon.

"Okay," he said, passing it over.

Janae passed the Sig over to Will, who tucked it into his belt, impressed with her talent. Janae took another drag from her Chesterfield, then flicked it off into the alley.

"Now," she said, "take us upstairs. We want to see the cargo and talk to Arthur."

"A-Arthur isn't here," Jim resisted. "He..."

"Yes he is."

"Yes he is," Jim repeated.

"Let's go upstairs."

"Okay." He was hers.

Jim took the key ring from his pocket and unlocked the back door. Will saw the car keys attached to the ring and held out his hand.

"That's your van, huh?" said Will. "I'll take those keys."

"What?" Jim snapped. "Fuck you, man!"

"Give him the keys." Janae's voice soothed and reassured.

"Okay..." And just like that, Jim passed the keys.

Will smiled and pocketed the keyring as they all went inside and closed the door behind them.

Above the pool hall was where Arthur Wyckoff did his real business. He sat behind a luxurious desk facing a panel of LCD security monitors. He puffed on a fat Cohiba cigar and drank a double of Gentleman Jack whiskey from a fine crystal glass. Across from his desk was a two-way mirrored wall at a forty-five degree angle, overlooking the billiards club below. From there, he could sit in his bird's nest and survey his world.

Round glasses rested on his round nose. His head was shaved to the brown skin. A garish, green bowtie had been loosened after a long day, and hung around the shoulders of his purple, silk dress shirt. A framed photo of him with his wife and kids sat on his desk.

Arthur smiled as he sat at his throne, adding up the numbers for the day.

Footsteps came up the stairs. Arthur swigged down the rest of his drink and stood up. He snatched the jacket from the back of his chair, preparing to leave.

"You ready yet?" Arthur said. "Let's go, playa'. It's a long ride to Savannah."

The door opened and Jim walked in, followed by Will and Janae. Arthur stopped, his eyes wide.

"What's in Savannah?" Janae asked.

"Who the...?"

Arthur froze in place as the two strangers took positions flanking Jim. The tall Cherokee had a gun in his hand. The confident young black woman had a smile on her lips.

"Is that where you sell the kids off to your buyer?" she asked, circling towards Arthur. He stayed behind his desk, his fingertips grazing the sawed-off shotgun underneath.

"She said... she... we work for them..." Jim's mind was in a fog, trying to piece together what was happening. Arthur snarled at his ignorance.

"What did you do, you idiot?"

"He's just doing what he's told," Janae said, her eyes burning into him. Arthur gripped the shotgun under his desk. "Hands where I can see them, Arthur."

The man snarled and obeyed her order.

Will nearly choked on the energy coming from the two men. Rancid and filthy. Black and moldy. There was no compassion in them that he could sense. Only greed. They were evil to the bone, but Will did not detect an animal presence, as he did with the others. "They're not skinners," Will said mostly to himself.

"Nah, they're just men," Janae said. "Just sick, twisted, piece-of-shit men."

"Who are you?" Arthur demanded. "What do you want?"

"You don't remember me, Arthur? I guess you wouldn't recognize me now that I'm all grown up. And there's been so many, hasn't there?" She crossed in front of him, fingers stroking the top of his desk.

Jim's senses were coming more into focus, his trance starting to dissipate. Sensing a threat, he lunged at Janae.

"Hey, wait a second, bitch!"

A strong, copper-tone fist cracked into Jim's ribs, and the henchman gasped in red, searing pain. Will could feel the bones snap behind his strike. He grabbed Jim by the back of the neck and shoved him to his knees.

"Stay down, you piece of shit."

Arthur's eyes were panicked, and he lunged for the shotgun in desperation. But Janae was a blur over the desk, switch-kicking him across the bridge of his nose, sending his glasses into the opposite wall and reeling him back over his throne. His full weight crashed to the floor with a shuddering thud, and Janae's boot stomped down on his clavicle.

"Twenty years ago. New Jersey. You were thinner then. You had hair..." Janae held back her rage as the flesh peddler groaned on the floor beneath her. "You weren't the boss-man back then. Just a grunt. But I remember you. I remember the day you *sold* me off... To be *raped! And tortured!*"

The leopard hungered to come out. It strained and trembled within her. Its growl rumbled in her throat. Its emerald eyes flashed within hers.

"Jesus, Lord... *You're the devil!*"

"That's right," said Janae. "And I've come to take you to hell." She stomped down on his face, shattering his nose beneath her heel. Arthur wailed and convulsed, and Jim once again jumped forward to help him.

"Arthur!"

Will swept Jim's legs out from under him, smashing him to the floor. He trained the X-Macro on his face, finger ready to squeeze. Janae held up her hand.

"Wait... Where are the kids?" Janae looked around, gesturing towards a locked door at the far end of the room. "In there?"

Arthur shook his head, quivering as she stood up, crossing the room to reach the door. She pressed her hand against the cool wood, but sensed nothing living behind the barrier. "No, not here..." Janae turned back to face Arthur, eyes on fire. "I know. They're in the *basement*, aren't they? Nobody hears 'em cry down there, police choppers with infrared can't see 'em..."

"Fuck you... Fuck you!"

"Who is your guy in Savannah?"

"P-Please... I don't know what you're talking —"

Janae roared, her face sliding into that of her spirit animal for an instant. Fangs bared, eyes blazed green and her snarl was thunder echoing through the room. Arthur gasped as the leopard warped back into Janae's face.

Jim whimpered on the floor, Will's gun never wavering from its aim between his eyes.

"Who is your guy in Savannah?"

"Oh, please! Oh, Jesus lord! *What are you?*"

"You better start talking, nigga'." Janae could barely restrain the leopard, and Arthur watched in horror as it flickered in and out of reality. Her fists clenched and opened, hooked claws sliding out, then disappearing again.

"I'd do what the lady says, asshole." Will's beast wanted to come out to play as well. But he shuddered, still afraid of it, fearful of losing control. Losing himself.

Janae reached down with both hands and yanked the

large man off the ground with unnatural strength. She seethed in his face, the tears in her eyes demanding answers.

"Talk."

"It-It's not just one guy! It's a whole network! Th-They use the railroads and shipping freighters! S-Send cargo all over the country, all over the world!"

"*Cargo...*" Janae hissed the word. "Who is the top guy?"

"P-Please! I can't! I — "

"Will?" Janae looked over her shoulder at him.

Knowing what she wanted, Will hesitated. He had taken life many times before. But not like this. If anyone deserved to die, it was this man, this destroyer of inno-cence — but he was no executioner. Janae saw him waver, and pulled out her own pistol, aiming it between Jim's eyes without a second thought.

She squeezed the trigger.

Thunder cracked through the room and Jim's head erupted in a spray of deep, crimson blood and gray brain matter. Will gasped, stunned. Arthur yelped, his ears ringing as Jim's dead body continued to twitch.

"H-Hendricks! Roy Hendricks!" Arthur said, weeping and trembling. "Their operation is huge! It's-it's global! You don't know what you're getting yourself into! Oh, God! Oh, *Jesus!*"

"You pray to Jesus all you want," Janae said, lifting Arthur off his feet and putting her face right up to his. "But Jesus *ain't* coming to save you."

Her ebony features melted into the snarling muzzle of the jungle beast. Her hands flickered away into large, powerful claws, digging deep into the flesh of his chest. The leopard queen stood tall, lifting the crying man over her head.

His blood ran through her talons, staining his nice purple shirt. She made sure the last thing he'd ever see would be the face of a snarling, raging beast with dripping, four-inch fangs.

She lunged in, wrapping her mouth around his neck and punching those fangs into his throat. Arthur thrashed, his eyes wide in panicked terror as she squeezed with her bone-crunching jaws. With one shredding snap, Janae tore his throat away and spat the bloody morsel across the room.

Arthur spasmed and watched a fountain of hot life spew from the wound. His eyes dimmed and his body went cold. He was, however, still conscious enough to feel himself lifted high over the cat's head.

He felt the moment of cold vacuum as she heaved him forward through the air, then the bone-crunching shatter of the two-way mirror overlooking his pool hall. He felt the shards of glass cutting from head to toe, and watched them shimmer as they fell in slow motion along with him.

He felt the splintering and snapping of his bones as he smashed into one of his pool tables. The wood frame cracked and the green, felt table top was splashed with his blood.

Janae stood in the shattered window above, a predatory cat, standing on two legs, tail thrashing and chest heaving. Triumphant.

Will walked up behind her, looking down to admire

her work. A dead pile of meat and bones, Arthur's twisted, dark aura dissolved and faded away.

"Praise the Lord," Will said.

23

CARGO

JANAE LED Will down the stairs to the basement.

A single lightbulb shined. They reached a steel door at the bottom. Janae inched up to it, putting her hand against the metal surface and letting out a sigh of validation. She could sense the little hearts beating on the other side, hear their trembling fear. She could see their ankles and wrists tied, their mouths gagged. Their faces streaked with tears.

She held out her hand and Will produced the keys taken from Jim. She took them and tried to fit each one into the lock, until she found the right one. The lock turned over and the door squealed open. They crept into the dark room.

Will ran his hand along the wall where he expected to find a light switch, but to no avail. Instead, a chain hung from the ceiling in the center of the room, and with a light tug, he turned on a lone-hanging bulb. The entryway was empty but for a stack of cardboard boxes, some cleaning supplies and overstock from the pool hall's limited kitchen.

The floor was a mottled concrete and the walls were cinderblock. The air was cold and stale. But there was something else. Another door at the end of the room. On it was a padlock and a heavy bolt, and it was blocked off by more boxes and two broken barstools. Will and Janae approached the door, both sensing the heat within.

"Can you feel them?" Janae asked.

Will nodded.

Janae flipped through the keys on the ring, finding one that looked the right size for a padlock. She inserted the key and it fit. The lock popped open. Reaching up, she slid the bolt open with a rusty shriek. She put her hand on the doorknob, looking back at Will. Again, he confirmed he was ready. Janae took a deep breath and pulled the door open.

Whimpers and cries in the darkness.

Will turned the light on and gasped. Six young children lay amongst the cold, dusty filth, bound and gagged. They winced at the light and squirmed, terrified. Four of the youngsters lay sideways on two stained, old cots, and the other two huddled on the floor against the cinderblock walls.

"Shhhhh," Janae said as she rushed inside. "It's gonna be okay. We're here to get you out." She flipped open a short knife and began cutting the bindings on their wrists and ankles. Will was right behind her with his own knife, his heart twisting in his chest.

They were all so young and innocent, the oldest only ten. Much like the energy exuded by young Dominic, there was a white light surrounding the children. There was a sense of wonder, a fresh purity and a cleanliness of spirit. But there were also hints of yellow, as well as a tinge of rust... It was the aura of fear. Part of their innocence had already been stolen, Will realized.

Together, Will and Janae cut the children loose, one at a time. Two little girls appeared to be Hispanic. There was a black boy who was the youngest, and the other three were snow white; A blonde boy, an auburn-haired boy, and a pale girl with long, black hair. Their eyes were full of tears and confusion.

Will suppressed his outrage, knowing that his own blood, his own brother, had been responsible for this.

"It's okay... It's okay..." Will said. "We're not gonna hurt you." Little arms and legs came free, and Will and Janae eased the gags from their mouths.

"I want my mommy!" The girl with the black hair cried.

"We're gonna get you back to your mommy, I promise," said Janae. "We're gonna get all of you back home, okay?"

The two Hispanic girls huddled together, terrified. "*No,*" one of them cried. Janae caressed the girl's cheek after cutting her loose.

"What's the matter, baby? Don't you want to go back home?"

"No!"

"Don't you want to see your mommy?"

"*No!* She g-gave us to the bad men!" the child cried. "She said sh-she loved us, but she needed the money!" The two sisters held each other tight, sobbing. Janae clenched her jaw, her blood boiling. She and Will shared a look, both disgusted.

"Well... We're gonna take you out of here, baby. Get you somewhere safe, okay?" The girls nodded, sniffling. "And we're not gonna let your mom or the bad men, or anybody else hurt you. Okay?" They nodded again, daring to glance up at her.

Will watched Janae, impressed with her tender care. Her gentle empathy was a light in the darkness, and the kids all were comforted by her warm energy. She knelt down and held out her arms, inviting them forward. Slowly, the kids stood to their feet, following her lead.

"Is this everybody?" Will asked the group.

"No," the shaggy-haired boy said. "Casey's not here. They brought us all here, but they left her behind..." Will and Janae looked at each other, concerned.

"Don't worry. We're gonna find Casey too. I promise."

"Come on, you guys." Janae picked up the young black boy, who couldn't have been older than five, and held him against her chest. She reached out with her free hand and the others began to follow. "Come on, now. Let's get you all out of here."

WILL DROVE THE GRAY PANEL VAN THROUGH THE empty night as Janae rode up ahead on the Ducati. Buckled in behind him sat the six kids. Will's heart pounded in anger and his mind could not stop racing. He thought of Janae talking to the kids, remembering the genuine honesty in her voice and the look in her eyes. A stark contrast to the two brutal executions she'd performed just minutes before.

They arrived at the downtown Chattanooga Police Department just after four a.m. Janae flipped open the kick-stand and hopped off her bike. She met Will at the van's sliding door and opened it, flashing a tender smile and reaching out her hand.

"Come on now," she said to the kids. "Let's get you inside. Get you safe." She helped them with their seat-belts and lifted them gently to the ground. With Will's help, she guided them around the van and up the front steps of the imperial, stone building.

"What are we gonna say? I mean, we can't tell them..."

"You just leave the talking to me, hot stuff."

The group entered the stately lobby, the massive seal of the state of Tennessee high up on the wall. A portly guard greeted them with a puzzled expression. "Morning, ya'll," he said. "What are you kids all doin' up this late?"

Janae wasted no time in pulling out her wallet, flipping it open and holding her driver's license up for the officer to see. "I'm special agent Jones, Federal Bureau of Investigation. This is agent, uh... Firewater." She gestured to Will, who did his best to keep his eyes from bulging out of their sockets. "We've just rescued these children from captivity. They've been kidnapped and were about to be sold into a trafficking ring."

"Oh, my goodness," said the officer, looking at her driver's license, yet seeing a legitimate FBI badge. He scanned the faces of the confused and traumatized children. "Are ya'll all right?"

"We need to get these kids inside. And I'm gonna need to speak with your lieutenant right away. Right now."

"Uh, yes ma'am."

"Go!"

"Yes, ma'am! I-I'll be right back!"

The officer performed his best approximation of running, disappearing behind the back door to fetch his superior. Will turned to Janae with a sly, dimpled smile.

"Cute little Jedi mind-trick you got there."

"Yeah, comes in handy," she said. "It's not full-on mind control. Just suggestibility. Doesn't work on skinners."

"I see."

"Are we going home now?" the little girl with the black hair asked. Janae nodded and stroked the child's head.

"The police are going to have some questions first, but yes. We're going to call your parents right away." She looked over at the two Hispanic sisters with a reassuring glance. "Don't you two worry. We'll make sure you are put somewhere safe. Nobody's going to hurt you."

"P-Promise?"

"I promise."

"What about Casey?" the little blonde boy asked.

Will stepped forward, touching the boy's shoulder.

"We're gonna keep looking for Casey, little man. We'll find her. Don't you worry." He looked up at Janae, both of them aware the statement was wishful thinking.

The door opened, and the portly guard returned with his Lieutenant. "Agent Jones?" the man asked.

"Yes, Lieutenant. Let's go on in back to talk," she said, the pupils of her eyes instantly hooking the man into a trance. "Agent Firewater will wait outside for me." She turned to Will and nodded. He stammered, but figured he'd best play along with her charade.

"U-Um, yes ma'am."

He nodded to the Lieutenant and began to back away. The blonde boy caught his hand, and he stopped to look back at him.

"Don't forget about Casey!"

"I won't, buddy."

"Casey Madison... She's our friend!"

Will looked the boy in the eye and nodded his head, accepting the challenge. He squeezed the boy's hand tight, then let them go. Janae escorted the children into the back room as Will sauntered outside to wait.

———

The air was brisk and the sun had yet to kiss the horizon. Janae emerged into the early morning hours to find Will leaning against the driver's door of the van. She trotted down the stairs and approached him, letting out a relieved sigh.

"They'll be okay," she said.

Will nodded.

"You wipe your fingerprints off the van?"

"Mm hm."

"Well then," she said, hopping onto the Ducati and grabbing her helmet. "Andiamo, shall we?"

Will lingered, kicking at the ground. "Do you think I'm stupid or something?"

Janae froze, watching him closely. He looked up at her. The air between them was thin and crisp.

"What are you talking about?"

"I think you know, Janae."

"Will, my little powers of suggestion only last so long. Pretty soon those cops in there are gonna come to their senses and start asking questions." Will pushed off the van, circling around her. He looked into her eyes, trying to see what might lay beyond.

"When I look at regular people now," Will said, "I know they're not skinners. I can *see* their... their energy. Their aura. It's different when I look at a skinner. Like those fucking monsters earlier."

"Yeah, so?"

"So, you expect me to believe that you just met me by chance? That you just happened to come to the dealership that day? That you seduced me and didn't know who I was? Bullshit."

"I didn't. I-I... You can't tell until someone has already changed. When the animal spirit is dormant, you can't tell — "

"Bullshit!" Will leaned in face to face, his eyes burning into hers. "You've been after my brother for years. You came looking for me, knowing full well what I was. You *wanted* to change me! You needed me to join your little crusade!"

"No, I-I..."

"Don't fucking lie to me, Janae!"

"Okay, so what if I did?" Her eyes glazed over. "I needed your help, okay? With my *little crusade!* I figured if anyone could help me take Mason down, it would be you!"

"So you just came along, pretending to like me, seduced me... And turned me into a fucking *monster!*"

"All I did was help you connect with what you already are! Now, if you don't want to help me, fine. Fuck you, then. But there are lives out there — innocent lives — to save! So yes, I used you to achieve the objective! I'm sorry! But taking these fuckers out is more important than you, or me, or..."

Her voice broke, a tear running down her cheek. Will's demeanor softened at this glimpse of vulnerability. Beneath her hardened, warrior mask, she was just a girl whose heart was breaking.

"I don't suppose I would've said yes if you'd asked me."

Janae laughed, throwing her head back.

"You could've just bitten me," he said.

"Why would I do that? I wanted your body. That part wasn't a lie." Will smiled, his wall of ice and anger crumbling. He stepped closer to her. Their eyes met. "Look, you don't owe me anything. You want to go, go ahead. I'm sorry I dragged you into this."

Will let out a sigh, thinking about all that had transpired. "You know, what we did tonight... What we saw tonight... I can't just let that go. I can't just go back to selling cars, punching a time clock. We really *did* something tonight, you and I. We really made a difference."

"Yeah, we did."

"My whole life, I've wondered what happened to my brother. If he was alive or dead... Now that I know... I can't just let it go. I have to stop him. *We* have to stop him."

"Okay," she said.

"But no more lies. Say it."

Janae sighed. "No more lies."

"Okay, then... Partner."

She smiled. "Well, hop on and let's get the hell out of here. I need sleep!" He leaned in and her lips parted. They kissed. Will pulled back, a wry half-smile on his face as he cocked his head and looked at her.

"All right. But just one more thing," he said.

"Yeah, what's that?"

"I'm driving."

"*Pfft*," Janae scoffed. "Oh, really? This supposed to be some kind of male dominance bullshit? Nobody drives this baby but me. So hop on the back unless you want me to leave your ass here, *agent Firewater*."

She smiled at him with sassy lips.

Will laughed and shook his head, climbing on the bike behind her as she started the engine. "Anybody ever tell you, you have a talent for getting your way?"

24

GROWING PAINS

CASEY MADISON LAY in the dark bedroom of the RV. Her hands and feet were bound by duct tape, her mouth gagged. From the silence and dark outside, she surmised that they had parked the RV far from civilization. Still, she could hear the crickets chirping and hopping in the grass outside. She could hear the gnats flying around and almost smell their sweat.

It was impossible, she thought, how sharp her senses were. A six mile-an-hour wind changed from north to northeast, and she could tell. The sky had clouded over the moon, and despite not being able to see it, she knew it.

What's wrong with me? she thought.

It had been several hours since they had parked and left her there alone, but now they were back, and the RV started up and took off again onto the road. She had struggled and writhed and strained, but could not free her hands or feet. She could not scream for help, and if she could, no one would hear her.

A new, incessant urge flashed in her mind. It wasn't a voice, but a feeling. A begging need from deep within —

FAST. FAST. FAST.

SHE FELT THE TIRES WHIRRING ON THE ASPHALT below, heard the whoosh and smelled the exhaust of each passing vehicle. The bedroom door was closed, but she could tell that two of her captors were up front, the big man and the woman. The little guy was driving another van beside them, and the fourth of her abductors, well, there was no sign of him.

No, wait... She could smell blood, his blood. It had stained the hand and jeans of the big man, gotten on his boots. She could smell its rusty signature.

What the hell is wrong with me?

FAST. FAST. FAST.

CASEY COULD NOT SHAKE THE URGE FOR SPEED. SHE wanted, _needed,_ to run, jump and scream. She felt something within her that had never been present before. A strength and power demanded to be set free.

Untamed and wild, it saw through her eyes and she felt it in every pore and vein. It demanded her to break free, to kill, to run away fast.

· · ·

FAST. FAST. FAST.

CASEY FELT SURE THAT ONCE FREE, SHE COULD sprint around the circumference of the Earth. But she was still just a tiny thing, unable to break the tight bindings. Her tears welled up with frustration, and she worried about her mother. She was sure that back at home, her mom was worried to death.

She heard the big man and the woman exchanging words. They were heading to Savannah. His voice was laced with anger and frustration; her voice was tinged with grief. The man screamed out loud, *"Son of a bitch!"* and punched one of the storage cabinets on the wall. The cheap wood shattered and splintered, falling to the floor with all the contents within.

"Fuck!"

She heard him swipe his arm across the table, sending everything on top flying across the room. Plates, silverware and bottles crashed on the walls and floor. A heavy three-ring binder and a large bowl of fruit smashed into the bedroom door, jarring it open. Casey's eyes squinted at the new light. She looked out into the living room of the RV.

Mason paced in circles, seething, fists clenched. He looked down at his hand and saw a trickle of blood.

"Shit," he muttered and held the hand up to his mouth, kissing the wound. Annette steered the vehicle down the highway, stiff and tense, wisely remaining silent as she took them all into the early morning light.

Mason turned and noticed that the bedroom door had come open, and there was Casey, tied up on the bed and looking out at him. Deflated, he walked across the room, picked up the three-ring binder from the floor and swung the door closed again.

The door did not click shut, still cracked ajar by a sliver. Casey heard Mason's footsteps walk back to the couch and his heavy body plopped down with a creak onto the springs. She needed to see more, needed to keep moving.

Wriggling and squirming, Casey inched herself to the edge of the bed, swung her legs over the side and used her feet to ease the rest of her body down. She crawled and scooted across the cheap carpet, making her way to the door. She sat against the wall and reached out, pressing the door open ever so slightly in order to peer into the next room.

Mason sat on the couch, his chest heaving.

His brows were furrowed and his eyes were fire. He stretched his neck from side to side and took a few deep breaths, trying to calm himself down. Casey watched from her vantage point as he breathed in through his nose and out through his mouth. His eyes closed and his body relaxed. She had seen her mother doing online meditation classes, and this looked something like that.

Casey's eyes scanned the room.

Broken dishes, papers, assorted fruit and silverware littered the floor. Pizza crusts, orange peels, a steak knife... *A steak knife!* The serrated blade lay on the floor a few feet from where Mason sat.

She needed that knife, but dared not go for it. The

hulking Indian with the graying hair and the black eyes would surely catch her. And then, god only knows what he would do.

Mason focused his thoughts.

His eyes closed, and he reached out with his mind's eye. He controlled his breathing, centered himself and let all around him slip away. The couch, the motion of the RV, the anger, they all faded into the background of his mind. His wolf brain took control. Like a predator, he pointed a spotlight on one thing and one thing only.

"Will..."

He whispered it again.

Casey watched him, eyes flicking back to the steak knife.

"Will..."

Mason followed the spotlight into a tunnel, moving through space and time, sliding through solid matter and alternate states of consciousness. While his body remained planted on the cut-rate couch, his mind flew. It soared through the tunnel, pinpointing its target.

——————

WILL SAT BY THE WINDOW IN THEIR ROOM AT THE inn. He worked a lolly-pop in his mouth.

The sun was rising. Janae lay in bed, fast asleep. Will held his Sig, ready for anything. He hadn't slept and didn't plan on it. His mind whirled and his nerves quaked.

His eyes darted through the window, surveying the parking lot outside from one end to the other. Checking for enemy insurgents. At any moment, his specialized skills and extensive training might be called into action.

He was ready for guns, IED's, air assault, all forms of attack. He had an escape route planned, braced himself for injuries and looked up where the nearest emergency room was, just in case. He was ready for anything.

Anything except...

"Hey, buddy."

Will bolted upright in his chair as Mason's deep voice whispered. He held his gun out, spinning left and right, looking for a target, but he and Janae were alone in the room. Still, it was as if Mason was right beside him. Not a flashing thought in his head and not a memory, Mason's voice was right there with him, in his ears, ringing in his head.

"How are you doin' this?"

"We all have our little talents, don't we? I can't see where you are, but I can talk to you. Been a long time."

"...Mason?" Will murmured.

"Remember me now, little brother?"

Will pulled the curtain aside and looked out at the parking lot again. Nothing. He looked back at Janae, still asleep. Not wanting to wake her, he ran across to the bathroom on his tip-toes, easing the door closed behind him.

"I remember the fire," Will said. "I remember mamaw and papaw crying, screaming your name. I remember people around Harlan talking about you, sayin' you was a killer."

"We're both killers now, ain't we?"

Mason was still seated on the couch in the RV,

speaking out loud to no one else in the room. Casey thought he looked like he was making a phone call, but without a phone. His eyes remained closed. Casey's glance ticked back over to the steak knife on the floor. She had to try. With slow and calculated moves, she inched the door open. There was a squeak from the hinges, and she cringed.

She looked up, but Mason hadn't noticed. She continued forward, creeping her way to the knife scoot by scoot.

Miles away, Will snarled.

He gripped his gun as he paced in the small bathroom, talking to his brother on their spectral phone call.

"I killed for my country," Will said. "You kill because you like it. There's a difference."

"Ain't no difference, buddy. Killin' is killin'."

"Bullshit, Mason! You killed Ma and Pa. You kill little kids. *Children*, Mason! How could you *do* somethin' like that to a child?" Will's jaw clenched as he looked in the bathroom mirror. He could see in his own eyes that the beast wanted out.

"Oh, Will," Mason said. *"I'm doin' this for the kids. I'm doin' them a favor. That way they don't have a chance to grow up and go to Hell."*

Casey stopped in her tracks as she heard Mason speak those words out loud. Her blood went cold. She knew what Mason would do if he caught her... But she kept crawling, inch by inch. The knife was only a few feet away.

"Don't pretend you care about these kids, Mason. All you care about is seein' a person take their last breath!"

Mason pondered. "*I care about... Things.*"

"I'm gonna stop you, Mason."

"*Y'know,*" Mason said. "*You joined the Army, went away for all those years. Then you came back, did another five years in prison... I wanted to see you, to invite you into the family. We're special, you and me. And now you know it...*"

Casey crawled closer to the knife, now two feet away.

"*We are alpha predators, Will. And alpha predators hunt... Tell me somethin'. How did that bitch change you? She didn't bite you, did she? Naw, she fucked you good, huh? Gave you some hot chocolate! Got you on 'er side, turned you against me. Against your own brother.*"

Casey grabbed the knife.

Mason didn't notice. Annette kept driving.

Casey crept backwards toward the bedroom.

"Mason," Will seethed. "It don't have nothin' to do with her. I will always stand against you. I've been preparing for this all my life. When the time comes... I'll be the one to end it."

"*Big words, little brother.*"

"I'm comin' for you, Mason."

"*I tell you what, buddy,*" Mason said. "*It's been real nice catching up like this. It really has. We should do this again sometime. Real soon.*"

Casey reached the door to the bedroom.

FAST. FAST. FAST.

. . .

"Next time I see you," Will said. "One of us is gonna die."

"Well then, come and get it... Brother."

Mason ended his psychic call. He pulled his mind back through the tunnel and into his head. Taking deep breaths, he eased himself back into his body.

Casey made it back inside the bedroom, closing the door just in time.

Mason opened his eyes.

"If it's too much, I'll call my doctor and ask her to prescribe the generic instead."

"Okay... Hey, Dom! Come on, buddy, use your fork and knife."

Dom was trying to eat the pancakes with his hands and had made a syrupy mess of himself. He flashed a devilish grin.

"Come on, baby," Annie said. "Let's wash those hands. You little goober!" Dom giggled as Annie led him over to the sink and started the water.

A knock at the front door.

Jackson's body tensed. He knew who it was. Crossing to the door, Jackson looked through the peep-hole. He sighed, unlocked the door and swung it open.

"Hey, Jax," Will said, Janae standing behind him.

Jackson composed himself and smiled. "Well, did y'all have a nice time last night?"

"Oh, yeah. It was a blast."

"Listen, uh..." Jackson glanced over his shoulder. Annie and Dominic looked back at him from the kitchen. Her eyes spoke of worry. "I'm fixin' to go to work in a minute, so..."

Dom beamed and waved his hand. "Hi, Uncle Will!"

"Hey, buddy."

"Y'know what, Dom?" Annie said, sensing the obvious tension and taking initiative, "Let's you and me go outside for a little bit! Play on the swings or some-thin'?" Jackson smiled at her, appreciative. Will looked down at his feet, in shame.

Annie led Dominic out the back door, patting him on

25

ROAD TRIP

WILL SHOOK JANAE AWAKE. She groaned and writhed beneath the cheap motel bedspread. She had slept in the nude, and her curves peaked through the tussled blankets and sheets. He shook her again and she groaned louder.

"C'mon, wake up. We gotta go."

"Mmmmm... What time is it?"

"Almost ten."

Janae stretched and twisted, her face contorting as she let out an annoyed, bellowing groan. "I just got to sleep a couple hours ago!" she yawned. "Will Shaw, you're fine, but you're killin' me!"

"Up up up! C'mon! We gotta go!"

She pushed up onto one elbow and shot him an incredulous look through the sleep crust in her eyes.

"Where we gotta go?"

"I need to go talk to someone," Will said, gathering up his things. "Fill in the gaps. I need answers."

"How about you just bring your fine ass over here

and get in bed…?" Janae said with a sinful smile as she leaned back and allowed the sheet to fall away from her firm breasts.

"Man, after everything that happened last night, how can you even think about that?"

Janae let out a sigh and rolled her eyes, her small afro smashed and molded out of shape. "Did you even get any sleep?"

"Can't sleep," he said. "Can't stop. My mind is spinning… Come on, come on. Get up, I'm serious, now."

"Okay, okay!" Janae wrenched the covers off and battled her way to her feet. She yawned and stretched her arms out, her toned, naked body displayed proudly before him. Will gulped and tried to look away, conflicting emotions betraying him. She slinked across to him, reveling in his discomfort.

"Wanna come take a shower with me?" She came in close, fingers tracing over his powerful chest.

"I already showered," Will said. "I'm ready to go."

She deflated. "Where? Where do we have to go?"

"Kentucky."

"*Kentucky?*"

"Harlan, Kentucky. I need to speak with my papaw."

"Your *papaw?*" Her face twisted in confusion. "Oh, right. Your granddaddy."

"That's right."

Janae chuckled.

"That's what I call him! It's a southern thing, I guess. Now will you come on, already?"

"Why do you need to go to Kentucky to see your *papaw?*"

"Because I think he can help us find Mason… And clear a few things up. I've been lied to my whole life, and I want some answers."

Janae pulled in even closer, her nipples grazing up against his chest, her hands on his shoulders. "Last chance for a shower," she whispered an inch from his face. He felt himself getting hard, but suppressed the urge.

"No," he said through clenched teeth.

"Fine," Janae threw up her hands and turned from him, snapping her fingers as she strutted off to the bathroom. "You're no fun. Just give me a few minutes. And I'm gonna want breakfast. And coffee! Fuckin' *Kentucky…*"

"Well, we do have one other stop to make first."

I WAS NEARLY 11 A.M., AND JACKSON COOPER WAS running late for work. It was a good thing he was the boss. He fixed his tie as he walked through the living room and into the kitchen, scooping up a piece of toast and taking a bite.

Annie was enjoying a breakfast of scrambled eggs, avocado and toast, while Dominic scarfed down his favorite, pancakes. Fromage the cat weaved between their legs, rubbing against them at his leisure.

"Can you pick up my prescription today if you have chance?" Annie asked.

Jackson threw on his suit jacket and took another of toast. "On my way back from work, babe. Sure."

the butt. Jackson turned back to face Will. Their eyes met.

Silence lingered.

"What's goin' on, Will? What are you into?"

"I can't really talk about it, bro. I just need to pick up my things."

"Yeah, I think you'd better," Jackson said. "How about you give me back that key too." He held his hand out. Will nodded, producing his key chain and removing the key to Jackson's house. "And you are?" Jackson pointed a glance at Janae.

"Lupita Nyong'o," she said.

"Mm hm. Okay."

"Here," Will handed over the house key. "Look, I'm sorry about everything, Jax. I really am. I can't explain it, I just... Can I just come in and get my stuff?" Jackson sighed and stepped away from the door to let them in. As soon as they entered, the hair stood up on Fromage's back and the animal hissed, scampering away to find a cat-sized hiding spot.

Will and Janae went for the stairs, Jackson in tow. "Will, I wish there was some way I could help you, man. If you just tell me what's going on... Is it drugs? Is she your dealer?" He asked Janae, "Are you his dealer?"

"Oh, please." Janae rolled her eyes.

They entered Will's guest room, and he began packing clothes into his duffel bag. Underwear, socks, toothpaste, Will made sure to get all the essentials. Jackson stood in the doorway, watching, frustrated.

"Come on," he said. "You gotta give me somethin'

here, Will! For fuck's sake, how long have we known each other?"

"Jax, I'm sorry. But the less you know, the better."

"Well, I'm sorry too," Jackson said. "But if this is how it's going to be, I think it's best that... that you don't come back. I have a family here, bro. Whatever you're into, I can't..."

"That's why I can't say anything. To protect you and your family." Will pulled out the black pelican case full of weapons and laid it on the bed. Jackson's eyes went wide.

"Oh, no... Uh, maybe you'd better leave those with me, huh bro?" Jackson said. Will flipped open the case, revealing the small arsenal to Janae.

"Nice," she said.

"Will, what are you fixin' to do...?" Jackson's eyes were red and glazed. He knew this could be the last time he would ever see his friend.

"Jax," Will restrained his emotions as much as he could. "I want you to sell cars, be a good husband, a good father, and have a good life, my brother. Never stop singin' stupid songs. Never stop bein' a dirty ol' bastard. Me, I... I gotta do what I gotta do."

Will snapped the pelican case closed and held it firm, slinging his backpack over his shoulder. The two men stood eye to eye in silence. Janae watched and waited, eyes moving between the two of them.

"Well then, go do what you gotta do, Will. I wish I could help you, man. But... I guess all I can say is good luck."

"Actually, there is one last thing you can help me

with, Jax." Will shifted uncomfortably. This would surely not go over well. "I need your car."

Jackson's eyes flapped open. "What, the *Challenger?* Are you fucking crazy? *No way!*"

"I need it, man."

"Fuck you! God, you got some balls, injun! Take the Acura again! Or come to the lot with me, I'll give you a clunker!"

"I need the horsepower, man. And I don't have time. I need it now."

"No fucking way! Absolutely not! *No! No! No!*"

———

The obnoxious-orange Challenger with black racing stripes zoomed up I-75 North, headed for Kentucky. They had stopped for gas, gotten Janae's bags from the motel and left her bike parked there. Later on, they would stop at Will's favorite old guns n' ammo store to buy some boxes of shells to feed his babies.

He hadn't been home in years, since after coming back from overseas, and before going to the penitentiary. He wondered what old ghosts might come out of the shadows to haunt him, what secrets his papaw might reveal.

Those old streets, the smell of the air, the feel of the small town; it all flooded his mind. He gripped the wheel and pressed harder on the gas pedal.

GO. GO. GO.

26

HOME

HARLAN, *Kentucky*

THE SMALL TOWN CROUCHED IN A NARROW VALLEY of the Appalachians. Black Mountain cast its shadow over the north, Little Black Mountain hugged around the south, and Ewing Spur flanked the west. Harlan was mostly hidden from the rest of the world, and that's how its citizens liked it. A teardrop-shaped outline tucked into the mountains, Harlan was an old-frontier backwoods mining town and a modern city all at once.

There were schools, a post office, a church, a courthouse and a movie theater. There were shipping companies, a bus stop, a supermarket and a bowling alley. Nearly every home was now equipped with high-speed internet, but the boys still loved their deer and elk hunting. Populated by just under two-thousand residents, over ninety percent white, Harlan was an antique remnant of the Civil War, a genuine slice of American pie.

The orange muscle car tore into town.

Heads turned as they exited off Route 421 and growled onto West Clover Street. Will's eyes flooded with new sights and old memories. Many buildings had been torn down, restored or repainted. New stores had been erected. People used cell phones, drove vans with auto-closing doors and listened to music through wireless ear-buds.

He hadn't expected it to remain exactly as it was in the late nineties, when he left, but it was still a shock. Everything was foreign, yet familiar. He definitely remembered the mosquitoes.

Janae took in the sights through her Gucci sunglasses. Will drove them through the cool afternoon air, heading toward the north end of town. The streets and avenues began to shrink as they moved into the residential areas. Trees lined the roadways and simple houses flanked them on either side. Together, they pierced through the Norman Rockwell-picturesque landscape and headed into a more rural area.

They cruised up Ivy Hill to Lynn Hollow Road, and Will stopped. This was it. This was where he grew up. Just around the corner sat his Papaw Jimmy's house. Janae looked over at Will with concern. The angst in his eyes was focused. The muscles in his jaw flexed and his hands gripped the wheel.

It had been so long since he'd been back, since he'd even called... And now to return under these circumstances. He wasn't even sure if his grandfather was still alive. Shame gripped him in its clutches and Will squeezed his eyes closed.

"You all right?" Janae asked.

Will nodded, opened his eyes.

He took his foot off the brake and continued rolling up Lynn Hollow Road. While the heart of downtown had expanded and modernized, the sleepy-old country lane remained virtually the same as he remembered, save for some fresh paint and new screen doors.

They reached the end of the pavement, curving onto a smaller dirt road. Years peeled away as they arrived at a weathered, wooden gate at the foot of a large driveway.

It was a two-story home that was once painted a bright white, but had since chipped and faded with the years. A beat-up old Ford pickup sat in the driveway not far from a weathered John Deere riding lawnmower. Wind chimes sang their songs and dreamcatchers stood guard under the shaded porch.

The shingles on the roof needed replacing, yet the large vegetable garden was lush and well tended to. The modest-sized property was surrounded by wooden fencing and shielded from the outside world by a wall of Yellowwoods and Black Walnut trees. Sparrows and Bluebirds dove and soared, harmonizing with the wind chimes.

Will stepped out of the car.

Janae stood up and stretched, looking around. The smell of hot southern cooking drifted in the air and she nearly swooned. She met Will at the front of the car, where he waited, pensive.

He clutched the car keys, shaking them in a nervous tick. Janae could see his face was strained, his eyes worried.

"It'll be okay," she said.

"What if... What if he's angry at me? What if he doesn't know? I mean... We could be putting him in danger..."

"Hey!"

A man's voiced boomed at them from the house. The screen door cracked and a white-haired old man with bronze skin peeked his head out. "Are ya'll gonna come in, or what? I'm fixin' a beef stew." The old man pulled back inside and the door clapped shut again.

Will and Janae looked at each other and nearly laughed. Will shrugged, shaking his head, and they walked the remaining distance up the steps, and to the front door.

Adorning the distressed oak door was a carved wooden plaque with the image of a proud brown bear perched on a mountaintop. Will pulled the screen door open with a creak and they stepped across the threshold.

The living room was old and worn, but clean and tidy. A couch, a love seat and a recliner circled an oval coffee table, and across from that, a football game flickered on a 1990's thirty-inch TV. At the end of the room was the archway that led to the kitchen, where Papaw Jimmy was throwing ingredients into a large stock pot and whistling to himself.

"In here," he called, so they ambled over to the kitchen door.

"Hey, Papaw..."

"Hey, boy! C'mere. Gimme a hug." Jimmy smiled and held his arms out, hugging Will as if he'd seen him last week. "Good to see ya. And this must be your girlfriend."

"This is Janae," Will said.

"Oh, she's mighty pretty," Jimmy said. "Here, come on. Take off your jackets, make yourselves comfortable!"

Will and Janae did as he asked, puzzled by his nonchalance. Jimmy had aged twenty years since Will had seen him, shrunk by two inches and had wrinkled like a prune. His hair was short, tussled and stark white.

He wore jeans and a simple buttoned shirt, and moved around quite well for a man in his mid-eighties. His brown eyes sparkled with life and intelligence. But Will noticed something else about Papaw Jimmy that he'd never seen before.

All around him was a backlit silhouette, a furry outline, as faint as a whisper. It walked with him, matched his every movement, anchored to his core. It had curved claws and a long snout, its outline only visible when he turned in the light a certain way. It was the shape of a mighty brown bear.

When Will squinted his eyes, the aura around him was a radiant and glimmering silver, accented with fresh greens and browns. Will shook his head, learning more about his grandfather in that brief moment than in his entire childhood.

"You're a skinner," Will said.

"Oh yeah, *hyeck hyeck!*" Jimmy cackled, throwing some chopped onions into the stew and stirring it. "And now you know you are too, don't ya? Yeah, I can see it in ya. A cat, huh? Black jaguar?"

"I thought it's a panther..." Will mused.

"Same thing, boy. Panther is any cat with a black coat."

"Oh, uh... Okay."

"And you too, huh Janie? Another cat!"

Janae smiled and nodded, not caring to correct his mispronunciation of her name. She had thought Will's Southern accent was thick, but it was nothing compared to Jimmy's deep, twangy drawl. "Should'a known you'd find out sooner or later."

"Why... Why did you keep this from me?" Will asked.

"To protect ye' of course... Uh, beer?" Jimmy glanced back at Janae. "Beer?" She and Will both nodded. Jimmy opened the fridge, adorned with faded, old family photos, and tossed them each a cold can of Heineken. "To protect ye', boy. The weight we carry... It's a big responsibility."

"I thought skinwalkers were like, evil witches or something?" Will said. "That's what all the tribal legends say."

"Oh yeah?" Jimmy scoffed. "What else ye' believe in, Santa Claus? Can't give no credence to that campfire talk, boy."

"But... Aren't skinwalkers a *Navajo* legend? It's not even a Cherokee thing..."

"The Navajo are a great and noble tribe, that's for sure," Jimmy said. "And they did coin the term 'skinwalker,' or as they call it, 'Yeenaeldooshi.' But lots a' tribes and cultures around the world tell stories about men who turn into beasts. The names and details change dependin' on where you are, but they're all talkin' about the same thing. And 'round here, we call folks like us skinwalkers, or skinners."

"We're not all evil, and we're not witches," Janae added. "But we do obviously have strengths and powers that normal people don't. As you've already seen."

"So, you... You knew I was coming, didn't you?" Will said, cracking open his beer and taking a sip.

Jimmy swiveled his head and shot Janae a wry smile. "He's good lookin', but he ain't too smart, is he?" Janae cracked up, laughing uncontrollably. She couldn't stop. Jimmy cackled along with her as Will fumed.

"Shut up," Will said, making Janae laugh harder. "Shut up!" He blushed, shaking his head and feeling like a fool.

"Boy, I knew ye' were comin', when ye' were comin' and what ye' wanted!" Papaw Jimmy turned back to his stew, stirring it some more.

A notification bell went off in Janae's phone. She checked the text without expression, then put her phone face down.

"So... skinners all have these... psychic abilities, so to speak?" Will leaned in, piecing the puzzle together.

"Not all skinners," Jimmy said. "Just like regular people, some got the gift, some don't. But when a skinner's got the gift, it's strong. Some can see the future, some can see the past, some can read minds..."

"I can see things when I touch something. It's weird."

"Yep yep, that's what we call a tactile. Neat little trick, yer lucky..." Jimmy smiled and checked his stew. "Okay, this should be ready 'fore too long... So, this pretty thing bit ye', huh?" Jimmy waved his hand at Janae, and they both blushed.

"Eh, no. Not exactly."

"Oh... *Oh!* Right, sorry. None a' m'business."

"Papaw, if you know why I'm here, then... Can you help me? How can I find Mason?"

Jimmy stopped stirring, his face turning solemn as he let out a pained sigh. "I don't rightly know, Will. He disappeared the day of the fire. Never came back."

"What about my parents? Were they skinners too?"

"Your mamma was. But she never used the gift. She and your daddy, they did their best to keep it from you boys. They wanted ya'll to have healthy, normal lives. But then ye' ran off to the Army, an' prison after that... Guess we couldn't keep ye' from trouble."

"Papaw..." Will searched for the words, "I'm sorry I went away like I did. Sorry I never called, never came back... I just, I always felt something pushin' me, something inside. Guess now I know what it was."

"We all have a beast inside, boy."

"Yeah, but it wasn't just that," Will said, pacing the kitchen. "It was the memories. The fire. My brother disappearing. The secrets and the lies... I need to remember my past, Papaw. I need to understand what I'm up against."

"I've been tracking Mason for years," Janae added. "He's built up a gang of skinners. They kidnap and sell children on the black market. They rape and murder the innocent. We have to stop him."

"You been trackin' him for years, huh?" Jimmy's eyes

narrowed as he sized her up. "You with The Council, ain't ye'? You workin' with Keonee?"

Janae's body tensed, her eyes shooting over to Will, uncomfortable. Reluctantly, she nodded.

"What council?" Will asked. "Who's Keonee?"

"Well, you weren't s'posed to know," Jimmy said. "But I guess now the *cat's* out of the bag, eh? *Hyeck hyeck!*" Jimmy howled with laughter, stomping the floor and punching the air at his riotous pun. "The Spirit Council, boy. The regulators of all skinwalkers, shapeshifters, witches, demons... They enforce the law, keep the balance."

"So that's who you were telling me about," Will said to Janae. "And who's this Keonee?"

"He's their leader now. Used to be just a warrior-brave like me when we were both coming up."

"Wait, you were a part of this once?"

"Oh yeah, back before I met your mamaw. I was a stud!"

"So, what happened?"

"Oh, y'know... Me and Keonee didn't always see eye to eye," Jimmy said, pulling out mismatched bowls from the cupboard and placing them on the table. "Always such a stickler for the rules... Janie, he really wanted you to change Will?"

Janae meekly took a sip of beer.

"He does know, right? Nobody gets brought in to the life without specific reason, and approval of the council."

Janae struggled, feeling the heat of the eyes on her. Now was not the times for lies. "I needed Will's help to find Mason," Janae said, clearing her throat and checking their faces for reactions. Jimmy's brow furrowed, incredulous.

"You're playin' with fire, girl."

"I did what I had to do."

"Hm..." Jimmy's thoughts trailed off as he recalled the past. "I wanted to start a family, to leave it all behind me. Keonee didn't much like that. You don't cross The Council." He shot a solemn look at Janae. "He called me a traitor. Tried to come after me. You don't just bring a skinner into the world lightly."

Janae stared down at the table.

"Then you go and have a daughter who turns out to be a skinner too," Will shook his head, taking a sip of beer.

"And she had two sons, both of whom also had the gift," Papaw Jimmy nodded as he placed napkins and spoons on the table, then went back to stirring the meaty stew. "Your mamma never made the change, but she knew she had it in 'er, and so did your pappy. And we all tried to keep it from you and... your brother. Especially him."

"You knew what he was capable of."

"I knew what he'd *done*," Jimmy said. "There's more than two ways for a skinner to unlock their powers, Will. Of course, you can get bit, and you can get... Well, *you know!* ...But there's another way: If ye' take the life of an innocent. When Mason was thirteen years-old, that little Krause boy was murdered, stabbed to death, body found out at the creek... Nobody knew who did it. But I knew. Mason had unlocked his powers, discovered what he was. I knew he had spilled innocent blood..."

Silence descended.

"Welp!" Papaw Jimmy clapped his hands, a hungry grin on his face. "Who's ready for some beef stew? C'mon, now. Sit, sit." Will and Janae took seats at the table as Jimmy began to ladle the steaming soup into their bowls. "And here's some bread for dunkin'."

"Thanks, Papaw."

"Eat up!"

They all picked up their spoons and went to work. Will moved slowly, his mind more focused on the information than sustenance. But he ate, scooping up the hot, meaty stew. Janae moaned, her eyes rolling back in her head.

"Oh my God, this is *so* good, Jimmy!" she said.

"Thank ye', Janie."

Janae glanced over at the framed photos on the wall. A black-and-white portrait of Jimmy and his wife in their younger days hung beside the light switch.

"Is that your wife?"

"Yes ma'am, that's her. Will's mamaw. The love of my life. Passed on nearly twenty-five years ago. Cancer." He smiled proudly and looked at the photo. In it, he was a strong, young Cherokee warrior like Will, and the woman beside him was a stunning, onyx-haired Indian goddess.

"She's so beautiful," Janae said. "What was her name?"

"Jimmie."

"No, I mean, what was *her* name?"

"Jimmie."

"Wait... I thought *your* name is Jimmy."

"It is."

"Well then... What was *her* name?"

"Jimmie."

"Okay..." Janae shot Will a confused glance.

Will shook his head and chuckled, ripping off a chunk of bread and dipping it into his soup. "He thinks he's funny."

27

MALE BONDING

HOT SOUP MADE way for hot coffee.

Will and Janae sat across the kitchen table from Papaw Jimmy, the old man patting his pot belly with pride. He and Will both took their coffee with cream and sugar, while Janae took hers black. They all sat, contented, digesting their meals.

"Yeahp," Jimmy said, sipping his coffee. "That was some good eatin' right there. If I do say so m'self!"

"It was delicious, Jimmy. Thank you," said Janae. "I'm so full." She glanced over at Will, and his thoughts were elsewhere, his eyes looking past the walls of the kitchen.

"You okay over there, boy?"

"Yeah," Will said. "Just thinkin'."

"I 'spect you are."

Janae glanced around the house, admiring the rustic decor. Family photos lined the walls, along with small wooden statuettes of animals posed on countertops. A large, oak bookshelf was jammed haphazardly with books, VHS tapes and CD's, in no particular order. On one wall was the mounted head of a wild boar, and across the room, the head of a large buck was perched in stoic silence.

"Bit of a hunter, I see," Janae said.

"Oh yeah, you could say that. That buck over there I shot? It was little Will's first time out huntin'. 'Member that, boy? How old must you a' been, twelve?"

"Hm? Oh, yeah. Yeah, that's right." Will nodded.

"I recall you near passed out when I cut 'im open, *hyeck hyeck!*" Jimmy cackled, the skin around his eyes crinkling into a thousand cracks. "Always was a bit squeamish, wasn't ye'?"

"Papaw, c'mon."

"Say, what d'ye say we go out and do a bit a' huntin' together tonight? Just you n' me?" Jimmy smiled.

"*Tonight?* Oh come on, in the dark?"

"Best time for it. 'Sides, you an' me ain't never been out huntin' together before."

Will's eyebrows crunched up in confusion. "Papaw, we used to go huntin' all the time."

"Not like *this*, we ain't." The gleam in Jimmy's eyes was wicked and suggestive. Will suddenly knew exactly what he meant. He shared a look with Janae, but shook his head.

"I don't... I don't think I can, Papaw..."

"Oh, come on, boy. You're hurtin' an old man's feelin's."

"Go ahead, Will," Janae encouraged.

"Yeah, see boy? Us men'll go out huntin' and let the

woman-folk take care a' the dishes! *Hyeck hyeck!* You don't mind, do ya' Jane?"

"Um, uh..." Janae stammered. She looked over at the pile of filth in the sink and her heart dropped. She'd been living in hotels nearly her whole life and couldn't remember the last time she'd so much as rinsed off a spoon. "Uh, okay..."

"*Ha-haaaa! Jack dog!*" Jimmy howled, slapping his knee. "C'mon, boy. Come take a walk with the ol' man. C'mon!"

Will knew his Papaw would never take no for an answer.

———

THE AIR OUTSIDE WAS COOL AND THE MOON WAS A three-quarter orb in the clear sky. Papaw Jimmy led Will through the backyard, which led into the woods, which led into the mountains. They had hiked and hunted this trail many times, but Will knew Jimmy had something different in mind this time. They carried no guns tonight. Will slowed his stride so that Jimmy could keep up with him, the old man's back slightly hunched, his hips and knees rusty.

"I know why yer so quiet tonight, boy. Ain't no secret."

"I don't know what to do with all this, Papaw," Will said. "I still can't hardly believe it."

"You just gotta learn to control it, son. The beast is just as much a part of you as your own hands. Your own eyes. When ye' become the beast, it's still you behind the wheel, ye' get me?"

"Yeah, it's just... It's just..."

"What, boy?"

"It's Mason. I have to stop him."

"I know ye' do," Jimmy sighed. "And I sure wish I could help." They headed deeper into the trees, working their way up an incline, the darkness swallowing them.

"You gotta know *something*," Will said. "Where he is, or where he's been. Maybe you know what he's thinking, like the way you knew I was coming today..."

"Naw, it ain't like that," Jimmy said. "I can feel him and I can sense what's gonna happen, but I don't know any particulars. I could feel you all these years, knew you were alive, felt you gettin' close. Knew you'd be comin' for answers, looking for your brother."

"You know what's gonna happen? Well... What?"

"You and yer brother are gonna find each other again. An' when ye' do... one of you is gonna die."

The trail grew steeper, smooth soil giving way to large boulders. Small trees and bushes transitioned into red spruces and Fraser firs. They walked in silence for a moment, working toward the next plateau. All forms of wildlife populated the green ecosystem around them, and Will's heightened senses could hear every scuttle and smell every musk.

"I only remember bits and pieces of that night," Will whispered. "And I see it in my dreams... Sometimes when I'm awake. These little flashes. The fire. Mom and Dad on the floor, all that blood... I don't remember seeing Mason there, but I saw something. Something with yellow eyes, in the smoke. It was reaching out to me, wanted me to come to him. Then you came and got me... I know now he was gonna kill me."

"Or change you. And try to make you evil like him."

"All these years, I didn't know if he was alive or dead. If he died in that fire, or if he was out there somewhere... You never saw him again? He never tried to contact you?"

"He spoke to me once," Jimmy whispered. "In my mind. He has the ability to do that."

"I know. He spoke to me too."

"He wanted me to let him come home. To let him pick you up and take you away. I told 'im if I ever saw 'im again... That I would kill 'im." Jimmy's usually jovial voice had flattened into a somber tone. "He killed m'baby girl, and your daddy. Tried to kill you. He wanted to destroy the whole family. So, yes son. I know... You gotta stop 'im."

Will and Jimmy stepped into the clearing they had set out for. Trees gave way to the vast sky above. Jimmy smiled as he looked up at the moon and stars, smelled the fresh breeze and felt the grass beneath his feet. "I like to come here," Jimmy said. "Far from the world a' men. Up here, I get to be m'self... You ready, Will?"

"I-I don't know."

"We gotta eat."

"I'm completely full!"

"The *beast* gotta eat too! C'mon, help an old man out. I'm getting too slow for this stuff. Now, just relax... And show me who y'are."

"I-I don't know how. I can't control it..."

"Ye' just relax and surrender to it, boy. Easiest thing

in the world. Just open the door and fall back, and let him slide right in. Like this..."

Jimmy closed his eyes and held his arms out. The moonlight shimmered over his form, his body beginning to ripple as if he was just an optical illusion. The light around him bent and warped in waves. Reflections of man moved in the light, becoming refractions of animal.

Within thirty-seconds, Jimmy had glimmered away like a desert mirage, and in his place stood a huge, brown bear. His amber eyes gleamed with wisdom. His coat was a deep-chestnut brown and peppered with nicks and scars. His claws were curved blades and he stood comfortably on his hind legs. Will watched in awe.

"Well, go ahead, boy!"

Will laughed at the surreal experience of hearing Papaw Jimmy's telepathic voice in his head, and coming from a massive brown bear. Will shook his head and sighed. He had to do it, needed to practice. Needed to control it. He took a few sharp breaths, psyching himself up. Jimmy's bear eyes rolled.

"Yer tryin' too hard," Jimmy growled. "Just relax."

Will nodded, slowing his breathing. He closed his eyes and relaxed. He let the world drift away, thinking nothing but *cat*. He focused on yellow eyes, black fur, sickle claws. He thought about power, dominance, freedom and speed. He visualized the cat and felt a warm sense of comfort come over him.

"Open yer eyes, ye' 'idgit."

Will opened his lemon-yellow eyes.

He looked down at his black-furred body, muscles

flexing in the moonlight. His nearly imperceptible, black rosette pattern caught the light when he moved.

His taloned feet dug deep into the earth. His hands flexed, sharp-crescent claws sliding in and out at his command. He felt his power, his strength, his freedom. He was still Will behind the ferocious mask, still in control.

He looked up at Papaw Jimmy, a bear and a black jaguar facing each other, all of nature stretched out before them. The muzzle of the bear smiled as he nodded at Will.

"How do ye' feel, boy?"

"I feel... *great!*"

"So what do ye' want to do?"

"I want *to run!*"

"So, run! The world is yours!"

Will sprang into action with a fierce roar.

He blasted across the expanse on two feet, not a man, not a cat. His arms pumped and his chest heaved. He reached the edge of the clearing in seconds, doubling back and sprinting around the circumference.

Papaw Jimmy ambled to the center of the open area, enjoying the show. He watched as Will jumped and spun, darted left and right, looked all around and breathed in the multitude of fresh scents.

Will sped across the field again, kicking up grass and soil, this time powering through the tree line. He ran through the trees, dodging around, leaping over obstacles. His feet smashed down onto an overturned log and his powerful legs thrust him back up into the air.

He latched onto a tree with his claws, climbing with

ease. He reached a branch twenty feet up, sprang away and hooked on to another tree. He climbed higher, breaking through the branches and leaves. He stopped, a clear view of the entire night sky and the mountain valley stretched out before him.

He bellowed out a majestic roar. It was all *his*.

STRENGTH. POWER. DOMINATION.

WILL RETURNED TO THE CLEARING WHERE PAPAW Jimmy waited in bear form. He was rolling in the grass and scratching his furry back on a large boulder. The black cat marched with a confident stride, meeting up with his grandfather-bear. His chest heaved and his claws relaxed. Jimmy flipped over onto all fours.

"Well, boy? Ye' hungry now, or what?"

"Oh, yeah!"

"You smell it, don't ye'?"

Will lifted his snout, breathing in the night. Crickets and sparrows, grass and trees and sap, mealworms and rabbits... *and an elk.* Will's eyes lit up. The distinct musk was unmistakable.

"To the east," Will said.

"Mm hm. 'Bout two and a half miles. Big 'un. You want to do the honors, or — "

Will was off like a shot before Jimmy could finish his sentence, bounding into the wild. Jimmy chuckled and followed behind, trying to keep up on his four old paws.

Will was a black streak, a shadow amongst the shadows. A silent and invisible hunter. Smooth as silk, he slid through the dark woods of Black Mountain. The thick pads on his feet betrayed no sound and no obstacle gave him pause.

The towering trees blocked out all moonlight, yet Will's electric-yellow eyes could see all. He breathed in the aromas of the land and could smell the elk less than a hundred yards away, over the next hill and down in the valley.

Will bounded over two fallen trees and whisked through the accompanying foliage with barely a whisper. His padded feet propelled him to the next ridge, where he slowed down and dropped to all fours. He crept to the edge, peering through the bushes. It didn't take him long to locate his prey.

The elk walked through the valley clearing in the moonlight. A large stag, he must have weighed nearly a thousand pounds. His formidable antlers gleamed as they reached for the sky. His body was massive and muscular, his scent clear and strong.

Will could even sense his heartbeat and hear his breathing. He was clearly the dominant bull in his herd, and would not go easily without a fight.

Good.

With a rustle of leaves, Papaw Jimmy crept up behind Will in the shadows, not nearly as stealthy as the young feline. He peered over Will's shoulder, his mouth watering as he appraised the upcoming meal. The cat and the bear shared a look. Will nodded his head in agreement and slinked off on all fours around the edge of the valley.

The elk grazed, casually meandering within his domain. The air was cool in his fur, but something in the light breeze made his head perk up. A scent he didn't like triggered his alarm. He was not alone. There was another animal there with him, something big.

He looked around on high alert, soon hearing the rustling of grass and the padding of four feet. The huge bear burst into a sprint from across the field, charging right at him, muzzle snarling.

The elk bolted with oiled precision, much faster than the old bear. He ran for the protective cover of the surrounding trees, hoping he could outrun the predator once inside the forest maze. Powerful hooves pounded the ground and shot him forward for the tree line, and he sprang for the first opening he saw.

A black shadow lunged out from behind the trees.

Curved claws dug into the stag's neck and flanks, throwing the beast to the ground. The elk groaned in shocked panic and pain as it landed on its side.

The panther pounced, but the bull was up again, swinging its royal antlers right and left. Will dodged the counterattack, a rolling grumble deep in his bestial throat.

The brown bear smashed onto the scene, knocking into the elk and shaking him off balance. The bull spun around in fury, stomping and charging and posturing his might. He shook his antlers and thrashed them back and forth.

Will and Jimmy circled the beast, avoiding the sharp, multi-pronged spears of bone. Will lunged forward again, digging his claws into the elk's body and biting at his throat.

The stag thrashed in alarm and released a haunting cry. A booming, high-pitch shriek like a flute being strangled came from its throat. Will held on with his hooks, sinking his fangs in to the thick musculature surrounding the beast's windpipe.

The bull was a mighty and proud warrior, whipping his head and bucking his hooves. The antlers grazed Will's shoulder and he leapt back, hissing. The bull stomped at Will, head stabbing forward, screaming his terrible, chilling, wraith-whistle cry of distress.

Papaw Jimmy jumped in from behind, grabbing the antlers with his massive paws and holding the elk back. The animal bucked and screamed, using its weight and all its strength, and the powerful bear struggled to restrain him. Will shot forward again, wrapping his deadly maw around its throat and biting down hard.

The bull shrieked again and again, struggling, desperate. But Will thrashed his head and sunk his claws in once more. Jimmy released his grip and let Will take the prey to the ground.

The black cat bit down harder, holding the grip. His vicious jaws crunched down on the spine and cut off the oxygen supply, and the elk's terrified eyes slowly rolled back in its head. Will ripped out the throat and beheld the gorgeous hemorrhage of blood soaking the grass and dirt.

With lust and hunger, Will dove back in, tearing away flesh and feasting on it. Jimmy joined the party, ripping open the torso and splintering the ribs, letting out the steaming innards.

The black cat and the brown bear fed.

Will looked up, his face spattered and dripping with crimson gore. Jimmy gulped down fresh, thick muscle and drank the savory blood. They shared a look and smiled.

"Hey, Papaw," Will said.

"Yeahp."

Will shook his head and laughed. "You're a *bear!*" he said, still in disbelief. They both laughed.

Papaw Jimmy threw his head back and bellowed into the night, a howl to match any wolf's. Will bared his teeth and roared at the moon. Together, they let their dominance be known.

Then, they returned to their meal.

———

Janae walked out onto the porch. Cool wind blew through the chimes and chilled her bare shoulders. She looked around into the darkness. All alone. She pulled out her phone and dialed.

She paced, holding the device to her ear.

"Janae?" It was a man's voice.

"Yeah."

"Is everything on track?"

"Yes, but..." she wavered. Her free hand rubbed at a knot in the base of her neck. "I don't know, I don't like it."

"This is necessary, Janae."

"But he's not a bad guy! He's really not — "

"You know the prophecy, child." The man's voice was deep, controlled and resonant. Even through a phone, it carried authority. "It has to be done."

"I know, Keonee, I know!" Janae said. "I just... I..."

"You like him."

"...Yes. A-And maybe he'll come work for us..."

"One of the Shaw brothers shall be the destroyer of The Council. It will be the end of all of us. Throw the world into chaos... *You know the prophecy!*"

"I know! There just... There just has the be a better way."

"I'm sorry," he said, his voice soothing. "Once you have confirmation that Mason Shaw is dead...

Will Shaw must also die."

28

FAMILY

"IT'S ALL OVER THE NEWS," TJ said, blowing a stream of smoke and flicking his yo-yo. "Arthur's dead. Jim Reid too. They got hit hard. The cargo was taken to the fuckin' pigs."

"Fuckin' bitch," Annette said almost to herself as she too puffed on a cigarette.

Mason paced in front of them, smoking a cigar. They stood in a mostly vacant Georgia truck stop in the dead of night. Two eighteen wheelers rested across the lot, and only the occasional motorist passed through. The Pack's RV and van had been gassed, and now the trio found themselves at a crossroads.

"Those kids are gonna talk," TJ said, jaw clenched in frustration. "And the pigs've got Moonshine's body now. They're gonna start puttin' things together. They're gonna be lookin' for us."

"And just what do you suggest we do, TJ?" Annette snarled.

"We disappear, that's what!"

"Oh, yeah? And do what? Split up, get jobs at convenience stores, wearin' little name tags and shit?"

"No, but we can lay low for a while. Maybe move somewhere far away, like Canada... or Mexico! With your bedside manner, I can see you doing well in some sort of customer service industry, maybe a hotel or a luxury spa..."

Mason cut in with a sobering, *"Quiet!"*

TJ and Annette snapped to attention as their leader paced in front of them, his eyes and cigar smoldering. "Nobody's runnin' anywhere. Nothing has changed. Roy wants to see us, so we're goin' to Savannah."

"I don't like it, Mase," TJ said. "It's like goin' to the principal's office. Roy never wants to see us. He always deals with Arthur..."

"Yeah, well Arthur's *dead*, TJ. And I'm sure Roy wants an explanation. So we're gonna give him one."

"We don't need him, Mase," TJ urged. "We don't need any of these fuckin' sheep, bro. We're *skinners*. We can go where we want and do what we want."

Mason stepped up to TJ, putting a hand on his shoulder. "I'm right where I want to be, doin' just what I want to do. Roy's the one with the money. I'd rather keep a low-pro and stay out of the spotlight. Just keep on bringin' in product like we always done... Plus, maybe him and his posse can help us deal with our new little problem. My brother and — "

"That *bitch*," Annette said.

Mason grunted.

"It would be better if we didn't come in empty handed," Annette added, gesturing over to the RV where

Casey remained. "I say we bring the girl in to Roy, Mase. She's pretty, he'll get top dollar for — "

"No!" Mason snarled, crossing over to Annette. "She is our responsibility now. She's one of us."

"Then we gotta take her out, Mase."

"*No!*"

"Once she connects with her power, once she skins for the first time... Come on, man. She'll be dangerous. She'll escape..."

"We'll bring her on into The Pack, that's what." Mason nodded, pacing, determined. "We'll teach her our ways, get her on our side. We'll build The Pack back up, find more skinners, become stronger than ever."

"Dude, she'll never just *join* us, Mason," TJ said. "We'll never be able to trust her."

"It will take time, but we can bring her over to our side. Think about what an asset she could be. We start training her young..."

"It's a bad idea, Mase. We're the monsters who kidnapped her, man — "

Mason grabbed TJ and thrust him against the side of the van, snarling in the smaller man's face. "Who's runnin' this crew, little man? *Huh?* Is it you?"

"N-No."

"That's right," Mason growled. His eyes gleamed with yellow. "We have a new daughter now. We're gonna take good care of 'er. And we're gonna make this family *strong.*"

"O-Okay, Mase."

"Good. Now, if you'll excuse me," Mason said. "I got some snacks to buy."

. . .

CASEY LAY ON THE BED IN THE DARK OF THE RV's back room. Tears had dried on her cheeks. Her wrists burned from the duct tape bindings, and her jaw ached from the gag. Her captors were still too close, and she was too far from anyone who might help. This was not the right time to make a daring escape, so she bided her time, thought of her mother, and tried not to cry.

Footsteps approached from outside and the RV's door swung open. The sound of heavy footfalls and the lurching of the shocks told her that the big man had come inside. The other two were still outside, silently smoking.

Casey braced herself as the footsteps drew near, and the thin bedroom door creaked open. Mason stood in the dark, his figure a massive silhouette filling the door frame as he looked in on her.

"Hey there, kiddo," he said.

Mason flicked on the light switch and Casey winced at the sudden brightness. Mason had a brown paper bag in his hand, stained with grease, and Casey could smell the hot bacon cheeseburger and fries he'd bought at the truck stop. In his other hand was a large soda.

He sat down on the corner of the bed, placing the bag of food down beside her. His bronze face had an earnest smile and the tone of his voice had softened. He opened the bag and began pulling out food.

"I'm sorry about all this," he said. "You must be hungry. Come on, now." He helped her sit up, then untied the gag from her mouth. She flexed her jaw with a groan of relief. Mason held the soda up to her mouth and she anxiously drank from the straw. He pulled out a French fry and held it up to her mouth.

"You gonna feed me like a baby?" Casey asked. "Can't I at least use my hands?"

Mason sighed, contemplating.

"I can't risk you tryin' anything."

"What am I gonna try? We're out in the middle of nowhere and there's three of you." Mason considered this sound logic. After a moment, he pulled the folding knife from his belt and flicked it open.

He held it before her for a threatening moment, silently warning her against trying anything stupid, then sliced the tape off of her wrists. Casey ripped the rest of the tape off, rubbing her raw skin and stretching her arms.

"When you're done eating, I'm gonna have to tape you back up." Mason's tone was apologetic.

"Why is that?" Casey said. "Aren't you trying to 'bring me into the family' now?" She looked firmly into his eyes. Mason laughed.

"You heard all that, huh?"

"I heard everything," she said, "I *hear* everything, I *smell* everything... I don't know what you all did to me, but everything is different. You kept saying 'she's a *skinner*, like us.' Well, what the heck is that?"

Mason searched for the right words. "You're like us. You're very special. You're not a normal little girl. That's why we had to take you the way we did. That's why we have to tie you up... For now. Because you're dangerous. You have incredible power inside of you."

"You're all monsters! That lady turned into a... A

snake or something, and bit me! Is that what a skinner is? Are you all snake monsters? *Is that what's happening to me?*" Tears burned in Casey's eyes and she struggled to hold herself together. Mason put his hands on her shoulders and used his best tender voice.

"No, sweetie, no. We all have our own animal spirit inside," he said. "Annette's is a viper. Mine is a wolf. Yours is yours, and you'll find out what it is soon enough. It's been with you all your life. And now it's... Now it's just ready to come out, is all."

"I want to go home! *I want my mom!*"

"Now baby, it's too dangerous for that right now. You don't know how to control it yet. You could *hurt* your mom, maybe even kill her. You don't want that, now do ya'?"

She shook her head, fresh tears rolling down her cheeks.

"That's why we have to keep you here, keep you tied up. For now. You could hurt yourself, or hurt others." Mason wiped the tears from her face with his massive bronze thumbs. "And that's what we do. We find special children who are about to change, and we take 'em away, to protect 'em. And to protect all the sheep out there — That's normal people — from knowin' the truth."

She wanted to call him a liar and spit in his face. She wanted to ask him what happened to the other kids that had been in there with her. Crying and confused, they were innocent victims. Staring at Mason's rugged countenance, she wanted nothing more than to claw his eyes out and *run, run, run.*

. . .

FAST. FAST. FAST.

She also knew that at least some of what he had told her was the truth. There truly was an animal within her, a beast pacing in a small cage. And it was not a snake. It felt completely alien and inhuman, and yet, completely natural. It truly had been a part of her all along. It was not something that Annette had put in her with that bite, but merely a door that had been opened. She truly could not control it, and she feared what might happen whenever it finally came out.

"I know this is scary," Mason reassured. "But we're gonna help you, okay? You have to trust me. You're one of us now, Casey. Part of The Pack! We will protect you, I promise. We're *family* now... Okay?"

Every fiber in her body told her to bite his nose off, to pull the hidden steak knife from her waistband and stab it into his throat. To let out whatever beast was inside of her, and let it tear him to shreds. But she held her tongue and played along. Casey was a smart girl.

She was going to be a doctor someday.

"Okay," Casey said, meekly nodding her head.

"All right then," Mason smiled, pushing the food closer to her. "Go on and eat, now. We got a long drive ahead."

29

NOT A MONSTER

WILL SAT on the edge of his old bed, in his old room. Another night had passed with no sleep. He stared bleary-eyed out his bedroom window, looking at the view he had grown up with. There was morning dew on the window pane, the branches of an old yellowwood just outside, and the South end of Black Mountain beyond that.

The furniture and decorations were the same as he had left them, including his *Friday The 13th* posters and his signed headshot of Salma Hayek. Most of his old clothes, sports gear and toys had been moved elsewhere, but he had found his favorite old six-inch action figure of The Hulk.

He held the little muscular green man in his hands, fingers tracing the contours of the plastic as his eyes wandered into the past. So many memories flooded his mind. So much urgency weighed on his present.

Mason was out there somewhere, and Will was running out of time. He'd cleaned and prepped his guns, loading every magazine. He'd stayed up, pacing, thinking, working The Hulk around in his hands.

After their little hunting trip, Papaw Jimmy had gone straight to bed. Janae slept on the couch downstairs, her snoring a light purr. Papaw's snoring was more like a rusty lawnmower, but Will didn't mind.

It reminded him of home.

Downstairs, he heard the sound of footsteps and the bathroom door opening and closing. Janae was awake. Soon, the door of Papaw Jimmy's room creaked open, and that familiar, halting gait came down the hallway. The footsteps stopped right outside Will's door. There was a moment of silence. Then...

"You didn't sleep a wink, did ye' boy?"

Will laughed at the muffled voice through the door.

"Well, come on downstairs," Jimmy said. "I'll put some coffee on."

"Okay," Will said. He turned his gaze to the mirror across the room. He studied his own face in the reflection. He looked at himself harder than he ever had before. Two eyes, a broken nose, a mouth, a stubbly chin, two little ears, and short black hair. He was a handsome man. A *man*. A human being.

He was still Will Shaw.

He was not a monster.

THE AROMAS OF SAUSAGE PATTIES AND HOT, BREWING coffee greeted Will as he trotted down the stairs. He held the Hulk toy in his hands, rounding the corner into the kitchen. Jimmy worked at the stove, cooking the sausages and getting eggs ready to scramble. Janae sat at the table, laughing as she stirred her cup of coffee.

"Hey there, *tiger*," she said, trying to hide the sadness in her eyes.

"Ha. Ha."

"Man, you really didn't sleep a wink, did you?"

"I'm fine. What are you laughing at in here?"

"Oh, Jimmy was just telling me about the first time you brought a girl home," Janae teased. "What was it, Deanna?"

"Diandra," Jimmy said with a chuckle.

"Oh, Papaw, please…"

"Girl was all over Will like flies on a picnic table, and he just did not have a clue. She wanted him to kiss 'er so bad, but he was waitin' for an invitation! *Hyeck hyeck!* You 'member that, boy?"

"Yes, Papaw." Will plopped down at the table, rolling his eyes and Janae couldn't help but laugh at him. Jimmy poured a cup of steaming coffee and passed it over to Will.

"Drink coffee," Jimmy said. "Coffee good."

"Mm, thank you," Will said with measured sarcasm.

"So, what happened, Will?" Janae asked. "Did you ever get some sugar from Diandra?"

"No," Will said, blowing on his coffee and pouring a heavy dose of sugar and cream into it. "I asked her at the end of the date if I could kiss her. She got all uncomfortable and was like, 'I don't want you to *ask* me to do it, I just want you to do it!' So that was the end of that one."

Jimmy cracked several eggs into a big bowl and beat them up, mixing in salt and pepper. He poured the whipped eggs in the hot frying pan and began to stir as they crackled and popped. "I'd ask ya'll to stay a couple days, spend some time," Jimmy said, "but I know ye' won't. Fixin' to head out, you'll say."

"He's still out there, Papaw. I've got to…"

"Yeah, I know, I know. Gotta do what ye' gotta do. Just wish I could've been more help is all." Jimmy portioned out the eggs onto three plates along with the sausage patties, then passed them over to Will and Janae.

"Mmmm, thank you so much, Jimmy."

"My pleasure, Jane."

Papaw Jimmy sat down with his own plate and they began eating. Will scarfed down his eggs and sausages, and Janae took her time. Silence descended as the three enjoyed their meal. Will gulped down his black coffee and slowly, the fog lifted from his head. He was coming alive again.

He smiled at his grandfather, remembering fondly his kindness and generosity over the years. Breakfasts like this were a daily occurrence, and Will couldn't help but appreciate all that Jimmy had done for him, especially in light of recent events.

Jimmy gestured to Will's Hulk action figure as he gobbled down his eggs. "Found one of yer old toys, eh boy?"

"Yeah," Will said. "Not much left in my room. All my old clothes and toys are gone. But I did find my buddy here."

"Well, I got plenty more of yer stuff in the basement. Your clothes, you and yer brother's toys. Got it all boxed up."

Will stopped eating.

"What?" Will's eyes intensified. "You said you got... some of *Mason's* old things?"

"Yep, somewhere down there, I think. Why?"

Will shot a look at Janae.

THE LIGHT TURNED ON IN THE BASEMENT.

Will clomped down the stairs in his rattlesnake-skin boots, followed by Papaw Jimmy and Janae. The dingy, cement cellar was even more packed than he remembered. Everything from lawn care equipment, to Christmas decorations, to decades-old weight lifting gear lined the cinderblock walls. Boxes of all shapes and sizes were stacked up, labeled in sloppy, black magic-marker writing.

"Over here," Jimmy said.

He led them through the maze into a dark corner near the old boiler, and clicked on an overhead lightbulb hanging on a chain. The old man began moving aside boxes, finally uncovering two large ones, aged by time and mildew. On the side was written *Boys stuff*.

"Here we go."

Will tore into the first box and began sifting through the contents. Inside, he met his memories face to face, in physical form. There were his high school yearbooks from junior and senior year. There was a worn baseball tucked into a short-stop mitt. There were three pairs of shoes, his framed high school diploma, his graduation cap and a small stack of comic books. Will rummaged while Jimmy and Janae watched.

"Wanna tell me what yer lookin' for?" Jimmy asked.

"Something of Mason's. Anything."

"Ah, right. Yer a tactile."

"If I touch something of his... I might be able to see where he is, or where he's goin'." Will reached the bottom of the box and found nothing.

He pushed it aside and started on the second box.

"You pick up things by touch," Jimmy said. "I can't do that. I get visions of what's to come, but not specifics like that."

Will dug through the box, this one filled mostly with toys from his younger years. Several Masters of the Universe figures were present, along with original Star Wars toys that would now be worth a fortune had he just kept them in the box.

He found his old BB gun and smiled. Freddy Krueger and Jason Voorhees were present, still locked in immortal combat. There was his favorite old baseball cap, a sloppily painted, vinyl model kit of The Predator, and... Will's eyes opened wide.

Mason's old slingshot.

Will reached down, hesitating for a brief moment, then picked it up. A spark jolted in his hand and a current shot up his arm and into his brain.

He spasmed and hung on for the ride as a flood of sensory information washed through him.

DRIVING. HIGHWAY.
SOME KIND OF BUS OR RV.

· · ·

"You okay?" Janae asked.

"I'm there... I'm with him...," Will gasped. He turned and looked back at them. "I can find him."

———

Janae loaded up the car with her bags as Will came back outside with the last of his things. Jimmy followed, a box of ammo in each hand, and the two men loaded everything into the trunk of the Challenger. Janae zipped up her leather jacket and waited for the boys, ready to roll.

She checked her phone.

Jimmy shot a smile at her, then turned back to Will. The two men faced each other, neither knowing what to say. Jimmy slapped Will's shoulder, a gesture of silent reassurance.

"You got everythin' ye' need?" Jimmy asked.

Will held up the slingshot in his hand. "Yup."

Jimmy reached into his jacket pocket and produced the small Hulk action figure. "Don't forget yer little green friend," he said, handing it to Will.

"Okay," Will chuckled.

"Don't forget who ye' are, boy."

Will nodded, then continued loading up the car. Jimmy walked over to Janae, who gave him a warm smile. "It's been a pleasure, Jimmy. Thank you for everything," she said, giving him a warm hug.

"The pleasure was all mine, Janie," he whispered in her ear. He pulled away, giving her a serious look. "Be careful, kid. You know what Keonee will do to you if he finds out about Will."

She flexed the muscles in her jaw.

"He won't find out."

Jimmy rubbed her shoulders and they shared a moment. He sighed, nodding.

"Take care a' the big lug for me." He hugged her again, then stepped away. She smiled and nodded in agreement, going to the car and getting in the passenger seat.

Jimmy turned back to Will, giving him a strong bear hug. Will hugged him back. "Thanks, Papaw," Will said, holding tight. "Love you."

"I love ye' too, boy. Come on back, soon. We'll do some more huntin' together."

"Will do."

"Now... Go," Jimmy whispered. His eyes misted over. "Go take care of yer brother, boy. Go make things right."

"Will do, Papaw."

Jimmy released his embrace and faced Will again. Will nodded, swallowing his Adam's apple. Jimmy slapped his shoulder and backed off.

"Go on, now!"

Will glanced over at Janae and nodded. He slid into the driver's seat and started it up. He placed The Hulk in the niche on the dashboard, letting his favorite hero look back at him. He held the slingshot in his hand, then placed it down in the center console.

He looked at Jimmy through the window and the old man smiled and nodded his approval. Will held up his fist and extended both his thumb and pinky finger into the "hang loose" symbol, a dimpled, sly smile on his face. He revved the engine and put it into gear.

Dirt and gravel kicked up into the air as Will and Janae ripped down the country road. An orange and black streak, the machine stalked into action.

The hunt was on.

BIG BOSS MAN

SAVANNAH, *Georgia*

THE GREAT SAVANNAH RIVER WAS A SPECTACLE OF natural beauty.

Built on its shores, a spectacle towered that was anything but natural. The Georgia Port Authority had constructed the largest single-terminal container facility of its kind in the United States. Comprised of Garden City Terminal and Ocean Terminal, the immense shipping port spanned one-thousand-three-hundred and forty-five acres and moved millions of tons of cargo every year.

Thirty-six massive cranes lifted and moved the rectangular steel containers from the docks to the ships and back. In ten years, they projected that number to be forty-two cranes.

Cargo was moved inland and overseas, wherever the clients wanted. The workforce was thousands strong; the whole operation was a monumental feat of engineering and commerce. Steel containers were stacked on top of each other like boxes of cereal, many of them five-high.

The facility was a booming city unto itself, moving billions of dollars in product per year. During normal business hours, the place surged with activity. Massive freighters came and went, cranes lifted and moved containers, and workmen in yellow vests and hard hats buzzed around like busy little bees.

Now, just after midnight, the work was significantly slower. Ships still came and went, and workers still performed their tasks, but third shift was much less busy.

Far fewer people worked the docks at night, most of whom were private, armed security. For the right price, they would look the other way, or even participate in some of the after-hours dealings that occurred on the docks.

Mason had parked the RV in lot B.

He had apologized to Casey for needing to tie her up again, leaving her locked in the bedroom as he, TJ and Annette drove the van deeper into the complex. They rolled up to the main gate, where an annoyed guard sauntered out of his booth and approached the driver's window with a cocky smirk.

Mason wanted to rip that smug look right off his stupid skull.

"Help you guys?" the guard asked.

"We're here to see Roy," Mason said.

"Roy who?"

"Hendricks."

"And you are?"

"Just tell 'im it's Mason."

The guard grunted and keyed the call button on his radio, calling inside. He relayed the information and the static voice on the other end replied in the affirmative. The guard mumbled "10-4" in response and turned back to Mason.

"Okay, I'll buzz you in," said the guard. "It's dock 19, the control tower. You turn left at the first — "

"I know where to go, thank you."

The guard stepped back inside his booth, pressing the button to lift the gate arm. Mason drove inside, slipping into the shadows of the industrial complex. Annette and TJ shared a look, both keeping their mouths shut as they moved into unfamiliar territory for them.

TJ couldn't help but smack nervously on a piece of gum.

Mason had been here only twice before, but he remembered every turn and his nose followed the scent of fear. They slowed to a halt as they approached the dock, a wide-open space where an enormous shipping freighter waited to be loaded with cargo.

Two eighteen-wheel trucks were parked, along with several other vehicles. Headlights illuminated the scene, and security officers worked hand-in-hand with what appeared to be plain-clothes mercenaries. From the trucks and cars, the workers removed their cargo...

Children.

They ranged in age from three to thirteen. They were all being herded towards a large, open shipping container, where a coordinator stood with an iPad, taking a digital inventory.

Several different groups were apparent, all working in-sync together. Independent contractors from all over the South convened in this spot, each dropping off their latest catch. Some brought in a few, some brought in many.

Two more guards carrying MP5 sub-machine guns approached the van and motioned for the trio to get out. "Hands up," one of them said. Mason let out an angered sigh, but obeyed, and his partners reluctantly followed. In an instant, they were being frisked for weapons.

"What the fuck, dude? You gonna buy me a drink first, or what?" TJ sneered and cackled at his own riotous jest. The guard doing the frisking found a .38 snub-nose in a holster on TJ's belt and a switchblade in his boot.

Both were tossed back inside the van. A blade was found on both Mason and Annette, and they too were chucked back in. Satisfied, the guards indicated they could lower their arms, then motioned for them to follow.

They were led to the elevator at the foot of the imposing steel structure, an industrial bird's nest to oversee the flow of traffic. From up there, controllers monitored shipments of everything from food, to toys, to furniture, to automobiles, oblivious to the secret traffic that flowed through the port after dark.

Mason, TJ and Annette stepped into the steel cage, flanked by the two guards. The door slid closed with a slam and the hydraulics whirred to life, lifting the metal box up into the sky.

Mason shared a calm look with his two cohorts as the

view of the outside docks craned upward. The cage carried them up with a metallic squeal, thumping to a halt when it hit the top. The door screeched open and the second guard nodded in the direction they were to go.

The group walked over the metal grating and the white-painted, steel sheet walls, lined with rivets. They may as well have been walking the deck of a battleship. TJ looked down and could see the activity below on the dock through the metal grating.

He took a deep breath, trying to stay calm.

At the end of the walkway was a door guarded by two other sentries. These men were not in uniform, merely a couple of sleazy goons plucked from the U.S. prison system. They rapped on the door and turned the knob.

Mason and his crew were escorted in by the first two guards and were met by a chill in the air.

Inside, the control room looked out over the whole operation, the sparkling lights of the city beyond visible through the wrap-around windows.

Sitting at a desk across the room was an older man, surrounded by a collection of thugs, guards, mercenaries and henchman. A dozen men in total waited for the new guests to be escorted in.

"Mason. Come on in," said the man at the desk.

Roy Hendricks was tall, thin and in his mid sixties. His clothes and manner exuded not the flashy and ostentatious bearings of a rich man, but the subdued nonchalance of a *very* rich man.

He wore basic beige slacks, a nice sweater and a modest wedding ring, but felt no need to show off more than that. The desk boasted several stacks of cash, piled nearly up to his chin, and bags filled with more green currency rested on the floor around him.

The two escort guards nodded dutifully and left the room, while Mason, TJ and Annette approached the desk. The guards standing post in the room eyeballed their every step, hands resting on their guns.

Mason sauntered forward, unconcerned with this collection of weak sheep and their posturing.

"Hey, Roy."

"It's been a minute, Mason," Roy said, barely paying attention to him as he finished counting a stack of money and put it into a bag. "Here you go, Rico. Thanks again. See you next time." Roy handed the bag of money off to the man standing by the desk, who thanked him before leaving the room.

"Yeah, it has," Mason replied. "This here's TJ and..."

"So what's going on, Mason?" Roy interrupted. "Why am I here talking to you? I don't deal with you directly, I deal with Arthur... Oh, right! Arthur's dead."

Mason didn't answer.

"And the product is gone too, am I right?"

"With the police," one of Roy's henchmen chimed in.

"Right, right," Roy said, keeping his cool. "With the police... And now you're here. Empty handed."

TJ shot Mason an *I told you so* look.

"We can get more," Mason said. "That ain't no problem."

"Well, the problem is that my guy in Tennessee is a corpse, and the PD out there is now investigating his whole operation. Plus, one of your boys made the news as well, didn't he Mason? High-speed chase, motorcycle accident... That was your guy, right?"

"Yeah, that was Moonshine."

"Of course, *Moonshine*... So can you please explain to me, Mason, what the *fuck* is going on?" Roy's eyes flared with anger. He was no skinner, had no supernatural power, and Mason could tear his throat out in a heartbeat.

But the man did have money, and he did have men, many men with firepower. Mason, TJ and Annette felt the heat of those guns all around them, their pulses speeding up.

Mason kept his cool.

"Someone took out Arthur," Mason said. "And Moonshine. They're comin' after all of us, Roy..."

"Oh, yeah? See, I kind of think they're just coming for *you*, Mason. You're a good supplier, but you're flashy. Sloppy. You let our business spill out into the public." Roy stood up and crossed around the desk, eyes never leaving Mason's. "And now you've got people after you. Threatening to expose us all. Expose *me*. I've got a family, Mason. That shit ain't cool, man."

"We'll take care of it."

Roy laughed, stepping closer to Mason. They were the same height, and Roy's cutting blue eyes looked straight into Mason's browns.

"You'll take care of it? Mason, we don't supply product to pimps and poor white trash here. We deal with high-end clientele exclusively. We can't risk *any* of this getting out! But hey, you'll take care of it!"

Roy's henchmen had slowly begun circling the trio. It

did not go unnoticed. Mason tracked their movements in the corners of his eyes. Annette and TJ could hear their footsteps behind them.

TJ was itching to burst into his hyena form, scare the shit out of them and tear their guts out.

But all it would take was one bullet.

"L-Look, sir, if we could just — " TJ started.

"*Shut up!* Who the fuck are you, monkey boy?" Roy paced over to TJ, glaring down into his eyes. "And swallow that fucking gum! *Do it!*" TJ obeyed, gulping down his gum like a child in the school principal's office. Roy stalked back over to his desk, shaking his head. "Disgusting... So who the hell is after you, huh? Other than the police!"

"Just a couple troublemakers," Mason said. "All we need is a little time. Maybe you can spare a couple men? Help us take them out..."

Roy clapped his hands and laughed out loud. "*Ha!* You need a little time? You need a couple of *my* men? Well, I'm sorry, but you shit-heels are *out* of time."

The henchmen and thugs raised their weapons behind the trio, cocking the actions on the firearms and clicking off their safeties. Mason, TJ and Annette tensed as the verdict came in, their sentences delivered.

AN ORANGE DODGE CHALLENGER SLOWED TO A STOP at the main gate of the dock complex. The annoyed guard sluggishly pulled himself out of the chair in his booth and sauntered over to the car with his smug face.

"Can I help you folks?"

Will had a cherry lolly-pop wedged in his cheek.

He remained stoic and silent as Janae leaned over him from the passenger seat, smiling at the guard as she teased out her hair. Her demure eyes pulled him in to their black pupils with a strange gravity.

He was spellbound.

"I know it's late," she said. "But me and my friend here would just *love* a tour around the docks. Please?"

31

BLOOD RIVER

THE HYPNOTIZED guard led Will and Janae through the shipping yard on foot, smiling vacantly as she pushed him forward, hand on his shoulder. They heard the sounds of workers and heavy machinery in the distance.

Will controlled his breathing.

His DPMS Ar-15 was strapped around his shoulder. His 1911 and Sig X-Macro hugged his ribs in opposing shoulder holsters. His two grenades were clipped onto his belt at the ready, along with his two Spyderco folding knives and his hidden boot knife. He had given his .380 and .38 snub nose to Janae, who also carried her own Glock 17. No matter how many times he went into combat, it never got any easier.

He could already smell the blood to come.

"It's right over here..." The guard led them between two rows of shipping containers, stacked five-high.

"Shhh," Janae pressed on the guard's shoulder.

They slowed to a halt before entering the area ahead. Will and Janae peeked around the corner into the halogen-lit work area. Before them stood the control tower, surrounded by cars and trucks, with workers and armed guards going about their duties. To the right, the colossal freighter SS Abbey-Faith waited at the dock as the next container of cargo was prepped for loading.

It sat there on the dock beside the ship, a solid steel shipping container. At least forty young children stood inside. Trembling and crying. Will and Janae tensed, their blood boiling. Up above, an industrial hook lowered down on a heavy-duty galvanized cable from a full-gantry crane looming overhead.

One of the armed guards stood atop the shipping container, and clasped the hook securely into place in the center. He whistled and twirled his hand around, signaling that the connection was secure and ready for transport, then climbed back down the built-in ladder on the side of the giant steel box.

Will's jaw clenched. These were bad men, each and every one. He could see their energies, dark and corrupt and twisted.

They all had to die.

"This is where the kids ship out of," the entranced security guard said. "Every Saturday night, like clockwork."

"Is that right," Janae said through gritted teeth.

The door of the container closed, the latch secured.

"We have to move," Will said.

The crane's mechanisms whirred into motion and the hook began to pull the shipping container up into the sky. Will and Janae shared an urgent look. No time to waste.

"You get the kids," Will said, "I'll get Mason."

She nodded. The guard casually smiled, gesturing ahead. "You guys want me to take you on up to the control tower?"

"Nah, we can take it from here," Janae said. "You've been very helpful."

In a blur of motion, Janae whipped a folding knife into the side of the guard's neck with a *shunk*. She yanked it out and the officer staggered as a fountain of blood gushed from his carotid artery. He fell to the pavement, dying, as the two silent warriors stepped up to the threshold.

"Ready?" Will swung his AR into position.

"Let's do the damn thing," Janae said, drawing her Glock and chambering a round.

Will took out the first of his two grenades, pulled the pin. Took a deep breath.

He hurled the explosive through the air. It clanked beneath one of the pickup trucks used for loading, and before any of the guards or mercenaries noticed, it erupted with thunder.

The concussion blast sent shrapnel into the crowd of thugs and the gas tank of the truck, igniting it instantly. The vehicle hitched up in a massive fireball, shooting flaming debris around the dock.

Will and Janae leapt into the fray, guns raging.

Guards and goons were peppered with semi-automatic fire as Will blew them down. Discombobulated, the men fired back in all directions, not sure where the attack was coming from. Five fell in a row, the high velocity impacts spattering their blood into a fine mist as they collapsed into dead heaps.

Janae charged forward, taking them out one at a time with her Glock. Her eyes whipped up to the shipping container, hoisting higher into the air, on its way to the freighter. No matter what, she could not let that ship leave the harbor.

Guards fired back at her but she was an elusive dark streak. Two bullets sliced through her jacket but did not break skin. She emptied the rest of her magazine into the closest man's skull and used his body as a platform to jump over the hood of the truck that stood in her way.

Shouts and screams mingled with gunfire.

Gunpowder residue filled up the night and a high-pitch ringing resonated as all other sounds went numb. Janae spat out an empty magazine and clacked a fresh one in, taking cover behind the wheel base of the truck as the hired guns opened up on her.

Will stormed at them, using the last of his magazine and taking down four of the enemies. One remained standing, and ran at Will with a raging scream before he could reload.

Will knocked the man's gun out of the way as it fired, pulling his favorite Spyderco knife from his waist band and slashing it across the attacker's belly.

The goon's eyes went wide in terror as he staggered back, his hands grasping at his stomach to keep his guts from spilling out onto his boots. Will ended the bout with a final security shot to the head.

He slapped in a new magazine and went back for more blood.

Roy's eyes were panicked.

"*Friends of yours?*" he hissed, turning from the window where the carnage ensued below and stared daggers at Mason.

"Not exactly," Mason said.

"Get on your knees!" Neither Mason nor his two cohorts obeyed. Roy jabbed a Smith & Wesson .45 into Mason's ribs. "*Now!* All of you, on your knees!"

A yellow hue burned within Mason's irises and a rumble from hell vibrated in his throat. Roy's face drooped in confusion and dread as he looked into those animal eyes.

"The wolf does not fear the sheep," Mason said.

His hand was on Roy's wrist in an instant, twisting the pistol away in his bone-crunching vice grip. Roy let out a pained grunt and watched in horror as a shimmer began in Mason's clenched hand and ran up his arm.

Flesh and clothing warped away, leaving muscle and gray fur in its place. Hand became claw, and as the shimmer swept up to his face, human features flickered away. Roy gasped for air, unable to scream as a horrible new visage snarled down at him. Not man, not wolf, but a demon born of both.

"Oh my *God!*" Roy cried. "What the hell are y—"

Mason yanked Roy's arm, heaving him across the room. The guards screamed and trained their guns on the beast, but TJ and Annette were already moving.

"Oh yeah, motherfucker!" TJ grinned. "It's party time! Come get it, bitches!"

In seconds, humanity rippled away in the warped bending of light and reality. The hyena and the black viper sprang into action, grabbing the gunmen and tearing into them. The others ran for cover, screaming.

Mason lifted Roy's metal desk overhead, stacks of cash still piled on it, and launched it at the man as he tried to crawl away. Roy dodged and rolled as the desk crashed down, money raining all around him.

The gray wolf stalked forward, but Roy turned to face him, firing his .45 from the ground in a panic. The shots went wild, except one, grazing the side of the beast's temple and drawing deep-red blood.

Mason snarled and jumped into the side room to avoid the barrage of bullets. Roy scampered to his feet, fleeing from the control room for his life. TJ and Annette finished slaughtering the other two guards in brutal fashion and moved on to the next.

———

Janae finished her last rounds in the Glock, shoved the pistol back in its holster and drew the .38. Two more guards stood in her way as she sprinted for the ladder leading up to the crane. The men opened fire and she returned it, one of her bullets hitting its target center mass. The man went down.

The other kept shooting. One of his bullets ripped through her side and she hissed at the burn. Her six shots spent, she chucked the empty weapon at the man's head. He ducked away from the gun flying at his temple, but Janae vaulted through the air with a battle cry.

She crashed into the gunman, knocking him to his back and wrestling for control of his firearm. Her dagger came up again and she brought it down once, twice, three times into his chest. He spasmed and spat up blood. Janae made sure to look into his eyes as he slipped away.

She staggered to her feet and clenched the wound on her left side. It burned and bled, but was only superficial. She turned to the ladder with urgency and began to climb up the metal rungs, desperately chasing after the storage container as it lifted into the night sky.

———————————

BOOM! BOOM! BOOM!

Will blasted his way into the ground floor of the control tower, slicing down three more guards with 5.56 green tips. He jumped over their smoking corpses and cleared the room. Finding the staircase, he peaked around the corner and aimed up.

He dashed up the stairs, hugging the wall, the muzzle of the AR-15 trained upwards. Two plain-clothes mercenaries charged down at him from two floors up, firing at the ascending dark shape.

The big Cherokee fired back, emptying out his last magazine. The first guard howled as the bullets seared through his vital organs. He fell over the railing and careened past Will on the staircase.

Will heard the man's body crunch as he impacted the floor. He tossed the now-useless AR-15 aside and drew his 1911, clicking off the safety. The second guard charged down, emptying out his own magazine as he drew near.

Will ducked and answered with the 1911.

One bullet struck the attacker's shoulder, the next in his stomach — but he kept coming. Using his downward momentum, the mercenary crashed into Will, head-butting him and straining for his gun.

Will pushed back, but the larger attacker had him pressed against the railing, threatening to throw him over and down the stairwell. The man grimaced in Will's face, sweat beading on his intense brow.

Will shot a knee up into his opponent's crotch, buckling him. He slammed the man into the wall, then whipped him around and threw him at the railing. As the shrieking goon toppled backwards over the rail, Will fired the 1911 three more times into his chest for good measure.

Rattled and bruised, Will charged up the stairs.

His leg badly broken, Roy Hendricks crawled across the steel grate floor of the long hallway. The elevator beckoned up ahead. Behind him, he heard the sound of heavy, padded footsteps. The beast stalked through the smokey shadows, taking its time.

Roy whirled onto his back, frantically thrusting his sidearm out in trembling hands. He fired his last three shots, all going hopelessly wild.

The wolf closed in, undeterred.

Roy turned onto his stomach and crawled ahead along the grate, gasping, crying as voices of gunfire sang close by. He felt the tremble of the grate as two bestial, clawed feet stomped down on either side of him. He wept, daring to look up. Mason stood over him, an alpha wolf toying with a lamb.

"P-Please..."

A clawed hand reached down and lifted Roy up by the back of his neck and into the air. The lamb trembled and shuddered as the beast held him up at eye level, face to monstrous face. Lips parted and a vicious canine muzzle smiled at him. Yellow eyes burned with intent.

A trickle of blood ran down the side of the beast's head from Roy's bullet that had sliced across. Mason delicately traced the features of his victim's face with his menacing claws.

Roy pissed his pants.

"P-Please, no! Mason, *please!* Oh god, this can't be real! This c-can't... b-be..."

The beast wrapped its hand around the man's head, its animal jaws still twisted into that terrible smile. He gripped the bald head with claws that were short and stubby, meant for crushing and tearing, rather than slicing. With increasing pressure, the bone-crunching claws dug into Roy Hendricks's skull.

Roy shit his pants.

He convulsed and squealed as he felt his head crush like a blood orange. Claws gripped and ground into his brain, his head collapsing into a pulpy mess as his body went slack. Mason snarled, satisfied.

Just then, Will emerged from the stairwell, gun trained ahead. He saw Mason.

Their eyes locked together.

The moment froze, lingered.

Brother saw brother. They both had been expecting

this, and both knew what had to happen. Will's warrior instinct kicked in, and he broke himself clear of his emotions, leveling his sights.

Mason gave Roy's limp corpse a vicious shake just for good measure, then tossed the dead weight through the air at his brother. The bloody body smashed into Will, knocking him down the stairs again.

He caught the railing with a single hand, pulling himself back up. Before he could find his footing, two of the panicked gunmen came from opposite corners, opening fire.

Buddabuddabuddabudda!

Will rolled backwards down a flight of steps to evade the barrage of lead. Mason felt a hot slug tear into his leg. Howling in pain, he sprang out of the corridor as the attacker chased after him.

Bullets flew and sparked as Will took cover in the stairwell. He shot back at the merc in the doorway, running out of ammo in his 1911 and switching over to the Sig. One bullet grazed his arm, and Will hissed at the sting, ire bubbling through his veins.

He roared in anger and charged up the flight of stairs, rapid firing. His opponent took cover, and Will used the man's brief retreat as a chance to spring through the doorway, firing three life-ending rounds to his chest.

TJ and Annette stalked through the offices and halls in their animal forms, dispatching the guards and thugs. Smoke and gunpowder residue whirled in the air. Annette swept her long neck left and right, using her big, black eyes to assess the carnage.

Through a cracked window, she saw a sight outside

that made the mottled black and green scales on her back bristle with anger.

Janae was climbing the ladder on the tower.

She had nearly reached the crane arm.

The snake hissed and smashed through the window, slithering out into the night after her.

Will charged through the smoky halls, pistol trained ahead at the ready. He stepped over bodies and through puddles of blood as he cleared each corridor, eyes laser-focused, adrenaline masking the pain.

Up ahead, he heard a scream. To be more specific, it was a horrified wail, a shrill vocalization that had no business coming from the mouth of a grown man. Through the haze, Will saw the thug up ahead in the room at the end of the hall.

Something unseen hurled him into the steel wall, crunching his bones. His face and body were slashed deep, rich blood pulsing from the wounds. Mason stomped into view through the doorway, a towering, raging timber-wolf.

He lunged at the thug, lifting him off his feet by the throat. The man yelped and choked, leveling the sidearm still in his grasp.

Pop! Pop! Pop!

The shots echoed down the metal hall, one of the rounds cutting deep into the wolf's abdomen. Mason howled and raged at the pain, swiping the gun from the man's grip and burying fangs into his throat.

He wrenched a chunk of gory meat away and spat it out, letting the goon slide down the wall to his death.

Mason staggered back, grasping the fresh wound burning in his stomach.

"*Mason!*"

The alpha wolf snarled and whipped his gaze down the hallway, where Will wasted no time charging at him. His Sig was fully extended, aimed at the inhuman beast. His finger moved to the trigger.

He began to squeeze.

The next thing Will saw was a wall of fur and muscle. It sprung from a room to his left, blindsiding him. He felt it smash into him. He heard the crash and shatter of glass as he went through a window.

He felt the brisk night air as he fell.

32

CLASH

GUNSHOTS WHISPERED IN THE DISTANCE.

Casey fished out the hidden steak knife from her waistband. It was now or never. She had to move. Angling the blade into the bindings on her feet, she began to saw through the tightly wrapped duct tape. That part was easy.

Getting her hands free was a trickier prospect. She realized that she couldn't use her hands to cut her hands loose, so she pinched the knife between her feet. Leaning forward, she rubbed the serrated edge against the tape binding her wrists.

FAST. FAST. FAST.

THE NEW PRESENCE INSIDE OF CASEY URGED HER ON. The knife slipped from position between her feet and fell to the floor. She scooped it up and tried again. Sawing deep into the tape, she managed to cut through some of it. The blade fell loose again and she cursed herself. She scooped it back up, sticking it between her feet and desperately kept trying.

"Come on!" she said through the gag in her mouth, beads of sweet on her strained face. She sawed and labored, making her way through the stubborn tape. Halfway through, she was able to twist her wrists, effectively ripping the rest of the bindings off.

With a few desperate yanks, she tore her hands free.

The first thing she did was pull that evil gag out of her mouth and rub her aching jowls. Then she pulled the rest of the tape from her wrists and ankles, standing up in the darkened bedroom of the parked RV.

As the firefight continued outside, Casey wrenched open the bedroom door and hurried through the living room of the mobile home. She reached the door and swung it open, peering out onto the parking lot.

Crisp, free air kissed her face.

She had no idea where she was, but she could smell a river and hear the sounds of murder and pain not far away. The only thing that made sense was to get away from the guns.

Casey stumbled down the two stairs and stepped onto the pavement of the nearly empty parking lot. She began to move as the insistent new voice in her head compelled her forward —

FAST. FAST. FAST.

WILL FOUND HIMSELF ON A CORRUGATED STEEL surface.

Shattered glass lay around him. His head was throbbing. Ribs were busted. He felt the brisk night breeze and knew he was outside, on top of one of the many shipping containers stacked on the dock.

He looked around to see the steel box he lay atop was part of two rows, ten-long and five-high. He peered over the edge as the whole world rang and throbbed in his head, registering the near fifty-foot drop to the pavement below.

His Sig was lost. The 1911 empty in its holster. Will lifted a trembling hand to his head and his fingers came back with blood.

An unsettling cackle echoed overhead.

The hyena above him leapt from the shattered window frame. Two imposing paws landed beside him, powerful haunches absorbing the impact of the fall. TJ circled Will, his spotted, coarse fur bristling with excitement and anger. His massive neck craned down, black eyes appraising his opponent.

"I'm disappointed, man," TJ's voice rang in Will's head. "I thought you were supposed to be some great war hero. A real badass."

Will put his hands against the steel beneath him and started pressing himself up. His arms and face had small shards of glass embedded in the flesh. His vision blurred into threes, his equilibrium buzzing and spinning.

He felt two broken ribs shift as he moved, and he

held the intense scream inside. He wouldn't give this mongrel the satisfaction of seeing him suffer.

"Oh shit," TJ said. "Broke your ribs, huh? Man, that must be *painful!*" The hyena kicked into Will's side, launching him through the air. He slammed down onto the next container over, his whole body spasming in agony.

Will cringed and held it in, struggling up to his knees. "Don't worry, Shaw. I ain't gonna kill ya. Just gonna soften you up a bit for Mason!"

TJ charged ahead at him, but Will lunged up and lashed out. His fist flickered into a cat's claw for an instant, slicing into TJ's abdomen. The hyena yelped and jumped back, circling around. Will staggered to his feet, head throbbing, vision blurred.

He tried to let go, to let his spirit animal come into this world and take over for him. The black jaguar came, but then went, flickering and shimmering in and out of reality. TJ giggled his twisted laugh as he circled the wounded opponent.

"Can't change, can you, Will? Kind of hard to skin when your head's all fucked up like that, ain't it?"

The cat roared, but in an instant, he was Will again, fighting just to stay on his feet. TJ screamed an animal war cry and jumped at him again. His bony claws slashed across Will's chest, then a backhanded swat sent him flying once again.

TJ laughed as he stalked after the downed warrior. "Oh, I'm just gettin' started!"

Janae darted across the steel, grate floor panels two-hundred feet overhead. She ducked under and around the angled i-beams and support railings as she ran further out over the harbor, nearing the end of the crane arm.

Down below, the mechanism was slowly lowering the shipping container of children towards the deck of the outbound freighter. Feeling the urgency boiling in her blood, Janae hopped around the obstacles on the narrow walkway and tried not to look down.

Behind her, the black and green serpent appeared.

"Where do you think you're going, huh?"

Janae stopped and looked back as Annette stalked down the crane's walkway after her. Her long, venomous fangs extended through gray gums and the mottled neon-green in her scales popped against the black of the sky.

The .380 was still loaded and in her waistband, but Janae wanted to handle the vile reptile with a more personal, hands on approach.

"Hey! Annette, right? How you doing?"

"Shut up, bitch."

"You best be careful who you callin' a bitch, *bitch*. I'm a' turn your ass into a nice pair of shoes. Or maybe a purse."

Annette snarled and hissed, charging down the grated walkway at Janae. A volcanic roar boomed from Janae's mouth and a moment later, her golden leopard burst into the physical world. She stormed at the snake, claws flared out, jaws open wide.

Cold blood and hot fury met high over the water.

Slashing and snarling and biting, they raged.

Janae sliced her talons through scaly flesh. Annette bit with her poison into the cat's coat. Clawed feet slid off the edge. They caught balance on support beams, whipping back onto the walkway, battling on. Annette used her tail as a whip, scorching across Janae's forearms as she tried to block.

"You're gonna pay for what you did to Moonshine, bitch!"

"Moonshine?" Janae played dumb. "Which one was that? Oh, that must've been that dumb-ass cracker we smashed up in the tunnel. *Roadkill*, that's what we call him. *Was that your man?*"

Annette hissed and jumped at Janae, tackling her to the grate with a smash. Janae held the syringe-like fangs at bay as she turned and peered down through the grate. The shipping container holding the kids clanked down into place on the freighter. Workmen were making their way to it, preparing to disconnect the hook that lowered it down.

Janae snarled, tucked her haunched legs up and dug her hind claws into Annette's torso, slicing deep into her. The viper shrieked and staggered. Janae pounced back up, her spotted-gold coat gleaming in the moonlight. She slashed. She clawed. She knocked Annette back, her green eyes on fire.

<hr>

WILL SMASHED DOWN ONTO THE STEEL OF ANOTHER shipping box, his head peaking over the edge. Below him, a fifty-foot drop to unforgiving concrete. Nothing existed except hurt. The gibbering, high-pitch laughter of his attacker taunted from behind. A stubby, canine claw wrapped around his ankle and pulled him back in.

TJ cackled and picked him up, enjoying the helplessness of his victim. Will was too hurt and stunned to transform, and the hyena knew it.

"Mmmm, I like my meat tenderized," TJ said. "I'm gonna fuck you in the ass and make you my *bitch*, Shaw! Sure, you're a little old for my taste, but that's okay! Such cute dimples!" TJ howled with laughter and tossed Will once again through the air. He landed with an echoing metal crunch.

A few feet away, his Sig lay waiting for him amidst the shards of glass. He pulled himself across the steel surface, slicing flesh on broken glass with each drag, desperately reaching for his sidearm. Heavy footsteps thudded from behind as TJ ran past him.

"*Hoo*, there we go," TJ said. "X-Macro? Nice!"

The hyena's thick, stubby fingers could not wrap around a gun handle, so TJ allowed his human self to skin back into existence. He adjusted his bowler hat, bent down and casually scooped up the gun, admiring and checking it out.

Will closed his eyes, tried to concentrate. He tried to let the beast back out. His physical form began to shimmer, light bending and warping around him. He felt his human body falling into the ether, that cozy, comfortable nowhere zone. He floated there, a baby in utero, drifting off into hazy comfort...

"Hey!" TJ kicked his boot across Will's face, and he snapped back out into the physical world. He spat up blood, his face lacerated and his strength fading fast. He had to do something. No way this mangy cur would be the death of him. "We ain't done playin' yet!"

TJ tucked the pistol into the back of his waist band and used both hands to lift Will off the ground by his collar.

Will frantically searched his belt for a gun, a knife, anything. TJ pushed his face into Will's, eyes maniacal and raging. "Yeah, you may have had some doggie-style back in prison," TJ giggled with glee, "but you ain't never had no *hyena*-style! *Ow!* We gonna have us some fun now, convict!"

TJ dropped Will back to the steel surface and took a step back. His body began to shimmer and flutter, and within seconds, he had drifted off into the ether, and the hyena once again stood in his place. His ugly mug split open a heinous smile. His bony knuckles flexed. He cracked his neck from side to side, licking his lips in anticipation of what he had planned for Will.

"Let's get those pants off, eh convict?"

Will laughed, spitting up blood.

"Somethin' funny?" TJ asked.

"Yeah," Will said. "I always wanted to do that."

"Huh?"

Will held up a middle finger, flipping TJ the bird. Hanging around his middle finger was a loop and a pin.

A grenade pin.

Deep within the ether, TJ's human body floated peacefully.

Will's concussion grenade was hooked to his belt.

The crazed beast roared and clawed at its own stomach, but the explosion inside the ether blasted TJ's human body into tatters, and the shock wave erupted into the physical world. The hyena screamed as it blazed into a ball of fire and bloody debris.

Will threw himself over the edge of the shipping container, catching the top wrung of the steel ladder. He gripped the ladder and slammed into the side of the box, taking cover as flaming hyena carcass rained all around him.

ANNETTE'S TAIL WAS WRAPPED AROUND JANAE'S throat. She cinched it ever tighter and held the leopard's wrists, when a booming fireball over on the docks caught her eye. With it echoed TJ's death cry.

The snake was distracted and Janae broke free, slashing across the scaly stomach again. Annette hissed at the sting of the razor slice, staggering back. Janae jumped on her, sinking her fangs into the snake's long neck and digging the curved claws of her thumbs into its black, soulless eyes.

Annette thrashed and screamed as her eyeballs burst with ooze and her throat ripped open.

Janae spun the reptile around, climbing onto its back. Annette hissed and shrieked in unearthly tones. Janae reached into the snake's mouth, one set of feline claws digging into the roof, the other into its lower jaw.

Janae roared and pulled with all her strength, wrenching the jaws of the serpent open. Annette thrashed and cried. Bones and ligaments popped. Flesh tore and bled.

With one final rip, Janae shredded the snake's jaws apart. Her head split wide open, Annette's body collapsed into a limp mass of black and green scales. Blood dripped through the steel grate and onto the freighter below.

With a roar of bestial triumph, Janae kicked the reptile's carcass over the side of the crane, watching it plummet to the inky water between the dock and the massive vessel. Her gleaming green eyes shot back down to the container being loaded onto the ship.

Frantic and terrified crew members disconnected the cable from the container and scurried back down to the deck as the mammoth freighter began to slowly angle away from the dock.

Janae snarled and slinked the rest of the way to the end of the crane in great haste. She climbed down to the Liftech galvanized rigging and swung out with her bloody claws, hooking a grip on the cable.

Sliding down the thick, steel tether, Janae watched as the SS Abbey-Faith crawled farther away with each passing second.

33

CAPTIVES

WILL CLIMBED down the rungs welded to the side of the steel container he hung from, making it to the pavement below. He gasped for breath and held his aching ribs. He was standing in a narrow alley, rows of shipping containers towering on either side like apartment buildings. Bloody debris of the hyena skinner littered the surfaces around him.

An unspooled yo-yo sat in a pile of viscera.

Will staggered down the steel corridor, a bloody mess, stripped of all functioning weapons. He peaked his head around the corner to glimpse at the open dock ahead. Dead goons and thugs decorated the pier with their blood.

The gunfire and shouting had died away, leaving only a constant ringing buzz in Will's ears and a massive throbbing in his head. He took deep breaths, his vision slowly coming back into focus in the aftermath of the vicious battle.

Gunpowder swirled in the breeze. The only sounds

came from the freighter, which was slowly pulling out of harbor. Men on board were frantically running and shouting, trying to pull away as quickly as possible. Will stumbled forward, watching the scene helplessly.

The shipping container loaded with children was on that ship. He could hear their screams and cries echoing within their steel prison.

A feline shape caught his eye, sliding down a cable.

JANAE REACHED THE END OF THE TETHER, HER HIND claws finding the hook at the bottom. The wind and the motion of the cable swung her back and forth, and the leopard watched as the freighter passed just under her. In another few seconds, it would be gone, out of reach.

She poised herself, waiting for the right moment as the cable swung to the end of its arc.

She pounced.

The she-cat landed on the freighter, sinking into a crouch as crew members screamed and ran for their lives. One guard pulled a gun on her, but she was on him before he could pull the trigger. The other men heard his panicked screams as she tore into him.

"Go! Go! Get the fuck out of here!"

Janae jumped down onto the deck, face dripping cranberry, and charged after them. The men hollered and yelped, jumping off the side of the ship to avoid certain death. None of them had ever seen an African leopard queen running on two feet before.

She dashed and sprang across the rows of shipping

containers, scaling the steel tower up to the bridge. She hopped over the first railing, flew up a ladder and leapt over the second railing. She reached the bridge within seconds, and could see five men inside through the panoramic windows. Their eyes were panicked as they locked and braced the door.

"Mayday! Mayday!" The first mate screamed into his radio. Janae lunged at the steel door, but it was bolted tight. She crossed around the windows, snarling at the men inside as they gaped at her in terror.

She scooped an industrial-size fire extinguisher from the wall and smashed it into the glass pane. The men inside screamed as the improvised battering ram shattered almost the whole way through. One more strike, and the monster would be in there with them.

"Shit! Get out get out get out!"

"What is that thing?"

The captain and his crew fled for the far door, throwing open the latch as the fire extinguisher smashed all the way through the window. Glass rained into the bridge as the imposing, spotted jungle beast sprang inside, lunging at the retreating cowards.

They screamed and flew out the door, scampering away down the stairs. Janae did not follow them. Instead, she slammed the door closed and faced the ship's controls.

She caught her breath, surveying the knobs and switches, dials and computer displays. It all looked like the inside of an alien spaceship to her, but one piece of apparatus stood out as refreshingly familiar.

A steering wheel.

"Fuck it," Janae said, wrapping her meaty paws around the wheel. As the freighter inched slowly to the left, moving further away from the docks, Janae spun the wheel to the right, holding it strong. The floating mass of steel groaned as it shifted coarse, angling back toward the dock.

MASON HAD SKINNED BACK TO HIS HUMAN FORM.

He limped from the control tower, grasping his wounded side as he negotiated around the decimated bodies. His belt was now an improvised tourniquet around his wounded leg, and each step sparked hot pain through his body.

The shot to his leg was a clean penetration, in and out, but the slug in his body was buried deep in his guts. With long, salt-and-pepper hair strands dangling over his pained face, Mason staggered outside, determined.

He grimaced, cursing under his breath as he made his way back into the vast parking lot. He could feel his two companions were gone; their psychic connection had been snuffed out. He was all alone.

It was just him and the little girl now.

He would get her out of there, teach her the way, start a new pack of skinners, even stronger than the last. With a determined, agonized stride, he saw the RV up ahead and pushed his pace.

Mason fumbled the keys from his pocket into his bloody hand, trembling as he reached for the lock. He stopped with a gasp.

The door of the RV hung ajar.

Mason's heart nearly stopped.

The girl.

Mason turned back to the parking lot, whipping his gaze around. Only a few vehicles were parked in the vast blacktop, and the night was silent. Mostly silent.

His ears picked up a panicked breathing in the distance ahead. He looked, and there she was. Casey had traveled nearly the length of a football field and was nearing the gate.

Little bitch!

A snarl turned into a roar in Mason's throat. He charged up the stairs into the RV and slammed the door. He jumped into the driver's seat and turned the key in the ignition. The vehicle growled to life and Mason hit the gas, burning rubber and hurtling forward.

Will's eyes were drawn to the motion.

He saw Mason speeding away.

He saw the girl running.

Will burst into a sprint for the Challenger.

———

JANAE HELD THE WHEEL TIGHT.

The massive SS Abbey-Faith had angled back toward the dock. Its course had no finesse and it was not slowing down as it should. A crash was inevitable. Janae braced for impact as she saw the unforgiving concrete dock fast approaching.

"Shiiiiiit..."

The starboard side of the ship smashed into the dock.

Steel crumpled and concrete shards exploded.

A robust rumble harmonized with the groan of steel as the giant cargo vessel scraped along the dock, finally shrieking to a halt.

Janae bolted out of the control booth.

Her muscular, spotted legs vaulted her over railings, down ladders and across platforms. The container holding the children was not hard to find. Their screams and wails were audible even through the steel doors.

Janae slid into the door with a thump, frantically throwing open the latch. She stopped. Seeing a leopard skinwalker with six-inch claws and a blood-stained muzzle standing in the doorway would hardly ease their shattered nerves.

She took a deep breath and calmed herself. She closed her eyes and beckoned her human form. The light hitting her body bent and danced around her animal self, and the leopard shimmered away like ocean ripples.

Janae became a woman again.

Beat up and bloodied, but just a woman.

She yanked on the heavy door and it creaked open. Multiple whimpering shapes huddled in the darkness. Janae could see the whites of their eyes and hear their sobs. She stepped gingerly into the doorway, holding up her hands.

"It's okay," she said. "It's okay. I'm here to get you out of here. Just follow me, okay?"

Janae held her hand out.

The group hesitated.

One little girl desperately ran forward, past the extended hand, and hugged her. She couldn't have been more than five years old. Janae scooped the child into her arms, where she buried her face in Janae's neck and sobbed.

"Is your name Casey?" Janae asked. The girl shook her head. "Are any of you guys Casey? Casey Madison?" More heads shook in silence. Janae sighed. "Okay, come on, let's go."

The other kids didn't need more encouragement, all getting to their feet and hurrying out into the night air. Janae led them across the row of shipping containers, found a ladder and climbed down to the deck level. The others followed suit, each taking their turn.

"Come on, one at a time! Be careful, now! We're gonna get you off this boat and call the police, okay?" Janae carried the crying girl to the bottom and made space as the others began to reach the deck.

She ran to the edge of the freighter, which was now pressed into the side of the dock, and hopped over onto the pavement. She put the little girl down and reached for her phone. "Come on now! Everybody off!"

The kids climbed across from the freighter and onto the dock. Janae heard the faint wails of police sirens in the distance. They were coming. "Everybody stay together until the police get here, you got that?" The group nodded and grunted their understanding.

Janae looked around. She saw Will jump into the Challenger and speed away. She saw the RV up ahead, and the little girl running for her life in the distance.

"Oh my God," she whispered as the last of the kids made it safely to the dock.

FAST. FAST. FAST.

CASEY RAN AS FAST AS HER LITTLE LEGS COULD TAKE her. Her lungs ached and tears flowed from her terrified eyes. She could hear the RV coming up from behind. She could almost smell the bloodlust of the man driving it. Something deep inside urged her to go faster.

Faster.

Mason stepped on the gas, raging forward.

The little lamb ahead of him thought she could get away. Everyone had left him, or died. He had nothing left. And now she wanted to leave too. Mason snarled, gripping the wheel tight as he powered forward.

In the rearview mirror, Will sped up behind him, the Challenger an orange streak in the night. Mason screamed and pressed the vehicle to its limit as the sports car zoomed up beside it. Mason smashed into Will's flank and the Challenger swerved.

Will got control of the wheel again, not letting up.

FAST. FAST. FAST.

CASEY GASPED FOR AIR. SHE WANTED, NEEDED TO GO faster. This thing inside of her demanded it. It needed to be let out, needed freedom. It needed her to open the door and give in. Just give in.

The RV pushed up behind her, intent on smashing her beneath its wheels.

"*Mason!*" Will screamed.

He slammed the Challenger into the side of the RV. Mason returned the favor. Both vehicles battled forward, crashing into each other as sparks flared and metal crumpled. Up ahead, Will could see the little girl, seconds away from being run over.

He battered into the side of the RV again and again, sending it onto two wheels as they veered to the left. Mason swerved and slammed the wheels down again, not letting up.

Mason raged, racing up behind Casey.

FAST. FAST. FAST.

CASEY FELT THE HEADLIGHTS BURNING ON HER BACK. Soon she would feel her body crumple and smash like a bug. She had to listen to the voice. She had to let it out.

She closed her eyes. She accelerated. She allowed her feet to fly faster than she ever imagined they could.

She relaxed.

A shimmer ran through her.

Light bent around her.

Casey fell back and drifted into the ether.

The cheetah within her was born.

Mason's eyes went wide as the little cat burst into existence. Her stride blasted with a shot of nitroglycerin and she zoomed forward, leaving him in the dust. He cursed and pounded the wheel as he watched her spotted, tawny-yellow coat dart out of his reach.

Casey felt the power in her legs. *Faster, faster!* Clawed feet blurred over the asphalt. Her whole body flexed and flowed. Her big, amber eyes cut through the dark of the night and she smiled with deadly fangs.

Will smashed into the RV.

Mason smashed back.

Both vehicles swerved and smashed and sparked and skidded. They sped towards a low concrete wall and the RV's right tires crashed through it. The hulking can of tin lurched onto two tires and fell onto its side, skidding along the pavement.

Will swerved to avoid Mason's wreck, cutting the wheel too far to the right. The sports car's center of gravity was lost, and in a flash, he felt weightlessness as the Challenger flipped and somersaulted across the lot.

Broken glass seemed to float in mid-air.

All noise faded away. The air itself went numb. Will could sense the impact each time the car flipped and crashed down, but felt more like he was watching a movie than actually being there.

Both vehicles came to a halt. The Challenger landed on its wheels, a crumpled wreck. The RV lay on its side not twenty yards away. Smoke rose from the wreckage.

Casey stopped running.

She turned and faced the damage in awe. She looked down at her hands, fingers now furred and padded, a claw on each digit. She didn't know what she'd become, but she felt that somehow, she was still very much herself.

The man driving the sports car crawled out the broken window. He fell to the pavement, a bloody mess gasping for air. Will stood up on quivering legs, focusing on the young cheetah in front of him.

"It's... it's okay..." he managed. "It's gonna be okay..."

A raging bellow echoed in the night.

A pair of hands reached through the window of the overturned RV, and Mason pulled himself out. He swung his legs over and jumped down to the ground with a pained grunt.

"Okay, now..." Mason snarled. "Ya'll both gonna die."

Will instinctively took a protective stance in front of the animal child. Mason stalked forward.

"Give it up, Mason. You can't have her."

"I'll have you *both!* Roasting on a fucking *spit!*"

Mason's humanity warped away in a fast, shimmering light as he skinned into his wolf form. The wounded beast stalked closer, murder in his eyes.

The police sirens were getting closer.

"Stay behind me," Will said.

His head had cleared and Will was able to focus and relax. He surrendered himself and his black jaguar came from the ether. Casey watched in amazement as the onyx beast stood before her. It was tired and wounded, but stood its ground.

The brothers glared at each other.

The beasts snarled.

Both were injured, bloodied, in pain. Both knew that this was it. One of them was not walking away from this. Each took a step forward. Fangs bared and claws flexed.

Tires screeched from behind them.

Janae swung up from behind in a stolen panel van from the dock, bullet holes pocked into its side, its sliding back door wide open. She skidded to a halt beside Will and Casey.

"Get in! Get in!"

The wolf roared and charged at them as fast as he could on his wounded leg. Will wasted no time, scooping up Casey and diving into the van as Janae peeled away. Mason was not fast enough, barely missing the van with his swiping paw as it sped toward the exit gate.

"Please tell me your name is Casey Madison," Janae asked, turning to the backseat.

Casey nodded her head, bewildered.

"Thank God."

A furious howl thundered from Mason's throat as he watched the van disappear into the night. The police sirens were getting louder, and their cherry-tops were now visible in the distance. They were on their way.

Mason gasped for breath, frustrated and bristling with anger. He gripped his wounded side, looked around for somewhere to go, something to do. He would have to run. He looked back at the wreckage of both vehicles, smoke rising from their destroyed engines.

He limped over to the Challenger.

Wrenching open the passenger door of the orange muscle car, Mason bent in with his canine snout and sniffed around. Laying on the floor was something oddly familiar. He reached in and picked up his old slingshot, regarding it with a curious grunt.

He opened the glove box and reached inside, skimming through the mess of legal documents. He came out with a small square of paper in his claws, the official seal of the state of Tennessee stamped on its face.

It was the car's title.

It was registered to one Jackson Cooper, with a home address in Chattanooga.

34

MOTHER'S EMBRACE

CHATTANOOGA, *Tennessee*

THEY DROVE ALL NIGHT.

Janae steered the van through Georgia and into Tennessee, across Interstate-16 to the 75-North. The bullet holes in its sides whistled in the wind. Will and Casey had skinned back to their human selves, and she cleaned his wounds the best she could with a towel and a bottle of water. The child had an endless supply of questions, and they did their best to answer.

The bullet holes in the van had attracted the attention of a state trooper, and they were pulled over in the dead of night. Janae explained to him that she was the Director General of Police in Tennessee, and a quick flash of her New York driver's license proved it to the man. He nodded apologetically and wished them all a good night.

Will's head throbbed and his multiple wounds and

lacerations stung and ached. Each intake of breath was agony to his broken ribs. Janae was also a collection of small cuts and bruises, as well as the grazing bullet wound across her side. Her shoulder was numb and swollen from the snake's bite, and she steered mostly with her left hand as a result.

Casey was physically unharmed, but her mind spun as her new existence was explained to her. She took solace when Janae explained that she wasn't an evil monster, but rather a spirit of nature. That she wouldn't be a danger to anyone she loved, but still bore a heavy responsibility. This was a secret she would have to keep and live with the rest of her life.

She was a skinner.

They arrived in Chattanooga just after sunrise.

The streets were nearly dead. Janae steered the van off the highway and into downtown. Casey's eyes welled with tears as they passed through familiar streets. She was going home. The van slowed to a stop as it rolled onto her street.

Up ahead was her house. The light was on in the kitchen. Casey's mother was up; more than likely, she had not slept at all since her daughter's abduction. Janae turned to face Casey with a caring smile.

"Here you go, girl."

"What... What happens now?" Casey asked.

"Now, you go give your mama a hug," Will said. "Go live your life. Be happy."

"But... what about you guys? What about..." Casey's tears rolled down her cheeks, looking at Will and Janae, now the only two people in the world who could understand her. Will dug out his business card from Cooper Auto, his cell number printed on the front. He handed it over to the child with a bloody grin.

"You take this," Will said. "You give your uncle Will a call anytime." She took the card and looked him in the eyes. Casey could see his aura, feel his sincerity and genuine goodness. She lunged forward and wrapped her arms around him. They held a tight embrace, then released. Will opened the sliding door, letting the cool morning air sweep over them.

"A-Are ya'll gonna be all right?" Casey asked.

"We're skinners, baby," Janae said. "We heal fast."

Casey reached around the driver's seat and gave Janae a hug as well. "Thanks, Janae."

Janae smiled and reached up to pat the girl's head. Her shoulder ached with the movement. Casey pulled away, smiled and shared a final look at both of them.

Will smiled and flashed his "hang loose" hand sign.

Casey jumped out of the van and ran up the street to her house. Will closed the sliding door, then moved up to the front passenger seat. He and Janae watched as Casey darted up the front steps and pounded incessantly on the door.

A moment later, an exhausted African-American woman opened the door and her heart melted. Tears immediately burst from her eyes and she fell to her knees. Casey ran into her mother's open arms. They embraced and didn't let go.

Will and Janae watched, their own eyes glazing over with tears. They could see the mother's lips moving, saying something they couldn't hear from this distance. But they didn't need to hear it. They knew.

Janae shifted into drive, and pulled away.

———

WILL AND JANAE PARKED THE VAN IN AN ALLEY A few blocks from the Red Roof Inn, where she was still checked in. They walked the short distance on weary legs, hurt and exhausted. They trudged through the parking lot, where her Ducati Monster 1200 sat right where she had parked it.

They entered their first-floor suite and it was just as they'd left it. Her bags of clothes and medical supplies, his empty pelican case and boxes of ammo. It was safe and for now, it was home. Their adrenaline had long since given out and they each felt their damages acutely.

"Please tell me you have some Tylenol," Will groaned.

"Here," she passed him a bottle of pills after taking two herself.

He swallowed them right down and peeled off his frayed jacket and torn shirt. He noticed a bulge in his jacket pocket, reached in and pulled out his bottle of Peroxidine. *Forgot I even had this,* Will thought. He reflexively went to open the bottle, but stopped.

He lifted up the container, giving it a long, hard look. *How long have I been slave to these little pills? How long have I used them to escape my fears?* He realized with a cold clarity that he didn't need the pills anymore. He tossed the bottle into the waste-paper basket and continued to undress.

Janae did the same, each of them moaning in pain as they peeled out of their clothes.

"Jesus, look at you," Janae said, appraising his collection of wounds.

Multiple scratches and shallow cuts patterned across his back, shoulder and arms, many shards of glass still embedded. A deeper cut went across his shoulder as the result of a bullet, and five claw marks angled across his chest from TJ's attack. His ribs were a mottled purple and yellow, as was his beaten face.

"I feel like a million bucks," he said.

"Don't worry, I'll clean you up." There was a sadness in her tone, and Will detected that her usual flirtatious banter was gone.

"I'll get you too. You're a bit dinged-up, cupcake."

"We're quite a pair, you and me," she sighed, avoiding eye contact.

Will pulled a lolly-pop from the shopping bag, unwrapped it and popped it in his mouth. Janae shook her head.

"Don't judge me."

They began with the glass embedded in Will's skin. Using tweezers, Janae pulled out each shard, dropping it into the wastebasket. Her mind was distant and she spoke in monotone. "Now we gotta wash off," she said. "Get ourselves clean. Then we can bandage up."

"What's wrong?" Will asked. "We did it!"

Janae clenched her jaw, troubled.

"Mason's still out there."

"And we'll get him. But think about what we did! We *saved* all those kids! We did it!" Will sighed. "Couldn't have done it without you."

Janae fought tears.

What the hell am I doing? she thought.

She couldn't look him in the eye.

They went to the bathroom, and she started the shower. He stood in his underwear, but hesitated in taking them off. Janae showed no such shyness as she pulled off her bra and panties with a cringe of pain.

She climbed into the shower, letting out a moan as the hot water hit her skin. Will sighed and kicked off his underwear, pulling aside the shower curtain.

There she stood, naked, stretching her lithe and wet body as the room steamed up. She was cut and whipped and bruised, but that somehow didn't detract from her allure. In fact, he found it strangely arousing. Will swallowed hard as he stepped into the shower, flinching as the water stung his numerous injuries.

"Shhh," she said. "It's not so bad. Most of these are just little scratches anyway." She found the bar of soap and lathered herself up, then passed it to Will.

Janae ran her hair under the water. Will wanted nothing more than to touch her. But she had grown so cold, distant.

Will lathered up his whole body, then put the soap down and stepped into the water to rinse. His body rubbed against hers, and she turned away. Bloody soap suds washed down the drain. Janae lathered herself up, still avoiding eye contact.

"What's the matter?" he said.

"It's just..." she whispered, pondering, "sometimes I don't like who I have to be."

"Oh, come on, now!" Will pulled her in, rubbing her shoulders and resting his face against her neck. "It's okay. You did nothing wrong."

"Everything I do, it's for the greater good..." She was talking more to herself than to Will, trying to justify what she knew she had to do.

Will caressed her, whispering in her ear, "It's gonna be okay..." Will couldn't hide his attraction. It swelled up and reached for her, begging her to touch it.

"I... It's time to get out." Janae abruptly turned off the water and brushed past him.

They finished their shower, stepping out into the bathroom, fresh and clean. Their wounds had stopped bleeding, and Will realized that skinners must indeed heal very fast. Still, his body throbbed with pain and had a long way to go. They grabbed towels and dried off, stealing glances at each other's naked bodies.

"Let's take care of these now, okay?"

Will nodded as she produced her bag of supplies from the pharmacy. She laid out the hydrogen peroxide, the Neosporin, non-stick pads, gauze and tape. He stood nude in the steamy room as she applied the stinging peroxide to each and every cut and scrape. She gently bandaged his more major wounds, leaving the small cuts and nicks to themselves.

Next was her turn, and she stood patiently as Will cleaned and dressed her injuries. He couldn't help his gaze falling to her coffee bean skin, following her curves, wanting to feel her warmth. She wanted him too, but held back.

Will sighed, trying to concentrate. "Almost done here," he said, bandaging her shoulder and the grazing bullet wound on her side. He taped the gauze and took a step back. They were both as good as they were going to get with what they had.

"Thanks," she smiled, repressing her feelings.

"Don't mention it."

She turned away to walk into the bedroom, when Will came up behind, gently caressing her back. Janae stopped, her heart pounding. She could feel his breath on the back of her neck.

"It's okay," he whispered.

His fingertips felt like decadence, luxury beckoning. She stood still and silent, not stopping him as he continued to stroke her.

"Jesus," she said. "We're both hurt..."

"Mm hm."

"And exhausted..."

"Mm hm."

He did not let up, tracing his fingers down across her butt. Her eyes closed as he melted. She could feel him getting hard. The hurting and aching and exhaustion faded away, and all she could feel was lust.

Will turned her around to face him. "I'm not waiting for your permission." He kissed her.

They kissed with a hunger.

Hands stroked and tongues met. They fell onto the bed, where Will's broken ribs sent a jolt of pain through him. He gasped, slowing down, taking it easy. He rolled onto his back, letting her get on top and do the work. They touched and kissed, ecstatic moans and wounded grunts becoming indistinguishable.

Their bodies flexed with passion, their multiple injuries ringing out as they tensed. Pain and pleasure became one and the same. Slow and sensual, they moved as one. Janae gyrated and worked her hips, hitting the right spot. She rode the wave of pleasure until she came, trembling and convulsing on top of Will.

He rolled her onto her back and assumed the top position, wincing in pain. He kept going until they came together. He collapsed, the two of them gasping for air.

Will Shaw finally slept.

THE WHOLE DAY PASSED.

Will and Janae lay in the tussled sheets of the motel bed, the curtains drawn. The sun rose and set, and neither of the lovers budged. Their hurt and weary bodies craved the rest, needing it more than anything.

Will dreamt of his childhood, of Papaw Jimmy, of the fire, of Mason. He dreamt of running through the jungle, leaping and dodging effortlessly through the branches and boulders and foliage. His subconscious was in dialogue with his beast. They could meet together now in his dreams. They were no longer strangers.

Just after ten p.m., Will's cell phone rang.

He and Janae both woke up with a wince. Will looked around, seeing the light of his phone on the dresser across from the bed. He grunted and pulled himself up as the irritating chime beckoned him. Will crossed over to the phone and looked at the screen, Janae sitting up in bed watching him.

"It's Jackson," Will said as he glanced at the caller ID. He swiped the touch-screen to answer the call, holding the phone to his ear. "What's up, Jax?"

"*Hey, buddy.*"

Will's blood turned to ice water at Mason's voice.

Janae shot up in bed, the look of dread in his eyes telling her all she needed to know. Will could not move or speak; he was frozen and in a state of shock.

"What's the matter, Will?" Mason said, his voice tinged with pain. "Cat got your tongue?" Mason laughed at his own bad joke. Will struggled to speak, forcing words from his lips as he trembled with anger.

"Mason... What the hell have you done?"

"*Your buddy Jax has a nice place, Will... Hnng! Cute wife too!*"

Will heard Dominic crying, and his heart seized up.

"Mason... I swear to God..."

"*I'd love to chat longer... Nng! But I'm fixin' to catch a train. Just thought I'd call and say hi, y'know.*"

"*Mason!*"

"*Let's catch up again, real soon. Always good talkin' to ya, little brother.*"

The call ended.

Will stood breathless, clenching his phone, fury in his eyes. He turned to Janae, who was already throwing her clothes on in haste.

"...Jackson..." Will muttered.

"I know," she said, pulling her boots on. "Let's go!"

35

HARD RAIN

A HEAVY DOWNPOUR fell on Chattanooga.

Janae and Will burned through the wet city streets on the Ducati, dodging around traffic as they raced to Jackson's house. Will held on tight, the cold wind and rain whipping into his face. His eyes were focused and desperate, his head throbbing.

Janae cut a path through downtown and into the suburbs, her face a portrait of resolve through her helmet's tinted visor. He had reloaded his 1911 and taken back his .380, and she had also reloaded her Glock.

They splashed into St. Elmo, swerved right onto Old Mountain Road and raced up to Jackson's house on the left. The lights were on and all looked fine and tranquil from the outside.

Will was off the bike and running before Janae could come to a stop. His ribs seized in pain and his whole body ached, but he did not care.

He charged up the front stairs and burst through the door.

"Jackson! ...Jax!"

Will crept into the foyer, his 1911 trained ahead, and could already smell the unmistakable odor of blood. He came into the living room, dripping wet, and stopped in his tracks. The home was ruined and ransacked.

Furniture was turned over, family photos were smashed and traces of blood were scattered throughout. A spatter on the TV screen, a smeared hand-print across the light switch. Will swallowed hard as his heart sank. At the end of the room, a motionless figure lay near the lit fireplace.

It was Jackson.

Fromage gingerly licked at his daddy's cheek, but hissed at Will and fled to find a hiding place.

Will holstered his gun and ran to his friend's side as Janae dashed in, surveying the damage with a gasp.

"Jesus Christ..." she whispered.

"Jax! Jax!"

Will dropped to his knees and scooped up Jackson, who was still breathing. His swollen eyes fluttered open and focused on Will, terrified. Three slashes ran across his face, deep crimson crevices that seeped blood. His body was torn, ripped and broken, and Will's first impression was that he looked like a dog's chew toy.

"W-Will..."

Janae came up behind them, looking down with angered concern. Will held onto Jackson, tears in his eyes.

"A-A man came, Will..." Jackson choked. "Said he was your b-brother... And he-he changed... He changed into... into..."

"I know, Jax, I know. Just take it easy, okay?" He turned to Janae and shouted, "Call an ambulance!" She didn't need to be told twice, dialing on her cell and calling it in.

"M-My back... It's broken... Can't move my legs..."

"Shhhh, don't try to move, Jax."

"Annie..." Jackson's eyes flooded with tears.

"Where's Annie, Jax? Where is she?"

"She's... sh-she's..."

Janae paced through the devastation as she spoke to the 911 operator. She crossed into the kitchen doorway and froze. She turned back to face them, her face tightening into a grave, somber mask.

"Will," she murmured.

Will looked back that way, and through the door to the kitchen, he could see the lifeless body of a woman. She had been torn to pieces, shredded into gory ribbons. Her head was bitten completely off and was absent from the scene. Blood had splashed everywhere and was now drying on the walls.

Will realized with certainty that this had been done while Jackson was forced to watch, helpless and paralyzed. The dread sunk even deeper at the grim realization that one member of the family was still unaccounted for.

"Dom..." Will turned back to Jackson, holding him tight. "Where's Dominic, Jax? Where is he?"

Jackson sobbed, "H-He took him! That... That *monster* took my baby boy!" Tears flowed down Will's cheeks as he clutched his broken friend, watching the man wail and cry. "I t-told him there were no such things as monsters, Will! I told him there were no such things as monsters! *Oh my God!*"

"Oh Jax, I'm sorry! I'm so sorry, man!" Will cried, not possessing the words to describe the anguish in his heart. "This is all my fault, man! This is all... Oh Jesus, I'm so sorry!"

"Y-You're like him, ain't ya, Will? That's what you've been hiding. You're a... a..."

"Will," Janae said. "They're on their way."

"You hear that, buddy? Help's on the way. You're gonna be fine, just hang in there. I'm gonna stay here with you, okay? I'm not goin' anywhere."

"No!" Jackson snapped. "Go! G-Go get my boy back, Will! Bring me back my baby!"

"I... I can't just leave you here like this, Jax..."

"God damn it, you stupid fuckin' injun'! *Agh!*" Jackson cringed in agony, spasming as the pain seared through his body. He grabbed Will's coat by the lapel and pulled him close, face to face. "I-I said go! *Hnng!* ...G-get that bastard, Will! Kill him for me! And bring me back my boy... I'll be all right!"

"He's right, Will. We're losing time."

"Do it." Jackson's eyes burned with tears.

"I will, Jax. I will."

Will gently laid Jackson back on the floor, placing a pillow behind his head before standing back up. His ribs ached, his head pounded and his multiple wounds demanded at least a week of solid rest. But it was time for action. It was time to end this, once and for all.

"I'll get him back... I promise."

Janae touched Will's shoulder and led him back

towards the door. He followed her lead, muttering one more time, "I promise."

They ran back out into the rain.

Lightning blazed. Thunder roared.

It was a mythical night. Janae kick-started her black machine and pulled on her helmet as the sirens of Hamilton County EMS and the sheriff's department approached the scene.

Will jumped onto the back of the bike.

"Do you know where we're going?" Janae asked.

"Oh yeah," Will said.

36

BROTHERS

WILL'S MEMORIES FLASHED—

"LOOK, DADDY! CHOO-CHOO!"

"THAT'S RIGHT, WILL. WE'RE GOIN' TO SEE THE CHOO-CHOO!"

DAD POINTING OUT THE WINDOW. "SEE, MASE? THAT'S THE BIG STEAM ENGINE I WAS TELLIN' YOU ABOUT. PRETTY COOL, HUH?"

"SURE, DAD."

MASON SHOOTING STONES WITH HIS SLINGSHOT.

MOM TURNING FROM THE FRONT SEAT. SMILING AT HER BOYS.

. . . .

THE RAIN HAD DIED DOWN, AND NOW THE NIGHT WAS dripping. A single headlight cut through the gloom, approaching the rural piece of land that hosted the Tennessee Valley Railroad Museum. During the day, families and tourists and railroad historians would come to walk around and admire the old trains.

They would buy magnets and bottle openers and t-shirts in the gift shop, pose for photos in front of historic locomotives and take rides on the well maintained ones with lunch services in the dining cars.

Camelback steam engines still chugged around the tracks, pulling around the tourists thanks to generous sponsors and preservationists. The train yard was far enough away from downtown Chattanooga to have a sense of peace and privacy. The gravel lot buzzed with railroad aficionados daily, but after nine p.m., there was not a soul in sight.

The perfect place for a clandestine meeting.

Or an ambush.

Will remembered coming here as a kid. It was one of his earliest memories, riding the train with his parents, eating a nice lunch and watching the lush Southern scenery pass by. Thirteen year-old Mason couldn't stop shooting at little animals with his slingshot. The sun was warm and his parents hugged and kissed.

It was a good day.

Will now peered around the dark, desolate train yard. It was cold, wet and joyless. Janae parked the bike and flipped down the kickstand, taking off her helmet. She killed the engine and they both got off, sharing a look. Will knew exactly where Mason would be.

Four rows of locomotives and box cars arched in a semi-circle in front of them. Somewhere inside, a monster held a baby hostage. Will could smell both of them. Mason was still bleeding, and Dominic was whimpering in hushed tones. Also stinging in their noses was the distinct smell of gasoline. The stage was set.

It was clearly a trap.

"Will, I..." Her eyes were troubled. Will could see the conflict within her. There was something she just couldn't bring herself to say to him.

"You don't have to go," Will said. "This is my fi — "

"Bullshit."

Janae drew her Glock.

Will sighed and drew his 1911.

They crept forward into the dark yard, the old, metal husks of steam trains towering around them. Their boots crunched on loose gravel doused in gasoline. Their heightened senses zeroed in on the sounds and smells of fear, leading them to the last row of trains.

They rounded a corner and looked left. At the end of the row was the oldest train on the lot, a restored 1864 locomotive hitched to three box cars, used for taking tourists around the valley and serving them overpriced lunches. This was the same train he had ridden as a young boy.

Mason sat on a lawn chair in the darkness.

His left hand held a lit cigar.

His right hand held Dominic by the back of the neck.

On his lap, his old slingshot.

"Hey there, little brother." Mason took a puff from his stogie and coughed a cloud of smoke. Dried burgundy was crusted down the side of his face. His shirt was stained with scarlet from the gut-shot he took, and a scarf was tied around his bleeding leg. He had lost a lot of blood, and even in the shadows, Will could tell his complexion was wan and ashen.

"Mason."

"Put the guns down right now, if you please."

Will and Janae glanced at Dominic, his hands and feet tied. Tears of terror and pain stained the boy's cheeks. The child whimpered as Mason's large, strong hand remained gripped around the back of his neck.

"U-Uncle Will..." Dom cried.

"*Uncle* Will? *Hnng!*" Mason laughed and winced in pain. "Looks like we're all family here, ain't we?"

"Mason, I..."

"Drop 'em *now!*" Mason shook the child and elicited a terrified shriek.

"Okay! Okay!"

Will held his 1911 out to the side, then lowered it to the ground, and Janae reluctantly did the same with her Glock. They held their hands out, unarmed. Janae's eyes flicked down to Will's waist band, where his .380 still sat holstered in the crook of his back.

Mason pulled Dominic in close, smiling. "You should be careful about your uncle Will, buddy. He has a habit of betraying family."

"Mason, just let the boy go, man. This is between you and me." Will's words did little to impress, as Mason took another pull from his cigar, coughing once again as he exhaled. He leaned in to speak into Dominic's ear, ignoring Will.

"You see buddy," Mason said. "I'm Uncle Will's brother. Uncle Mason! And for years, I tried to track down Uncle Will. To get the family back together again. You see, we both have the same gift... *Hnng!*" Mason grunted in pain, but continued. "I just wanted to see my little brother again. Wanted us to run together. Wanted him to join me, to live free, be kings of the land... *Hnng! Ahh!* ...But uncle Will, see, he decided to betray me instead. To kill my friends. To join up with that black *cunt* over there to try and take me down!"

"Fuck you," Janae snarled.

"Mason," Will pleaded. "You're hurt, man..."

"You look a little worse for wear yourself, *brother.*"

"Come on, Mase. You're dying, man. Look at you. We can talk about this. Just please let the boy go."

"We can talk about this?" Mason grunted. "*Hnng!* You said next time we met, one of us was gonna die."

Mason stood up from the chair with a groan, still holding Dominic by the back of his neck. The slingshot fell to the gravel at his feet. He took another pull from the cigar, appraising the ground around them. Lines of gasoline had been poured all around the train. Mason smiled. He could feel the bullet in his torso burning, and knew Will was right.

He was dying.

"Just let the boy go."

"You want the kid?" Mason limped to the doorway of the boxcar beside him and tossed Dominic inside. The boy cried as he crashed down into the empty passenger car. "Come get him."

Mason flicked his cigar into a trail of gasoline.

Flames shot up and spread out, circling the train.

Will and Janae watched as the trails of fuel combusted, sending up barriers of fire all around the train yard. Orange, flickering light washed over the lot, sparkling in the wet sheen of the fresh rainfall. Mason sneered at them, standing his ground, blocking the entrance to the train.

Dominic wailed for help inside as the flames licked up all around him. Janae's eyes moved back to the .380 behind Will's back and made her decision. She grabbed the gun and whipped it out, clicking off the safety and opening fire on Mason.

Pop! Pop! Pop!

A hidden .45 in Mason's belt was in his hand in an instant, and he fired back. Janae's shots went wild, but Mason connected, a hot slug tearing into her shoulder. She gasped in shock as the .380 fell from her hand.

Janae dropped to her back, and Mason aimed again for a kill shot, but Will was already on him. He slammed into his brother, fighting for the gun in his hand.

They smashed against the side of the train, careening into the flickering flames. They hissed at the scorching heat and the .45 plummeted to the gravel. Mason threw Will back and they faced off, both shimmering in metamorphosis. Light bent and reality distorted.

The wolf faced the panther.

Will snarled, his black coat now etched with a scatter of maroon cuts and gashes. He stood ferocious and defiant. No matter what his condition, he couldn't let this monster get away again.

Mason growled and gnashed his bone-crunching

canines. He limped on his wounded haunches, his gray-and-black fur streaked with dried scarlet-brown blood. His eyes were empty and bloodthirsty. Will looked into those eyes and saw nothing but a foe.

His brother was gone.

They lunged at each other. Black cat and gray wolf slashed out with claws and fangs. More blood spilled. They smashed into the side of the train, then spun to the gravel, then back up again.

Janae held her bleeding shoulder as she sat up, cringing as she watched the beasts duel. Inside the passenger car, she heard Dom crying, helpless as the flames began to engulf the tin can.

The predators whirled around each other, claws digging in. Mason lunged at Will's throat, but Will caught him with curved talons and threw him to the ground. Will dashed for the passenger car to save Dominic, but Mason's vice grip was on his ankle in an instant, yanking him back down.

The black jaguar crashed back to the gravel and his ribs shrieked in agony.

Mason lunged on top of him, salivating jaws snapping an inch from his face. Will pushed back as the larger, stronger opponent bore down, digging his hooks into the black-and-gray wolf's hide.

The two beasts thrashed through the wet gravel as raging flames rose around them. Will felt the urgency of Dominic's cries as the passenger train began to heat up like a crock pot.

"Look at it, Will," Mason said, gazing up to admire

the inferno. "I always did love a good fire. Beautiful, ain't it?"

"Go to hell, Mason!"

Will rolled to his side, his ribs screaming, and slid out from under Mason's mount. His left claw whipped out, all five hooked fingertips flexed, and slashed open the right side of the wolf's face.

Mason staggered back and Will shot forward, launching a front kick to his solar plexus. The wolf fell back, hitting the track behind him with a bone-cracking wail. As Mason thrashed and contorted, Will dashed for the passenger car.

"Dom!"

He bounded through the blanket of flames and up the three steps into the doorway of the passenger train. The bleeding, giant black cat landed with a resonating thud in front of Dominic, and the child screamed in terror.

Will hadn't considered that the boy wouldn't recognize him in this form, or that he wouldn't know the difference between the good monster and the bad. But there wasn't time for that now.

He dropped to his knees to start cutting the crying child's bonds loose with his claws.

Mason was on him in an instant.

The two beasts staggered forward in a whirl of smoke and dancing embers. Will braced himself over Dominic to keep from smashing down on the wailing boy.

Mason dug claws into the cat's shoulders and wrenched him off the floor, hurling him to the far end of the car.

Will crashed over two rows of seats and collapsed. The wolf limped down the center of the metal tube, flames rising around them outside the windows. Smoke rolled into the cabin. Dominic screamed as the beasts whirled in deadly battle.

37

INFERNO

JANAE PUT her arm in an improvised sling made from her leopard-print scarf. She lurched to her feet, watching as the rising fire kissed and licked at the hull of the train. The door was still open. The child was still inside.

She pulled her blouse up over her nose and ran forward. Through the open doorway, she saw little Dominic writhing on the floor, crying in hysterics as he lay bound within the giant frying pan.

"Shit... Shit..."

Janae summoned her courage and dove through the wall of flames, charging through the blistering heat and up the stairs. Inside, she winced as smoke stung her eyes and the sweltering inferno drenched her with sweat. Dominic looked up at her, tears streaming down his face.

"Get the boy out of here!" Will commanded from the far end of the car, locked in combat with his brother and holding the beast at bay. Janae wasted no time, kneeling down and scooping the child up with her good arm.

"It's okay, baby! Come on now! Come with me..."

Janae cringed as she picked him up, agony shooting through her body. Mason lunged after them, but Will sank his claws in, holding the berserker back.

"Hang on!" she screamed.

Janae dove back through the open door, through the flames, landing with a gravelly crunch outside the train. She held the baby close, running around the side of the box car and jumping over the lines of fire that now criss-crossed the whole yard.

She found the museum gift shop, and not wasting a second, shot her boot into the handle. Wood splintered and glass shattered as the door broke in. Janae ran inside, putting Dom on the floor and cutting loose the rest of his bindings.

"It's okay, baby. It's okay. You're safe now..."

Janae looked back at the inferno, gasping for air. The shrieks and howls and roars of the two brothers echoed through the growl of flames. She gritted her teeth, hating herself for what she knew she had to do.

"One of the Shaw brothers shall be the destroyer of The Council. It will be the end of all of us."

She remembered Keonee's words.

"Okay now, you stay here, okay?" Janae stroked his head, reassuring the boy as tears streamed through his big, almond eyes. "You gotta stay here where it's safe, okay baby?"

"No! Don't go! Don't go!"

Janae scooped the wireless phone off the counter, turning it on and dialing 911. The dispatcher came on the line after two rings with a calm and controlled voice.

"Hamilton County 911. What is your emergency?"

"Come quick," Janae said, and put the phone back on the counter, leaving the line open.

"Hello? Ma'am? Are you still there? Hello?"

Janae turned back to Dominic, looking him in the eye. "I gotta help uncle W— I gotta go. You just stay here now, baby. Help is on the way, okay? Just stay here."

Janae left Dom sitting in the darkened museum gift shop and ran back into the fiery train yard, blocking her eyes from the pluming smoke.

MASON SMASHED WILL THROUGH A ROW OF SEATS, snapping the bases off their bolted mounts. Will snarled and pushed back, lashing out with razor claws. They clashed in the big can, a roasting skillet on a camp fire. Smoke stung their eyes and burned their throats.

They locked in a dead heat, holding each other at bay. Neither could move, retreat or advance. Mason painfully cackled a maniacal beast's laugh and threw his head up, howling up to the skies. They would die together, two brothers in a fire, just like their parents. Mason delighted in the morbid poetry.

Janae ran back to the train.

She covered her face and jumped through the fire.

"You know the prophecy."

Running up the stairs and into the open doorway, she could barely make out the silhouettes of the two skinners through the thick smoke at the end of the car. She watched as they battled, both injured and in horrible pain, but neither giving in.

Mason was on top, his clawed hand wrapped around Will's throat. Will held him at arm's length, choking and fading fast.

He sensed Janae and looked back at her.

She stood frozen in the doorway, Keonee's voice echoing in her head —

"Will Shaw must also die."

Her face was a portrait of turmoil.

"J-Janae..." Will reached out for her, waiting for her to charge in and knock the vile hell-hound off of him.

Janae stepped back outside the door, tears in her eyes.

"...I'm sorry, Will..."

She closed the door.

Will's eyes blazed as the steel slammed shut. He heard the heavy latch clank down on the outside, locking them in. His heart sank as the sobering realization hit him harder than any punch ever could.

She was leaving him to die.

"Janae!"

As Will furiously roared, repeating her name again and again, Janae staggered outside. Sobbing, she jumped over the lines of flaming gasoline, running back to the parking lot where her Ducati waited. She started the machine up, revving with her good right hand.

She looked back at the burning pyre, tears in her eyes.

"I'm sorry."

She flipped up the kickstand and throttled out into the night, leaving everything behind her to burn.

Will seethed, bristling with rage.

Mason crunched down on him, his mangled wolf's snout a dripping mess of bloody tatters. He laughed and coughed up blood, burning through his strength reserves to hold his brother down. He began to hum and sing in his distorted, garbled animal voice, eyes closed and a twisted smile on his muzzle.

"Just you and me, bro... Just you and me, bro... Mmmm, mmmmmm, mmmm... Hnng!" Mason hummed, welcoming his fate.

Will growled, reaching out with his hooks. He found the bullet wound in Mason's side. Digging his thumb's claw deep into the bullet wound, Will slashed across, slicing Mason's gut open from liver to kidneys.

Mason bellowed in shock.

Will lashed out again, slashing the wolf's throat.

Blood gushed in a cranberry fountain and Mason fell back to the hot floor. Will staggered up, gasping for air as he charged ahead to the exit door. He tried the handle and confirmed what he already knew. Locked. He snarled and pounded on the sizzling metal portal.

"Janae! Janae! God damn it!"

He ran to the back of the car, leaping over destroyed seats and his dying brother, slamming into the back door. This too was locked. Will whipped left and right, smoke everywhere, roaring fire wrapping up around the windows. Mason gurgled a bloody laugh as he lay on the floor, trying to hold his intestines in place as his blood boiled on the scalding surface.

"W-Way to go, Will!" Mason said. "You won! P-Proud of you, buddy..." The wolf groaned and convulsed on the floor, burning and choking and bleeding. "Looks like this is how it ends, *brother!*"

"Fuck that," Will said, grabbing one of the crumpled

seats and holding it over his head. With a determined roar, he smashed the padded metal chair into the window. The glass cracked but didn't break.

Again and again, he slammed the seat against the glass, finally shattering the window and knocking loose the dividing bar. Flame and smoke sucked into the vacuum and Will ducked away. He ran over to Mason, scooping him into his arms with his last reserves of strength.

"Oh come on," Mason coughed. "Are you kidding me? *Hnng!* Leave me here, damn it! Just go!"

"No fuckin' way, Mase! Come on!"

The black jaguar rose to his feet on mighty haunched legs, holding the dying timber-wolf in his arms. He squatted down, putting one foot up on the window sill. Every fiber in his being was suffering. He braced himself for the jump.

"*Hold on!*" Will screamed.

He jumped.

They sailed through the wall of fire, soaring through thick smoke and into clean night air. Will lost his grip and the two beasts smashed to the ground, spitting gravel in all directions as they rolled to a halt.

Will lay face down, wheezing and gasping pained breaths. He pushed himself up, looking around at the carnage. A few feet away, the wolf lay motionless in the gravel, shimmering and warping out of this world.

In a moment, he was a man again, flesh and bones smashed and ruined. Clothes tattered and bloody with gore. Will saw the small movement of Mason's chest as he continued to draw shallow breaths.

Will closed his eyes and focused his breathing.

He concentrated and pulled the jaguar back into the ether. In moments, he was Will Shaw. Short hair, beard stubble, dimples and copper skin, he was a man again. His face and body bruised and bloodied, he was out of energy, desperate to collapse and just sleep forever. But he pulled himself up and crawled over to his brother.

"Mase...? M-Mason...?"

Mason gurgled blood.

Will reached his brother, pulling him into his arms as fire and smoke plumed in the wet Tennessee night. Mason looked up at him. Will's eyes were filled with anger and tears.

"Why?" Will asked.

"W-Why what?"

"*Why*, Mason?"

Mason coughed and choked on blood as it streamed through the gash in his throat. They both sat in the growing puddle of scarlet oozing from his gut. Mason fought back tears as he looked up at Will, contemplating the question.

"There ain't no *why*... I-I would have loved to... to be like you, Will. But I guess... I just am what I am... I-I'm sorry, little brother..."

Mason's eyes rolled back. His body went limp.

Will watched Mason die in his arms.

He cried and screamed from the depths of his soul. Within arms-reach, he saw Mason's slingshot lying on the ground. He picked it up and placed it on his brother's chest, folding Mason's hands over it.

"Dominic! Dom!"

Will staggered through the fiery, smoking train yard. To try and narrow down what hurt most would be impossible. All he knew was pain. Every inch of his body ached and burned. His heart and spirit screamed of loss and betrayal.

Blood caked his face. The crimson stains continued down his arms, his hands, his shirt and tattered, filthy pants. He held on to consciousness with one thought, one final responsibility.

"Dominic! Where are you? It's me, Uncle Will!"

Through the haze and heat, he heard a mewling cry. He followed the sound around the engulfed train yard to the museum gift shop, where a familiar aura of innocence was crouched behind the cash register. Will limped inside, zeroing in on the child, doing his best to calm his own voice.

"Dom? Are you there, buddy?"

A sniffle came from behind the register.

Two big brown eyes peeked over the counter.

"U-Uncle Will...?"

"It's me, buddy. It's me."

Dominic rushed around the counter, running into Will's arms. They held each other tight and wept.

"I got you, buddy. I got you."

38

SUNSET

THE SUN DIPPED down behind the mountains.

Casey Madison walked through the scenic, rolling hills of Tennessee River-Park. Young couples watched their kids in the playground and older couples watched the sunset from the bridges and park benches. Casey smiled, breathing in the crisp air as she admired the green of the grass, the orange and red tones in the sky and the smell of the water flowing up ahead.

Humanity looked different these days. She could sense the energy and life force of every person — She had learned it's called an *aura* — and read their thoughts in an abstract way she had yet to understand or master.

It was a new world.

She approached the riverfront, the water shimmering reflections of the dying light. Sitting on a park bench, a silhouetted man looked out at the beauty of nature. A lolly-pop was in his mouth. She approached the bench and sat beside the man.

"Thanks for meeting me."

"No problem, kiddo," Will said.

She studied his face. Wounds that were now only two weeks old appeared mostly healed. The swelling and bruising had gone down, leaving only faded scabs.

"You look great," she said.

"I guess skinners really do heal fast... Ribs still hurt a bit, though." He turned to her, a dimpled, half smile on his lips. "So, what'd you tell your mother?"

"That I'm at a friend's house, studying." Casey chuckled to herself, kicking at pebbles on the ground. "She dropped me off, then I had to sneak away. She's super protective these days. Won't let me go anywhere by myself."

"Can't imagine why."

"Look at this," she said, reaching into her purse. "Look what she gave me." Casey took out a bottle of pepper spray, shaking her head. "She's taking no chances."

"She's smart, and she loves you."

"*Pfft.* Anybody messes with me now, pepper spray is gonna be the least of their problems!"

Will looked at her with sobering eyes. "No, Casey. That's the wrong way to think. You have to *control* this thing inside of you. You can't just let it out and tear apart everyone who gives you shit. Remember..."

"I know, I know," Casey sighed. "It's a secret, and a responsibility."

"Is that why you wanted to talk?"

"I just... I don't know." Casey searched for the words. "It's like, I just want to let it out now! To be free! To be me! I feel like, when I'm the cat, I'm like, even more myself! But I... I just don't know, like... I'm seeing things and hearing things... Everything is just... *different*, y'know?"

"Mm hm."

"I just... Don't know how to be."

"You think I do?" Will laughed. "This is all pretty new to me too. Everything has changed."

They sat in silence for a moment.

"How's your friend?" Casey asked.

Will sighed. "He'll never walk again. And Dominic is all right... Physically. But what they both went through... Their lives are changed forever. Scarred. And it's all because of me. I have to live with that now. Anybody who gets close to me... They're in danger."

"What about me?"

"Well, we're practically family now." Will smiled. "You're the only person who knows my secrets. You and my papaw."

"What about Janae?"

Will's face tensed and his eyes went cold.

"I still can't believe what she did," Casey said. "I thought you two were... y'know..."

"So did I."

"So, what happened? Where is she?"

"I don't know, kid. But I'm gonna find out."

"You're like, the old wise man," Casey cracked. "You're supposed to have all the answers."

Will erupted in laughter, pulled the lolly-pop from his mouth.

"*Old*, huh? You better watch your mouth, smart-ass."

He lovingly pushed her shoulder and she laughed.

"I mean, you're pretty old," she pushed. "Look at all those gray hairs on your chin."

"Yeah, keep talkin'..."

The sky grew darker, a bloody hue.

"So, what now?" Casey asked.

"Now," Will stood up, pacing around and kicking at the ground. "Now you get real good at lyin'. Nobody can know your secret. If anybody finds out, you're in danger and so are they. That means your mom, your friends... Anyone you love."

"Yeah, I can't really tell her I'm sneaking out to meet up with creepy old men in the park."

"Exactly." Will leaned against the railing overlooking the water. Casey stood up and approached it as well, hanging on to the rail as she looked out at the sunset. "You have a secret life now, and you're gonna have to learn how to live with it. You need to figure out who you are and what you want to be... And so do I."

"Sounds like you're just as lost as I am," Casey grunted.

"Well, maybe you and I can help each other out."

They looked at each other and smiled.

"So, what time do you have to get back?"

"My mom's picking me up at my friend's house at ten."

Will nodded. "Sounds good. You want to go get something to eat?"

Casey perked up, beaming a smile.

"You buying?" she asked.

"Actually," Will said, gesturing to the green, rolling

hills across the lake. "You see those mountains over there?"

"Yeah?"

"Lots of wildlife."

"So?"

Will wore a devilish grin.

His eyes flashed yellow.

"Well, what do you say... we do a little hunting?"

ART GALLERY

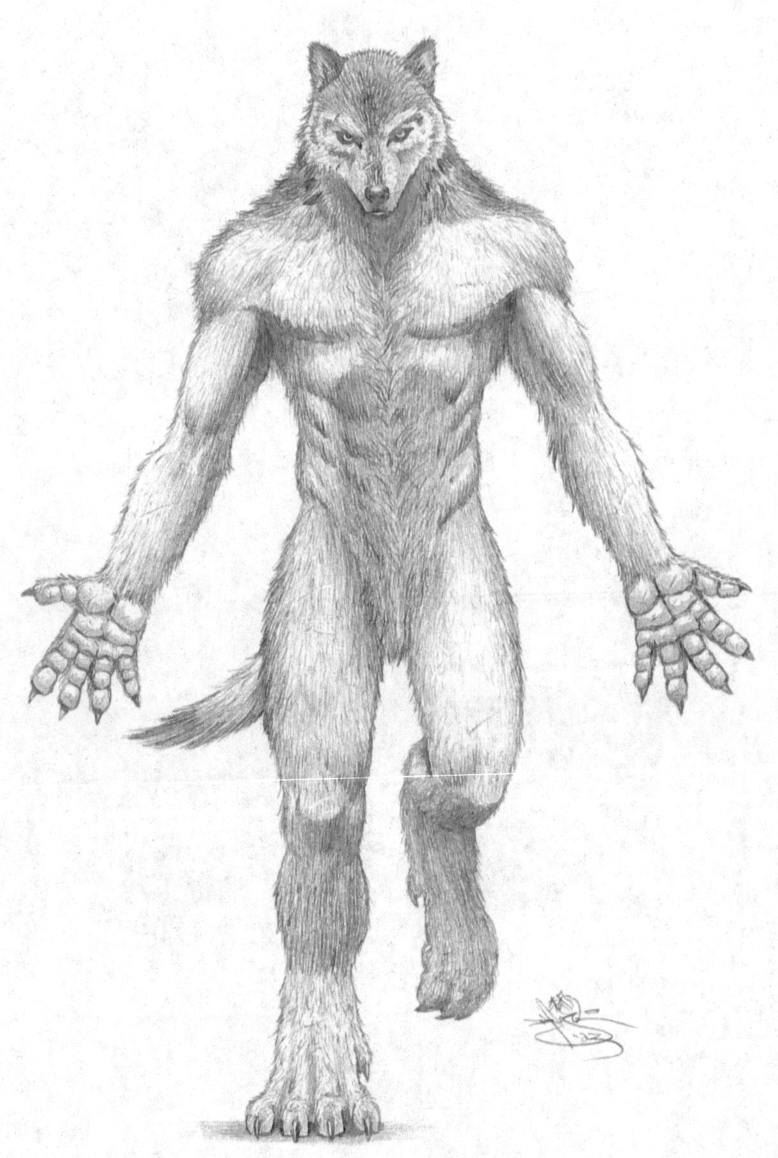

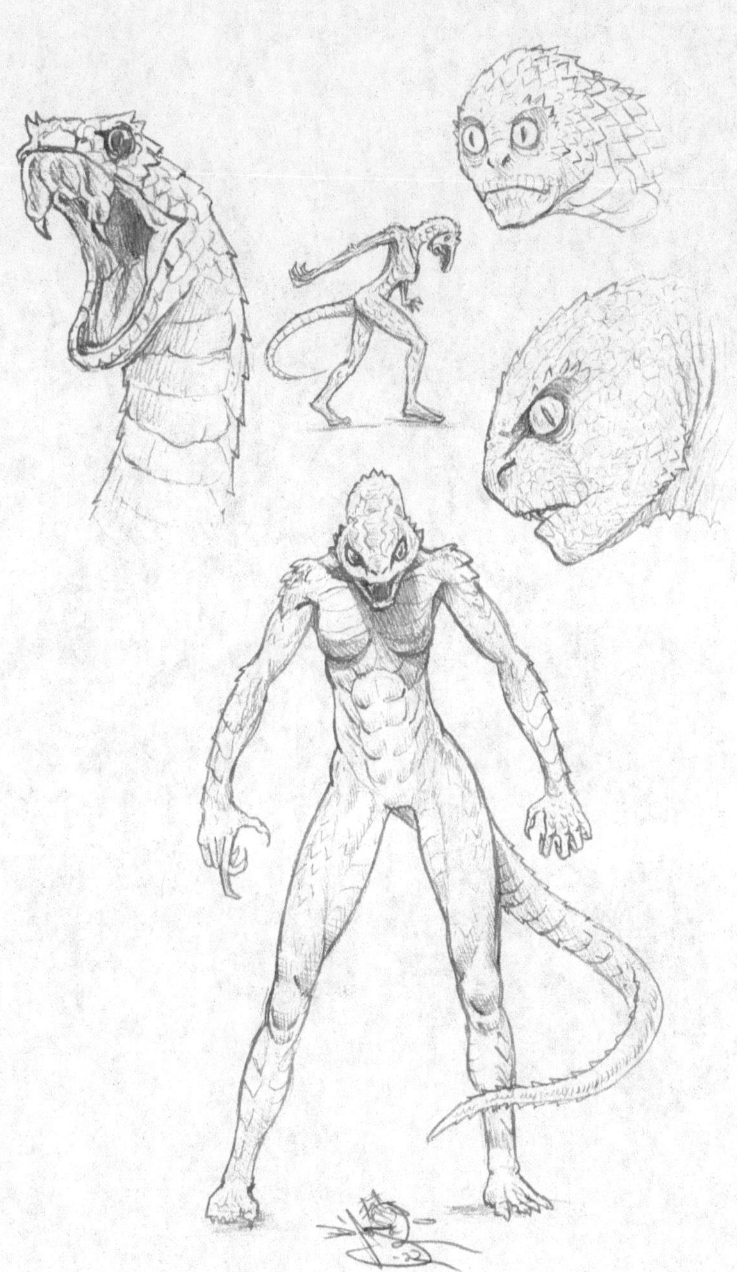

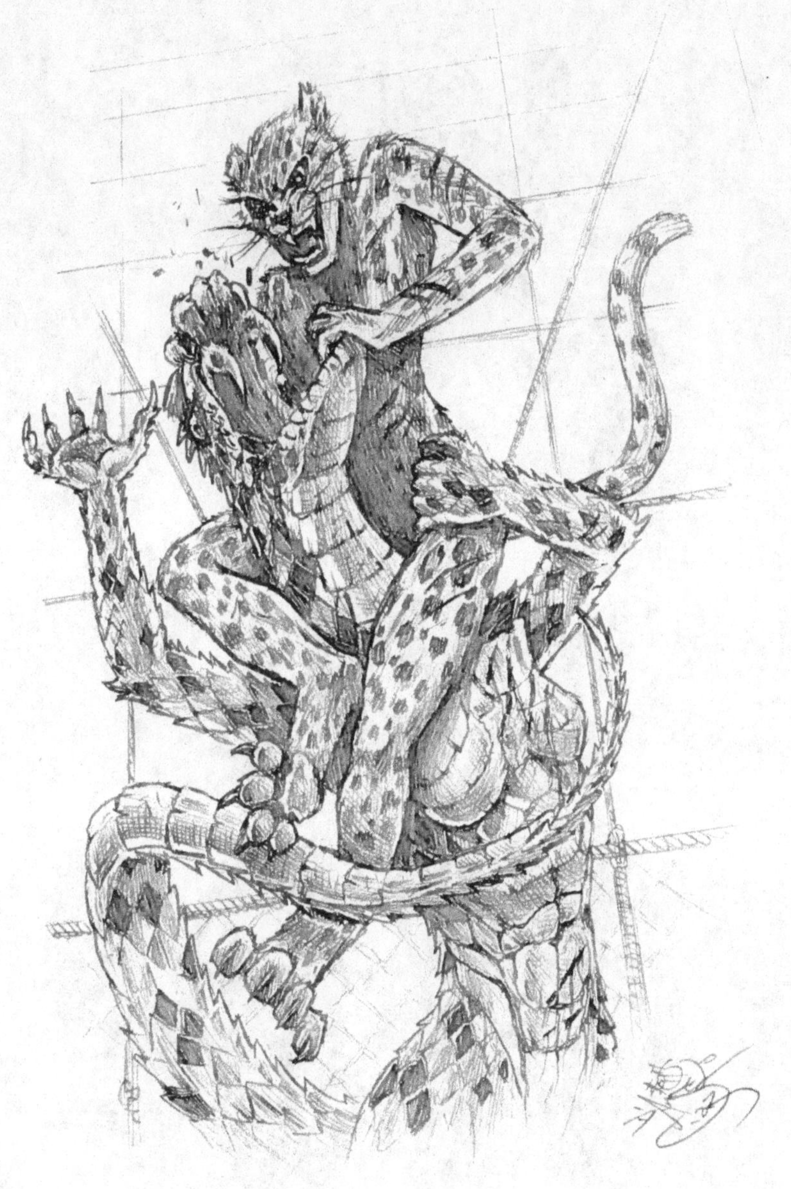

WILL SHAW RETURNS IN

BLACKBIRDS DANCE

THE SKINNER SAGA PART 2

BLACKBIRDS DANCE

Cherokee reservation, North Carolina

The baby was getting fussy.

He was only a week old, and it had been a long day. Grandma and Grandpa had come to visit along with the cousins, and everyone wanted baby time. He had been passed around and cooed at, serenaded, cuddled. He'd been fed, had his naps, enjoyed a delicate luke-warm bath in his special baby tub. All attention was on him, little Benny. Seven pounds-four ounces, brown eyes, a tuft of fine black hair on his head, he was the angel that Mommy and Daddy had been praying for.

Now his little face crinkled into a grimace and he squirmed in discomfort as Mommy paced the nursery, rocking him gently as she hummed soothing tones. Daddy leaned in the doorway, smiling proudly. They were a handsome young couple, healthy and fit, each with copper skin and long, jet-black hair.

"There we gooo... Sleepy baaaaby..."

It was working. Benny's eyelids drooped and his flailing slowed. Soon he was asleep, blissfully warm and snug in his mother's embrace. She took her bundle to the crib and eased him into place. A stuffed animal monkey lay beside him in case he got lonely and a carousel hung overhead in case he got bored. On the wall behind the crib was a large dreamcatcher, more for decoration than any spiritual superstitions.

The young mother gave her son one last tender kiss on the head, then switched on the baby monitor. If he made a sound, they would hear it. She crossed to the doorway and her husband slid his hand across her hips, pulling her close. He kissed her cheek and they remained there for another minute, just admiring the miracle they created.

"I still can't believe he's ours," she whispered.

"Come on. Daddy needs a drink," he said, playfully smacking her butt.

She giggled as he led her out of the room, closing the door behind her but leaving it open a crack. They continued to talk as they moved down the hallway, their voices fading away as they left young Benny on his own. He shifted in his crib, enjoying his baby dreams and the comfortable feeling of being protected and loved.

There was a stranger on The Rez that night.

It was a presence, neither male nor female, not physical or spirit. Anyone who saw it would only catch a momentary glimpse, and even then they would be unable to describe it. They might say they saw a shadow, or simply that they felt a malevolent chill in the night. That they saw nothing but darkness but somehow knew that someone, or something, was there.

It moved down the silent streets in the dead of night.

It didn't walk, it didn't creep, it didn't float... It moved. It was an intangible, elemental force. It had no name, no home, no soul of its own. But it did have hunger. Moving down the dark streets, it tasted the air and smelled warm, fresh nourishment.

Someone was coming. A man walking his dog.

The presence sucked in its breath and pulled its extremities inward. Tentacles and tails and wings and whatever else this abomination was made of folded up. It sucked in its breath, forcing its form into another shape like a black octopus, no spine or skeleton to restrict it. The black wraith stretched into a vertical form, then bulged out an oval knob on top, then a protrusion on each side. Next, two tentacles stretched to meet the ground and more came to fill out the shape.

The man with the dog walked past on the dark road. He saw the dark figure walking across from him, just some man in the shadows taking a late-night stroll. The dog-walker couldn't make out any features, nor could he focus on them in this heavy darkness if he tried. But he raised his hand for a polite wave, and the man across the street replied with a simple nod. The dog growled but its owner tugged at the leash to silence it. They made their way back home and thought nothing more of the stranger walking in the gloom.

The dark presence released its posture and allowed its crude human disguise to unravel. Tendrils and black viscera spread out like a drop of ink in a glass of water. Stretching to its full size, it continued down the roads and alleyways, tasting the air. Looking for something very special.

It passed into a residential area. Small houses and run-down shacks dotted the landscape, not a single light on inside. A tractor sat out in a field to the left, burned-out husks of old cars in the fields to the right. Some homes were simply trailers while others were nicer and more maintained. None of that mattered to the dark entity. It flicked its tendrils into the night, letting them graze across mailboxes, picket fences, parked cars.

It glided over to one house, tasted the air. It ran its feelers across the walls, sensing the energy inside. It lingered there for a moment, then decided no, not this house. It moved on to the next and passed it by, then the next. It moved across the street and stopped, deciding to look at another house more closely. Black tentacles silently swirled out, caressing the walls and windows. It tasted the air, a translucent black tongue flicking in and out. No, not this house. It moved on.

It reached a cross street and saw a cul-de-sac up ahead. It plunged forward, looking closely at each abode nestled into this dark pocket of the countryside. The air tasted fresh and clean and the being knew it was close. One house had a swing set out front as well as children's toys scattered in the yard. The black wraith closed in on the house, tasting the air, stroking the walls... No, not this one.

The next house was small and simple, nondescript. A single sedan was in the driveway. The lights were all off. An energy pulled the black shape forward, something it sensed inside. Tendrils felt at the walls, that horrible tongue licked the air... Yes, this was it. The entity crept around the structure, feeling each surface, scanning as it closed in on what it was looking for. And there it was.

It stopped at a window. The energy was ripe and fresh, clean and pure. This was it. What the dark creature wanted was just beyond the meager pane of glass. Mouth watering, it pressed itself against the window pane, smashing its formless mass against the cool surface. From an outside glance, it would appear to be a big mound of black goo just stuck there, transparent, not quite physical but not entirely black smoke either. But to look closer, something else was happening.

The entity was finding its way in. Through cracks in the wood, between the very atoms in the pane of glass, the blackness slowly pushed and squeezed. Smoke and dark tendrils worked through every microscopic gap until after a minute, it began to seep through like juice pulp through a strainer. The puddle of black goo on the inside of the window began to spread, and soon, half of the entity's form had passed the threshold, writhing and undulating with the effort. It grunted and hissed, pulling the rest of its non-corporeal form through. After nearly five minutes, the creature slipped the last of its tendrils through without even cracking the window.

Little Benny slept peacefully in his crib.

The dark being drew in a breath, tasting the sweet aroma of innocence. Its ghostly form billowing in the shadows, the foul thing drew itself closer. Its black mouth watered somewhere within its swirling folds. It peered down on the child resting peacefully, swathed in a sky-blue blanket with printed monkeys and elephants. The infant's skin was soft and smooth, his little chest moving with each tranquil breath.

Closer. The darkness moved in slowly. Tendrils and swirling black membranes stroking the edge of the crib. A baby monitor sat on a table, its red light on, ready to alert the parents for when it's time to change a diaper or sing a sweet lullaby. An acrid stink filled the sanctuary of youth, a nauseating marriage of battery acid and rotting garbage.

Closer. Benny stirred in his sleep.

The dark creature gripped the crib, leering over the edge. It moved in, its form undulating over the sleeping newborn. Slimy black lips parted to reveal not rows of sharp teeth, but gray, diseased gums. The sinister jaws spread open, forming an O shape, creeping in closer. Closer.

It pushed the carousel away and the device crashed to the floor with a plastic thump. Benny kicked and mewled. He began to fuss and stir, squeaks of infant discontent coming from his pink lips. The black came down and found those lips, parted them open, and gave little Benny a kiss.

Then it began to suck.

The young mother and father were sound asleep when the strange static sounds came through the monitor's speaker. They both groaned and stirred in bed, and the father began to push his blanket away, but his wife's hand touched his arm and stopped him.

"It's okay, I got him," she said, kicking her legs off the bed and lurching to her feet. She stretched and made her way around the bed, wearing only panties and one of her husband's oversized t-shirts. Baby sounded hungry. But no, actually, he sounds different, she thought. It was not his usual clear, sharp cries; it was muffled and sounded like the crib was shaking around.

She crossed out of the dark bedroom and into the hallway, running her fingers through her hair and untangling a knot. The sounds from the nursery stopped, but she kept going to the end of the hall. She reached the door, adorned with cut-outs of cartoon characters, and twisted the knob, pushing the door open.

The young mother stepped into the room and felt a cold chill shoot up her spine. The awful odor stung in her nose. There was slight ambient light in the room, but around the crib, all she could see was darkness. Undulating, evil darkness. She drew in a sharp breath and the foul creature suddenly pulled up and away from the crib, shrieking a horrible, high-pitched wail.

It spread out its membranes like great black wings and suddenly launched itself backwards. No time to seep slowly out through the window, the creature instead smashed through the pane, flying out into the night.

The horrified mother ran to the crib.

Little Benny lay lifeless, his pink flesh turned gray and shriveled, all the life and spirit drained out of his little body. His mother dropped to her knees, trembling, shivering. Tears burned in her eyes and her mouth gaped open, and at first no sound would come out. Then she screamed. And screamed again.

She screamed for the rest of the night.

Jesse D'Angelo was born in New York and raised in Los Angeles, working as both a writer and an artist in the film and television industries. His credits include "Sky Captain and the World of Tomorrow," "Species," "Hellboy," "Underworld," "The Cave," "CSI: New York," "Kingdom" and "Ancient Aliens."

He currently lives in Chattanooga, TN, with his lovely wife and son. He has a blue belt in Brazilian Jiu-Jitsu, makes pizza from scratch, is the proud father of three feline daughters, and gets teary-eyed when he watches cheesy 80's movies.